Tyrants and Traitors

Joshua McHenry Miller

BLUE INK
PRESS

Published by Blue Ink Press, LLC

Printed in the United States of America

Cover design by Greg Simanson

www.blueinkpress.com

ISBN: 0-9968673-2-5
ISBN-13: 978-0-9968673-2-0
Library of Congress Control Number: 2016948066

To Josh and Angie Hoffman.
They provided the perfect blend of encouragement, criticism, and lamb shawarma.

Prologue

This was the first step toward revolution; an adventure bards would retell for generations. It was also, technically, stealing.

My brother Isaiah and I hid behind a set of wine casks, the midday sun beating down on our necks. The covered, travel-worn wagon carrying our intended plunder waited at the other end of the alley.

"Niklas," Isaiah moaned softly, not wanting the cargo's current owners to overhear us, "this is a bad idea."

A smile split my face. "This is the best idea I've had all month."

Sweat dripped into my brother's eyes, forcing him to squint. "We have disturbingly different definitions for that term."

Chuckling, I rested my curly black hair against the wood and playfully shoved him. "We've got this. It's no different than any of our other plans."

"Your plans," Isaiah corrected me. "Ever since Mom nearly twisted off our ears for swiping a honey cake before dinner, they've always been your plans."

In stark contrast to my older brother's reservations, my fist clenched in excitement. "Think of what we could do with one of those weapons. There are only two swords in our entire kingdom."

"And why is that?" Isaiah asked. His fingers began rearranging the simple three-piece puzzle box he took everywhere. Four times he

1

made a mistake in solving it, a sure sign my brother's sharp mind was terrified by my plan. "Oh, that's right, because every time the Philistines catch one of our people with a sword, they drag him behind a horse for a week."

"I'm not suggesting we go brandishing it about town," I told him. "Subtlety would be key."

The comment caused his vast belly to jiggle from laughter. "If this plan depends on subtlety from you, we're already sunk."

"That's your job, ensuring I don't get myself killed."

Isaiah's genuine laugh morphed into one of panic and his fingers stopped working on the puzzle. "You're really going to go through with this, aren't you?"

"Yep," I said, peeking over the barrels and anticipating my next move.

We hid on the far side of an alley. The large covered wagon was parked at the other end. The owners of the cart, four traveling, scum-eating Philistines, sat on the street at the wagon's front. Waiting for the heat of the day to pass, they had already guzzled down three flasks of wine.

We had discovered the weapons earlier. Our eldest brother, Eliab, had left to negotiate the price of this season's wool, and Isaiah and I were exploring the streets of Lachish when we overheard the Philistine thugs bragging about their cargo.

"With this new shipment of blades from Persia, we'll finally be able to wipe the Israelite swine from our lands," one of the travelers had boasted.

The comment got my attention, and I had hauled my brother after me to investigate. What we found was better than my most fantastical dreams: a topless crate, filled to the brim with steel swords, rested at the back of their cart. The mission was amazingly simple: a dash and grab which I had practically perfected a year after I started walking.

I patted Isaiah's shoulder. "You don't have to do anything," I assured him, "just keep a lookout and shout if one of them catches wind of me."

"You're meeting with Uncle Benjamin as soon as Eliab gets back," he said, his hazel eyes pleading with me. "It's not worth the risk."

His sincerity was moving. For all of Isaiah's constant worrying, his heart was always in the right place, and he didn't want me to ruin my chance at an apprenticeship under our uncle. But this was bigger than my carpentry aspirations. Just one of those swords would almost double our nation's fighting strength, and with so many blades, the Philistines wouldn't even realize it went missing until they had returned to whatever backwoods cesspool they'd crawled out of. This was needed, and it was doable. Stealing wasn't my preferred method of mischief, but I'd be lying if I said it was beneath me.

"This will take five minutes," I said. "If things go bad, disappear down the side street. I'll run straight out the back and make sure they follow me." Then, before he could add another reason to abort, I ducked out from behind the casks.

Staying low to the ground, I crept up toward the rear of the cart. These lowlifes seemed so inebriated I probably could have walked up singing and dancing a jig without them noticing, but for Isaiah's sake, I played it safe.

I reached the cart without any alarms going off and considered my options. My hands just barely reached the top of the crate which held the swords, but I doubted one could be removed from this angle without it banging against the other weapons. If I climbed into the cart, procuring one became significantly easier, but I feared how much the wagon would creak from my weight. After a moment of thought, I decided climbing in would be the least likely way to draw attention to myself.

Mounting the back end of the wagon as gently as I could, my feet touched down on the platform without so much as a floorboard shifting. I pumped my fist in the air and shot a glance of victory to Isaiah, who in turn rolled his eyes and motioned harshly for me to hurry up.

I waved him off and took another step toward the crate, but my luck faltered. Wood groaned beneath me, and shivers of fright shot from the soles of my feet to the top of my head. I immediately lifted my sandal, frozen and awkward on one leg, like some kind of oversized bird, standing in a pond.

"Did you hear that?" said a slurred voice from the front of the wagon.

"Huh," said another.

Feet shuffled. "I heard something in the cart," the first man explained.

Terror produced sweat, and beads of water dripped over my eyes as I struggled against toppling over.

"Sit down, Backus," said a new, arrogant voice. "It's probably just our new pet getting bored. The Israelites wouldn't dare provoke us. You could throw a pile of gold into the street, and as long as we ordered them not to touch it, a year from now it would still be laying in the middle of the road, waiting for us. A nation of cowards, every one of them."

A burst of laughter erupted from the men, and I heard someone settle back to the ground.

Anger replaced fear, and I had the urge to grab one of the swords and see how cowardly the man thought we were with a blade in his gut, but I found smug satisfaction in doing precisely what he deemed us so incapable of attempting.

As I stared down at the stash of weapons, my eyes went wide. I had never seen a steel sword up close, and before me there had to be at least fifty of the blades. They were as long as my arm, with simple, leather-wrapped hilts and edges that gleamed in the sun. My fingers tightened around one of the handles. The grip felt right, and I began lifting the sword out from the crate.

"All right, Lahmi," said Backus, "we've carted it halfway across the continent. Will you finally tell us what's under those blasted wrappings? My bet is some kind of spear."

"Ha," said Lahmi, the owner of the arrogant voice. "Fine, as long as you promise to keep your lips shut. It's a surprise gift from King Achish. A weapon he commissioned to be crafted for my brother. A sword with no equal."

"A sword?" said a new voice in disbelief. "It's at least five feet long!"

"We all know my brother is unique. It's his gift for slaying over one hundred Israelites. With it, I bet you he matches that number in the first year alone."

Another chorus of howls went up from the men, but their voices were drowned out by my dark thoughts. For generations, the border skirmishes between our two countries had taken a heavy toll on our people. Almost every household had lost at least one of their own to a battle, and our family was no exception. Was my cousin one of this monster's victims?

No longer was it enough to simply steal one sword of many. Our nation needed to make a more personal statement. I inspected the other contents in the wagon. There were a dozen boxes stacked unevenly toward the front, a set of thick, purple carpets propped up vertically in the corner, and a large square crate completely covered in a dusty burlap cloth was right behind me. Then I found it—pressed against the sidewall, a long bundle lay on the floor.

Kneeling down next to it, I reverently unwrapped the end. The golden handle stretched at least two feet, and the blade was nearly as wide as my forearm was long. My heartbeat quickened. With a weapon like this, a warrior could become legendary, and a legend could change the course of the entire conflict with the Philistines.

I threw the covering back on and tried to pick it up. *Sacrificial lamb!* The thing was heavy. Bracing myself, I tugged again but realized it was lodged too deep. I needed a better grip.

I unwrapped the hilt again and grabbed hold with both hands. Pulling with all my strength, about three feet of the blade abruptly came free before it snagged again. The force flung me back, sending my body crashing into the covered crate behind me.

The crate turned out to be a metal cage, and whatever creature resided inside it did not appreciate being disturbed. It growled and then slammed into the other side of the bars. I let out a yelp, one that distinctly did not sound like that of a five-year-old girl, and clapped a hand over my mouth.

"An Israeli thief is in the wagon!" Backus shouted.

"No," growled Lahmi. "It's an Israeli corpse. We just haven't informed his body yet."

Score one for Isaiah. This was a bad idea.

***

My stomach dropped. I've jammed myself into an impressively high number of tight spots over the years, but if I didn't find some wiggle room quick, this one could serve as my tomb. Most of my ideas, at worst, left me with a sore backside from the discipline of my father. These men would settle for nothing less than separating each limb from my torso. Fighting four grown warriors was out of the question, no matter how many swords I had access to, which left only one option—tactical, albeit terrifying, retreat.

The first goon's body appeared around the corner of the wagon, and I leapt off the end of the trailer and soared over his shoulder. I landed awkwardly, but I scrambled to my feet and used the pure terror coursing through my blood to fuel my escape.

"Grab him!" Lahmi shouted, and I heard their boots striking the dirt after me.

I bolted past the wine casks and saw Isaiah still pressed against the wood. Burn it all! Why hadn't he ducked out the moment I was discovered? I jerked my head for him to disappear down the side alley but didn't dare stop with the Philistines so close.

As long as I kept them focused on me, he should be fine, but for an added assurance I craned my neck around. "I heard Philistines were easy marks," I shouted back to them, "but it's ridiculous how little effort it took to play with your toys!" Then with my head down I focused on increasing speed. As I turned the corner, the sound of wood tumbling over echoed behind me, followed by cursing from one of the men.

An elderly woman wrapped in a thin shawl stepped out right in front of me. She carried a basket of wheat stalks, and I barely managed to sidestep her. Yet the shock of our near collision rocked her on her heels, and she fell to the ground, her bundle spraying across the street.

I grimaced. Terrifying old ladies wasn't the outcome I had envisioned at the onset of this escapade. "I'm so sorry!" I yelled without turning around and continued my flight.

After running straight down the empty road for another two blocks, I chanced a look back to assess the situation. Only three men still followed me. All were shirtless, wearing nothing but long brown aprons and sandals. Two had disheveled beards and brown hair, but the largest of the bunch had the fiercest black mohawk I had ever seen. His nose pressed unevenly against his face, giving me the impression there may have been inbreeding with a boar somewhere in his family tree.

"Get him!" the boar-man yelled, and his voice identified him as their leader, Lahmi.

The only thing I cared about though was that I had gained at least another fifteen paces. I allowed the small success to spur me on and started working on my exit strategy. If I turned enough corners, I might be able to shake them, but with three of them pursuing me, if one fell behind and took a different route, he might accidentally cross paths with me again. There had to be a place for me to hide. I refused to sneak into a house and risk a family being brought into my mess, and the forest was too far out of town, especially if the missing man had left to grab a horse. I needed something here, something to get in their way...

A devilish grin crossed my face.

I headed to the far side of town, where our family's flock waited to be sheared in a large pen, nearly two hundred ewes. Sheep may be the dumbest creatures ever created. Given the opportunity, they'll follow each other off the face of a cliff, and they'll literally eat until their stomachs explode, and they are completely defenseless against the weakest of predators. They're crops with legs that crap everywhere.

The gate to the pen was only three feet high, and I easily vaulted over it and into the gathered herd. The sheep barely all fit into the area, leaving almost no room for them to move about. I waded into the center of the corral, their bleating voices all around me, and waited for Lahmi and his men to come into view. The moment they did, I waved at them, winked, and then ducked down among the animals.

"Find the brat!" Lahmi ordered.

The gate squeaked open, and the sheep around me began to shift about as the men attempted to get to the center of the pen. I crawled to the sidewall of the corral, knowing the sheep were already too disturbed to give away my location.

"This is ridiculous, boss," one of the men called. "I've already

7

stepped in at least three loads of—"

"I'll stuff your mouth with it," their leader interrupted, "if you don't shut up and search. He's here, find him."

I shuffled along the wall of the fence. If I could just make it another twenty feet without being spotted...

"Come out now, you little Israelite brat," Lahmi goaded, "and I promise we won't kill you. I'll send you back to your dog breath of a mother with little more than a few bruises."

My neck tensed when he mentioned my mother, but I withheld from taking the bait. And Eliab said I'd never start maturing.

"If I have to find you," Lahmi said loudly from far behind me, "I promise it will be worse. The runt has nowhere to go. We just have to find..." His voice trailed off. "Blood and ashes, turn around!"

He had figured out my plan, but it was too late. I already had crept out the front gate and was ten feet outside of the pen. I popped up and sprinted back into the city, hooting in victory. It would take them at least a minute to free themselves from the sheep, by which time my disappearance would be permanent. I dashed between several side streets before finally slowing down and tucking myself behind a green tapestry drying on a clothing line.

Bracing myself against the mud wall of a house, it took a moment to catch my breath. A mixture of exhilaration, relief, and accomplishment washed over me. If that had gone almost any other way...I shook my head to fling the ugly possibilities from my thoughts. Now, the important thing was to grab Isaiah and get back to our meeting spot with Eliab.

I checked the street and darted toward the alley Isaiah had escaped down. I wondered if he had any water left in his flask. The adventure had left me parched. It might take a little convincing, but I'm sure I could—

"Boss, I caught one!"

My body went rigid, and I whipped my head around but quickly realized the call hadn't been directed at me. It came from the next street over.

Sneaking down a side road, I peeked out to see what he was talking about. My heart sank. The Philistines had captured Isaiah.

***

Lahmi and his men were returning from their failed pursuit, while Backus waited for them with Isaiah kneeling at his feet, the thug holding my brother firmly by the back of his neck. He tried to wiggle free, but Lahmi's lackey tightened his grasp, and Isaiah erupted in shouts of protest.

"This bugger," Backus explained, "was the one who pushed the wine casks in our way during the chase."

"The little thief's accomplice," Lahmi said, as he walked up to them. He squatted down next to my brother and poked him in the stomach. "I can see why his partner left him behind. This fat rat would be almost impossible *not* to catch."

Isaiah looked up at Lahmi, his eyes filled with fear. He opened his mouth to speak, but the moment he did, the Philistine backhanded him to the ground.

"I didn't say I was ready to hear you squeak yet, fat rat," the cowardly pig-faced leader said, at ease again. "I'll let you know when it's time to beg. First, we need to remind you of an Israelite's sorry place in the world." He nodded to his men, and they closed in around my brother and began ruthlessly pummeling him with kicks. Isaiah's puzzle box tumbled out from the circle, and Lahmi gazed at it with scorn, before crushing it beneath his boot.

The cries of my brother paralyzed my thoughts. I could just barely make out his body, curled up in a ball, trying to defend himself from the savage attack. I despised the Philistines for their brutality, but that anger paled in comparison to how much I hated myself for putting Isaiah in this position.

I burst out onto the street. "Stop it!" My outcry was high pitched and broken, as I shouted over the men's assault.

The thugs abruptly stopped, and Lahmi examined me with a cruel, almost giddy glare. "How noble," he laughed, "the would-be bandit returns to rescue his friend."

I walked slowly up to the men. Isaiah lay whimpering on the ground, but at least they had halted their attack.

With my brother temporarily relieved, my brain started functioning again. Our options were incredibly limited. Calling for help would be useless. Though my people would sooner rip off a toenail than assist a Philistine, Lahmi had been correct in saying almost no Israelite would openly oppose him and his men. After being beaten down for years, our people were too weary even to attempt rising up.

With preparation, I probably could come up with some scheme to get us out of the predicament. The Philistines certainly weren't known for their wealth of scholars, but with Isaiah already trapped and wounded, there simply was no time to devise a complicated plan, which left only one option.

Raising my arms high above my head, I kept moving forward. "It was all me!" I pleaded. "My idea, my actions, my everything. My brother even tried to talk me out of it." Reaching the men, I inhaled deeply and looked their leader straight in the eye. "It's not fair to punish him for my mistake."

Isaiah shifted his broken body to see me. "Niklas, no."

Lahmi raised an eyebrow and glanced back at his men. "Tried to talk you out of it? Your brother is pretty smart. Too bad he wasn't better at talking. Though to be honest, after today, that particular problem won't be much of a concern for him." He paused. "In fact...," he trailed off.

The Philistine pulled out a long, curved knife from his apron and pointed it at Isaiah. "Get him to his knees and open his mouth."

The men roughly grabbed my still moaning brother, and I rushed forward. "Please don't do this! I'll do anything, just leave him alone."

Lahmi held up his hand to stop the men, and he stared back at me. "'Anything' is a big word."

"Anything," I repeated, breathing deep.

Lahmi paused in thought for a moment, and then a cruel smile spread across his lips. He yelled at Backus. "Pull the wagon out here."

The man appeared confused by the order, but he nodded and left to move the horse-drawn wagon forward.

"Israelite scum!" The Philistine leader announced loudly. "Come out of your rat holes and into the street. If enough of you refuse to join us, my men and I will be forced to start dragging you out, and you'll join these two! You have one minute."

At first, nothing happened, but then a door hinge slowly opened, and a cowering mother and her two young daughters stepped into the street. Soon others joined them, probably fifty men, women, and children combined. They formed a large circle around us and the wagon, mostly keeping their heads down, terrified.

Lahmi addressed them all, slowly moving in a circle. "Two of your people attempted to steal our cargo. Obviously, this was a very poor choice, and choices have consequences. However, one of them wishes to take the punishment for both. We Philistines are merciful, so I will allow it." He stopped and walked to the back of the wagon. "But we are also just; thus his discipline must be doubled." He grabbed hold of the burlap cloth covering the cage and tore it off. Inside, a male lion sat crouched, glaring at the crowd. Dark brown remnants of past wounds covered his body; a shabby black mane surrounded his gaunt neck, and a long scar traced his right eye socket. A low, rumbling growl emanated from the beast.

Gasps rose from the crowd; parents pulled their young children closer and an unnatural hush fell over the street.

Lahmi walked over and grabbed me by my shoulder. He pushed me toward the cage and bent down to whisper in my ear. "We haven't fed him for two days. Be thankful, this should be quick."

We approached, and I swallowed hard and caught Isaiah's glance. One of his eyes was already swollen shut, but the panic in the other was unmistakable. I tried to keep up a brave front but knew it failed to convince him or anyone else. Death by lion seemed like a particularly unpleasant way to go.

As we neared the beast, Lahmi motioned for one of his men to grab the handle of the cage. "Open it on my mark," he said softly to the man, before returning to address the crowd. "Remember this day well, when you were shown the penalty for trying to rise above your pathetic station."

He roughly pushed me forward, the lion watching me approach with his scraggly mane cocked to the side, curious. My breathing quickened, and I dug my feet into the dirt, terrified. I swept my eyes around, frantic for any idea to help me escape. The crowd stood transfixed. Most of them appeared as horrified as me. I struggled to release myself from Lahmi's grip, but his strength easily outmatched mine. It was only a matter of time.

The man at the cage tensed as we drew nearer, readying himself for the signal. He had already released the latch, and all he needed to do was open it long enough to stuff me in. Then it dawned on me, my chance, but I would only get one shot at it.

I redoubled my efforts to force myself back. "Too afraid to fight me one-on-one, huh?" I challenged, trying to distract him.

"That's it, exactly," Lahmi said dismissively, as he continued shoving me onward. I kept up the fight for another moment but then launched myself forward. The sudden change in force stunned my captor, and I flew out of his hands.

And right into the man standing at the cage door. My momentum tore into him, and together we tumbled away from the wagon, though not before his hand accidentally ripped the door to the cage wide open.

The lion didn't waste a second. He bounded out of the cart and onto the ground, surveying the crowd, a cold fury in his gaze. How long had this king among beasts been confined and humiliated in that cage? The golden feline stalked forward, but his left front paw snapped up as he stepped down on it. He tested it again and grunted in painful protest. From my viewpoint on the ground, I noticed the dark discoloration of his left paw. He was injured.

The moment was broken by the defensive bark of a stray dog, yipping beneath the main gate of the town. Despite his injury, within seconds the lion closed in on the mutt who dared challenge him, and with one powerful bite, broke its neck. Its prize and meal secured in his jaw, the lion dashed straight out of the gates, disappearing out of sight.

Relief washed over all of us, yet I quickly remembered how laughably precarious my position still was, and I struggled to untangle my limbs from the thug, trying to get to my feet. He recovered too fast, and in a matter of breaths, he rolled on top of me, pinning my body to the ground.

He replaced one of his hands with his knee. "You're going to pay for that," he promised, and then he moved his free palm to my throat.

No strength remained in me to push him off—my luck had run out. My lungs constricted, and the street started going black.

Then something slammed into my would-be executioner, and fresh air soared back into my chest. I coughed several times and glanced up. My oldest brother Eliab, The Bear of Bethlehem himself, stood over me.

Eli made an impressive sight. He was almost as tall as Lahmi, but his frame was more imposing. His shoulders expanded both wide and deep; his barreled chest was layered thick with muscle, and his arms resembled the trunks of cedar trees. He wore a white, sleeveless tunic that reached his knees, and his whole body was covered in tangled brown hair. At his side, he carried his weapon. While the Philistines restricted swords in Israel, they permitted axes for forestry. His was the largest double-sided iron axe I had ever seen; its blades were two feet wide, and its shaft four feet long.

He held his axe inches from the man who still pinned me down and spoke softly. "Get off him."

The Philistine snarled and opened his mouth to reply, but Eliab kicked the lackey again, this time in the center of his chest, punting him several feet off the ground and away from me. He rolled multiple times before he came to a rest, clutching tightly to himself.

Everyone watching responded differently. The crowd stood frozen in shock. Clearly apprehensive, Lahmi and his men swept their eyes between Eliab and themselves. For the first time, the savages were unsure of their next move. I had witnessed similar events with the bullies from my hometown. Cowards masquerading as warriors rarely do well when someone is brave enough to stand up to them. I pushed myself up and looked to my brother. This was the first time since the black night three years ago I had seen Bethlehem's hero take a stand against our enemies.

"Thanks for—" I started before being cut off by a harsh wave of his hand.

He kept his eyes locked on the Philistines and tightened his grip on his axe. "It's time for you to leave."

Lahmi twitched like a rabbit, and his breaths came out uneven, anger raging in his eyes. "These two boys attempted to steal from us.

By Philistine law, they must be properly maimed."

"Did they actually steal anything?" Eli asked.

The Philistine pointed his knife at me. "We interrupted them before they could."

"So they were simply trespassing?"

"By the law of our land—"

My brother stopped him mid-sentence by simply lifting his palm. "Ah, but we are not in your land, we are in Israel, and our laws state that a child shall be disciplined by his family. You have done enough."

Lahmi stalked forward. "We lost a prized fighting beast because of them."

"Did they release the lion?" Eliab raised an eyebrow. "I was under the impression your own incompetence caused that."

The insult was too much. The mohawked Philistine leader went to strike my brother, but Eliab caught his arm inches from his cheek. He held it there, no sense of strain showing on his face.

"It's time for you to leave," he repeated.

Lahmi's voice was quiet, but it dripped with malice. "Do you really think you can take all four of us alone?"

Eliab slowly surveyed the crowd, and then his voice boomed. "I am not alone!"

It seemed like a spell of magic descended upon the street. The submissive fog evaporated from the men's eyes around the circle, and one by one they stood up straighter, stepping closer to my brother. Twenty men, who only moments before were but shadows of their current selves, stood alongside us.

The shift in numbers was not lost on any of the Philistines. My brother still held Lahmi's arm in his grasp, the man unable to pull it free. Finally, Eliab let go, and the Philistine backed up slowly.

He gathered his men and they warily entered their wagon.

"Eli," I said, scrambling to whisper in his ear, "they have over fifty swords in the back of their cart. If we attack now, we can take them all."

The hard glare my brother leveled at me caused me to take several steps back. "Niklas, you *also* have done enough," he said. "Trust me. You don't need to add anything else to your punishment."

I swallowed hard and watched as the wagon bustled down the road. Maybe I should have stuck with the lion.

Part One: The Judge

Standing alone atop a nearby roof, the old man's gray eyes watched the standoff's conclusion between the Philistines and three brothers with interest. For fifty years, the Israelites had called him a seer, and for an increasingly rare moment, what he saw pleased him immensely.

The hero—Eli, his brother Niklas had called him—helped the boy up and then swept his eyes across the crowd that had gathered. "Thank you for your courage, brothers." The men nodded in approval, their shoulders tall with pride.

"Yes," Alvaro said to his unseen companion, "this man could do it. He could lead all of Israel."

A satisfied smile crossed the ancient seer's lips. For a man such as this, Alvaro would risk his life against the Mad King.

The smile disappeared. "What do you mean, 'He's not the one'?" His question boomed loudly enough that the others below him might notice his presence on the roof. He didn't care. "Which brother then, the pudgy one?" he asked doubtfully.

Alvaro's eyes went wide, dumbfounded, his long beard shaking back and forth. "You must be joking. The petulant boy?" He barked out a harsh laugh. "No. I will not do it. Not for that—that child!"

Terror gripped his chest like a vice. He needed to sit down, and he threw his hand back, searching for the ledge to rest on. This must be some kind of joke; first Erik, the Mad King himself, and now some immature, prepubescent brat?

Eli at least stood a chance against Erik once the king found out he had performed another anointing. The eldest brother was the type of man people could look up to, flock to even. But this Niklas would be slaughtered the moment the king found out, fed to his 'pets.' And Alvaro would share the same fate soon after. *Maybe it would be best if I just stayed retired*, the seer thought to himself.

The silent, unheard voice spoke. The old man's shoulders sagged, weary from the final question his unseen companion had asked him.

For a moment, the seer kept his gaze to the ground, and then he placed his hands on his knees and pushed himself up, resolute. "I will do it," Alvaro said. "I will anoint him as the next king of Israel." He turned away to leave the rooftop, doubtful the boy would live long enough to see a crown.

Chapter 1

The sling spun parallel to my body at blurred speeds, like a frantic wheel moments away from craning off its spoke. As I released my grip, the small stone flew into the air. Arching high, it quickly soared out of sight, and as I waited for it to come back down, my attention turned to Blackfoot, the obstinate sheep grazing a hundred feet behind the rest of the flock. The stone plummeted back to the earth and stuck the ewe on her hindquarter. Startled, she squealed and jumped into motion, awkwardly scampering forward like an overgrown mothball to catch up with the rest of the herd.

I wrapped the slingshot's hemp rope around my arm in a crisscross pattern, bent down to grab my father's oak shepherd staff, and continued leading the flock onward. For the last three days, Dad had woken me up an hour before dawn, and I ran the same routine over, and over, and over again. Go to the pen. Count each sheep. Shepherd the flock five miles to a fresh grazing pasture. Return flock to pen. Repeat until dead.

Isaiah was built for the job. Caring and patient, the endlessly disobedient flock never fazed him. He found pleasure in watching over them, a purpose completely lost on me. In the beginning, I considered the job merely a timed crucible to endure, an apt punishment for my behavior in Lachish. However, after the first night, my parents sat me down, explaining that until further notice, all carpentry plans were on hold.

They might as well have said I was doomed to an eternity of shepherd duty. Career changes after a man turned seventeen were as typical as angel sightings. Everyone knew Eliab would manage our household. Sham and Abin would direct the work in the fields. Nathaniel and Rabbi had learned to run the village granary. That left Oz and Isaiah to shepherd. Seeing as I was fifteen and the youngest son in the family—Isaiah was eleventh months older than me—it gave me the perfect opportunity to strike out on my own.

But now Oz, the golden child of my family, the brother who always does his chores with pep in his step and a thank-you on his lips, was being sent to my uncle. "As a trial," Father assured me. They even loaned him my new carpentry tools.

It was only a matter of time before this whole shepherding exercise went up in flames. Didn't anyone else see it?

Huh. If it was only a matter of time, and if failure was guaranteed, what good would it do to prolong the inevitable? At least with planning, I could control the fallout. I obviously didn't want to do anything that would permanently harm the livelihood of my family, but it would have to be a large enough debacle to ensure my parents never attempted this experiment again. The scheme required the perfect balance of shrewd failure and deliberate incompetence. I needed time to think.

It took two hours, but the flash of inspiration eventually struck. It required multiple pails of wet mortar, a dozen empty water jugs, and several hours of uninterrupted work. If all went according to plan, the flock's wool would be matted and unworkable for weeks, and all notions of my shepherding career would be banished from Father's thoughts.

My smirk returned for the first time since evading the Philistines, and I reclined my back against the trunk of the fig tree. With most of the flock getting sheared in Lachish, all that remained were the twenty-two newborn lambs and their mothers, and at this age they required rest every couple of miles, allowing for the one positive aspect of the job—nap time. I closed my eyes and faded off, confident the plot resolved all my problems.

There's something blissfully surreal about waking up from a nap naturally, absent the urgency of chores forcing me up, or worse yet, my parents catching me, and Mom getting a hold of one of my ears. Enjoying the rarity of the situation, I was tempted to drift back asleep.

Then the clicking started.

At first, I held out hope that the sound was simply the last remnant of a dying dream, but when the noise started coinciding with the slight pricks digging into my open palm, that hope died rather abruptly. One of my eyes peeked out to search for the source. Then came the terror—so much terror.

An Israeli deathstalker scorpion sat atop my hand.

As a rule, I avoid encounters with insects that have either *death* or *stalker* in their names. Such experiences tend to end poorly. And painfully.

The pale yellow scorpion was a solid four inches long, and its poison-tipped tail was raised high in the air, daring any movement.

Fright locked up my reflexes. Deathstalkers are nasty. A single attack rarely caused death if treated quickly, but its venom incapacitated the victim, and it could be hours before someone thought to look for me. If struck with its stinger, the best case scenario left me unconscious and my arms and legs bloated like overfilled wineskins. Worst case, the venom reached my throat, and I suffocated.

The little buggers were lightning quick, meaning any attempt to brush off or kill the insect would end with its stinger lodged in my hand.

The only good news was it couldn't consider something my size food, so as long as I didn't play the aggressor, it should move on—eventually. The smart thing to do now was to wait and keep still. My hand, however, apparently didn't agree with my grand plan, because it was all I could do to keep it from shaking from panic. A bead of sweat dripped into my eye and burned my pupil, but I refused to blink, focusing on my palm, fighting to hold it steady.

Finally, after what was by far the most drawn-out, horror-filled sixty seconds of my life, the deathstalker skittered off my hand and back onto the grass. It was leaving.

The breath I had held since waking up escaped my lungs. The sound was a beat too soon. The scorpion flipped around in an instant and crouched low, a single moment from springing up in attack.

A mere inch away from my flesh, there was no way I could escape its reach. My eyes shut tight, expecting the worst.

Instead, a sudden, dull squishing sound thudded into the ground.

Peeking out, I discovered a teenage girl in a silk, cherry-colored dress kneeling down beside me, clutching the shortened blacksmith's hammer that had crushed the insect's body. Her blue eyes sparkled at me from under a rose-colored shawl, and her white smile contrasted with a dark cinnamon complexion.

"Niklas, didn't your mother ever teach you the old proverb?" Deborah asked, straightening the purple sash around her waist. "A little folding of the hands, a little midday slumber, and a deathstalker poisons your blood."

Still in shock, I simply gawked at the now green smear on the ground. A single leg spontaneously flipped over, and I slammed myself further against the trunk of the tree.

Deborah chuckled, rose to her feet, and offered me her free hand. It took a moment for me to tear my attention away from the dead insect, but she waited until I grasped her hand.

My friend pulled me to my feet and then moved in close, her face inches from my mine. With a smile, she grabbed hold of the bottom part of my tunic and used it to wipe the entrails off the mallet her father, Bethlehem's blacksmith, had designed personally for her.

"Ack," I said, and took several steps away from her. "I'm not your personal cleaning rag."

She regarded the hammer before tucking the tool's handle under her purple belt. "I promise you, scorpion entrails come out of wool much easier than silk. And you're welcome."

I opened my mouth to argue but then caught myself. "Yeah, thanks."

She nodded and went to retrieve a basket outside the shade of the tree. "You're lucky I was here. Mother sent me to deliver dinner to the workers in the fields. If I had visited Niclem first, you would have puffed up so large I could have rolled you back to town."

"Ha, ha," I said, and shoved the mental picture from my mind. "Why are you delivering food, anyway? I brought a lunch, and even with my break, once Oz comes to help, I'll be finished by supper."

"About that," she answered, and then turned her back to me and sorted through the basket. "He's not coming."

"Why? Father didn't send him to Lachish already, did he?" My newly minted plans burned to ash.

"No, he's still here, he's just not coming." Deborah paused. "Nobody is."

I rounded on her. "Why isn't anyone coming? What's happening in Bethlehem?"

She looked up from her basket, her eyes betraying guilt with a touch of pity. "I'm sorry, Niklas. A judge came to town this morning, and he's gathered the village together for a ceremony. Some of us need to stay in the fields, though." She again averted her eyes.

"A judge," I repeated in awed disbelief.

Judges were where myth met reality. For centuries, their exploits had become something of legend in our country. They always arrived during Israel's darkest hour, and then they proceeded to kick darkness right between the tailbone. A single judge once killed a thousand Philistines with the jawbone of a donkey! Deborah's own great-great-grandmother was one of the famed leaders for over forty years. It was her namesake she carried, and the purple sash around her waist an heirloom passed down through generations.

"I didn't even know Israel still had a judge," I said, more to myself than to Deborah. "I wonder what he's like."

Deborah returned to her feet and shoved a sandwich into my hand. "My grandmother said judges are just like regular people. They simply accomplish irregular deeds now and again."

I paid no attention to her comment. This was a once in a lifetime opportunity. I needed to see this man. All I had to do was—

"Stop it!" Deborah chided me.

My head snapped up.

"Just stop it. Whatever you're scheming, whatever grand plan you just concocted to convince yourself you should leave, let it go."

"How did you know—" I stammered.

Deborah's scoffed. "Because you're Niklas, the Prince of Plotting and the Magistrate of Mischief himself. And you hate sheep. Ever since that ram bit your pinkie toe off, you've acted like they have leprosy."

"The bloody thing permanently maimed me!" I snapped.

"You were trying to prove to Isaiah you could fit a stick between its legs. You're fortunate he didn't take your whole foot," she continued, rolling her eyes. "You've probably spent the whole afternoon plotting how you're going to get out of shepherd duty."

The accuracy of her statement left me feeling eerily exposed. "How did you—never mind. Look, the shepherd thing isn't for me. I don't have the temperament for it. I don't have patience for it. I don't have the passion for it. Give me tools, give me a battle, give me something to do, anything other than guarding these pathetic creatures for the rest of my life." I held the shepherd's staff away from my body, frustration covering my face.

Deborah's expression morphed into one of understanding. "Do what you want, Niklas, but you won't find what you ultimately desire by running off after a judge."

A gentle breeze passed between us.

"And what's that?"

"Purpose," she answered, and straightened my tunic. "My grandmother taught me a quote passed down in our family. 'True greatness in a man'—or a woman," she added with a smile, "'isn't measured by the deeds they accomplished, but by the decisions they make.'" Deborah walked over to the flock and knelt down next to them. "You can choose to leave them here, but that choice puts their lives at risk. It puts your family's livelihood at risk." She finished petting one of the lambs and started walking further into the fields, glancing over her shoulder. "Choose to be great."

I studied the flock for a long while. My disdain for them didn't lessen, and my phantom toe began to itch, but I saw them in a new light. They were under my care. My father had trusted me with the responsibility of guarding the most vulnerable aspect of our wealth. Maybe it meant something.

I clucked my voice several times, a trick Isaiah taught me. The mother sheep knew what the signal meant and rose to their feet, spurring their young lambs into action. They waited eagerly for me to set a course, and I began the journey back home, if not content, at least less embittered.

We had climbed the first hill when my brother Oz, a.k.a Golden Boy, a.k.a Job Stealer, came sprinting hard up the other side.

"Nik," he said, panting. "You need to get back home, now."

He reached me and motioned for my water flask. He took two long draughts of it and then continued.

"The judge...he's demanding to see you." He paused. "And he's upset."

Chapter 2

A judge had sent for me.

The news spurred me onward, and the journey back home flew by in a blur. I felt like a starry-eyed child, about to receive his first ride on the village mule. Judges represented all that was exciting about our nation's history. When one arose, the world trembled. While I was growing up, the entire village would sit at the elders' feet, awestruck as they recounted previous judges' exploits.

So what did he want from me? They had no typical operating procedure. Sometimes they acted alone. The tales of Shamgar, Son of Anath, were famous for their brevity. "He struck down six hundred Philistines with an ox prod. He too saved Israel." Talk about dual-purposing farm equipment.

Others would gather together smaller fighting forces, leading them into battle after battle, etching their victories into the holy writings of our people. Is that why the holy warrior had come, to raise up a new army to fight for the freedom of Israel?

The appearance of a judge inevitably meant one thing—someone was about to impersonate the Angel of Death with Israel's enemies. The Philistines wouldn't know what hit them. And if this man had indeed come to Bethlehem to begin a campaign against our sullied neighbors to the west, I wanted in. Father would understand, a veteran of past wars himself. When a judge mobilized for war, we needed all able-bodied men to rise to the call. If Dad's aspirations of my shepherding career met a swift end, well, it was an unfortunate but necessary casualty.

Then another possibility gave me pause. Some judges served a more internal objective, cleansing the unrighteous and evil from our own midst. Yahweh, our God, had given us this land hundreds of years ago, but our people regularly found themselves hedging their bets, secretly worshipping the deities of our neighboring countries, just in case one of those deities might protect them better. That never ended pleasantly—think death by boils meets swallowed by earthquake. While I didn't keep a trove of idol statues stashed under my bed, my religiosity paled in comparison to some of the more pious — cough, hypocritical, cough—residents of Bethlehem.

I entered the city through the north gate and found only one man standing at the entrance. While attacks on the walls of Bethlehem were exceptionally rare, normally at least three or four men guarded each gate. Most enjoyed the opportunity, an excuse to drink wine and talk with friends. Whatever ceremony the judge had in mind must have required the whole city.

Oz said that he would wait for me at our house, though, so I began winding my way through the narrow streets of Bethlehem, ruminating on the best way to be recruited onto Team Philistine Extermination.

"This task is going to get me killed!" a man sneered, his comment ripping me from my train of thought. He stood in the middle of the road cloaked in a dark brown robe, the back of his head facing me. Dusk had covered the street in layers of dark shadows, making it difficult to locate the man's companion.

"The only hiccup with that," he continued, speaking to the empty space in front of him and running his fingers through gray hair, "is our current leader would sooner turn me into a chew toy for his pets than permit me to perform another anointing!" He cocked his head to the side and then barked out a harsh laugh. "You're not the one who has to stand in front of the hyenas!"

I grimaced. The village had several old men like this, trapped in the memories of their pasts. Talking with them was a lesson in patience, if not utter futility. Better for both of us if I simply passed without notice.

I took several soft steps behind him before my ankle caught on a dowel, sending the large loom it was attached to clattering to the ground.

"Ahhh!" cried the elderly man. He whipped his body around to face me and simultaneously back-stepped. The two actions mixed poorly. The robe entangled his legs, causing him to tumble to the ground.

"Jireh, protect me!" he pleaded and raised a hand above his face, eyes frantically scanning every direction. Finding only me, relief washed over him, and he let out a deep sigh.

The man was older than I had first assumed. Spotted flesh hung loosely off his slender arms, and his wispy gray beard had a white streak running down the middle of it. He looked up, and as the last rays of sun shone down upon him, gray eyes locked on to mine.

"You look like a brain-addled heifer, standing there with your mouth open," he said gruffly, completely lucid. He waved me near. "Well, help me up. Don't they teach respect for your elders in this town?"

I scurried toward him and offered him my hand, and he grabbed my forearm. The strength of his grip shocked me—far more powerful than I would have expected anyone his age capable of. The moment we touched, his silvery eyes ignited with fire, and his hold on my arm doubled in pressure.

I gritted my teeth. Was this some kind of con? Often thieves would work in tandem with children or the elderly to catch their mark unaware. I swept my vision from left to right, expecting an accomplice to appear around a corner. None emerged, but the man pulled himself off the ground and dragged me close.

"So, him?" he asked, studying me.

I tried to pry his bony fingers off my wrist, but he held fast. "Him who?" I said, my voice cracking from fright.

"But he's a child," the man said, ignoring my plea and shaking his head. "He'll be slaughtered."

Slaughtered? Perfect, not only did I happen upon a loon of unnatural strength, I found the serial killer variety. If he had a knife...

The man paused and glanced down at my arm struggling to pull free. He blinked hard and snapped his head up, letting go. I stumbled back several feet and put my shoulder between us, clenching my fists.

"What was that?" I shouted and again surveyed the street. Though he was stronger than me, there was zero chance he could catch me in a footrace, and our house was only a block away. It was time to go.

A hand touched my shoulder from behind. His accomplice!

I spun defensively and discovered my second-oldest brother, Abin, standing behind me.

"A bit twitchy today, are we?" he accused, raising his eyebrows in amusement.

Abin was my favorite brother. Not nearly as uptight as Eliab, he had been my first teacher in the art of mischief. He shook his shaggy head as I regained my composure. "Everyone's waiting for you," he said, and he glanced over my shoulder. "You already met the judge. Perfect. He refused to begin, well, whatever he has planned until you got here."

I turned around in disbelief.

The ancient man walked up to me. "I'm Alvaro, son of Elkanah," he said, "the final judge of Israel."

Chapter 3

I gawked.

This senile, most likely psychotic grandfather, couldn't be the man our hopes rested on. Less than sixty seconds ago, he was arguing with an imaginary friend. I groped for Abin's arm, trying to catch his attention.

"I'm not insane," Alvaro said dismissively. "There's no need to discuss it with your brother."

I took a step back. How did he know what—?

"Because I do." He answered my question before I completed the thought.

The gawking began anew. "You can read my mind?"

"Ha, no!" he answered, laughing harshly. "I assure you, my own thoughts cause me more than enough grief without your adolescent, hormonally fueled musings plaguing me, too. My Master, however, does have that burden, and sometimes He gives me the abbreviated version."

"He's been at this all day," Abin said. "Answering people's questions before they ask them, telling obscure secrets. He's eccentric for certain, but Dad insists he's the real deal. Something about seeing him chop off a foreign dignitary's head."

"His Highness, King Agag," the judge muttered in disgust. "Bloated, insufferable goat." He straightened up. "Never mind. It is

29

past time we began the ceremony. Lead me back so we can get this over with."

Abin raised his eyebrows at me, his deep dimples showing amusement, and the three of us walked home in awkward silence.

I watched Alvaro out of the corner of my eye. If this man was truly the savior of our people, a supposed legendary judge, what hope did we have? The Philistines had stronger weaponry and vastly more experience in war. Without some supernatural factor to give us the upper hand, we'd be slaughtered. The judge was said to be that edge, but this man had seen enough winters to qualify us for a handicap.

Maybe the fabled stories of past judges were just that—fables.

We reached the courtyard of the house, and my entire family waited in the square. Father stood in the center, telling a story to mother and my younger sisters. "And you know who's buried in that cemetery, right?"

All of my brothers and I answered in unison. "Dead people."

Father chuckled. "Told that one before, have I?" He ran his fingers through his brown beard, now sprinkled with streaks of gray. Lean, taut muscle covered his arms and legs, and the blue cord braided into his hair showed him to be one of the elders of Bethlehem. Corny as he was—and he ruled the Kingdom of Corny—everyone respected him. He was a war hero in his own time.

Abin joined his new bride, Rachel, and the rest of my brothers stood together. Isaiah played with the new five-piece puzzle box I had bought him in apology for the beating he had taken from the Philistines. Only Eliab sat apart from the rest of my family, sitting cross-legged on a mat and talking quietly to his wife, Sari. Even reclining, Eli appeared massive, his hulking axe resting against a wall. Someone like him should be leading our nation. People would follow him. I would follow him.

Three years ago, he had attempted just that.

In response to the never-ending terrorism of the Philistines, Eliab and about a dozen other young men from our village created their own makeshift militia. For months, they repelled groups of bandits who ventured too close to our borders. The group made quite the reputation for themselves, with my brother leading the charge, the

Bear of Bethlehem.

However, one night during their patrol, the Philistines laid a trap. A treacherous scout reported there were half a dozen horse thieves lurking in a nearby cave. In reality, it hid over five times that number of Philistine soldiers. A horrific fight for survival ensued, and Eliab returned with only two other men—my brothers Abin and Sham. The body of our cousin Abraham, Eli's best friend, along with ten others, was never found.

Abraham's corpse was not the only thing lost in the cave. Every ounce of courage disappeared from my brother that night. Now he refused to entertain any mention of an uprising, accepting a life under the heel of the barbarians' brutality.

Clenching my teeth, I turned to the elderly judge. I refused to cower. "Oz said you wanted to see me. How can I help?"

"He's eager," Alvaro said smugly, again mocking me to his invisible companion. He must have noticed the skewed looks on our faces, because after sniffing loudly, he answered my question. "I've been tasked with performing a ceremony, and your participation will be required. Privacy was essential, so I ordered the rest of the village elders to host an impromptu harvest prayer for your city. It should give us more than enough time."

"A ceremony?" my brother Sham asked.

Alvaro nodded and shuffled to the far side of the courtyard, where a young ram was tied to the post, loaded down with various gear. He pulled off the pack saddle, a wooden cage on one side and an earthen, plastered horn tied to the other. He carried both of them to the center of the villa and knelt down on the ground. Opening the top of the cage, the judge removed a white dove. He stroked it gently, pulling it close and murmuring something calming into its ear. Then, without warning, he snapped its neck. The bird spasmed and went lifeless, and he tenderly placed it on the ground.

Then came the weird stuff. He unsheathed a serrated, ivory-handled, ceremonial blade and proceeded to saw the entire dove in two, from skull to tail. Cleaning and preparing hunted game was one thing, but this was a bloody mess. The action caught the attention of everyone in the courtyard, and my father stood up and moved close to the judge. The gruesome job finished, Alvaro took the two halves of the dove and placed them three feet apart.

My dad stared at the scene. "A covenant?"

Alvaro nodded.

Color fled Father's cheeks, and he turned to my mother. "Take the young ones to the town square and wait for us to join you." His hands began shaking, and only stopped when he grasped them tightly around the belt of his robe.

I had never seen him scared. His positive demeanor was always unflappable. Whatever the judge had in mind terrified him, and his fear infected the rest of the family.

Mother didn't ask any questions but quickly gathered my younger sisters and the wives, ushering them out the front gate.

"But mommy," Yeva, my six-year-old sister, said, "Daddy promised to—"

"Hush," my mother replied gently. She glanced apprehensively over her shoulder. "He'll be right behind us."

After they had disappeared, Dad called the rest of us to stand by him and then gestured for Alvaro to continue whatever strange ceremony had shaken him.

"What you are about to witness," the judge began, "requires the utmost secrecy. The fate of our very nation may depend on it. Should the wrong people find out about what transpires here, you, your whole family, and quite possibly this entire village could be put at risk.

"Since the times of our earliest forefathers, our people have had a way of entering into a covenant, a binding contract. An animal is sacrificed, and its remains are placed in two portions apart from one another. Then, all those who wish to participate in the agreement must walk between the two halves, signifying that if they break the covenant, they agree to forfeit their lives in the same manner."

He paused to let us reflect on his words, the brutal sacrifice fresh on our minds. My stomach twisted and tensed. What could possibly be this important?

"If you stay," Alvaro continued, "until the day of my death, you must swear never to speak of this event to anyone, except for myself or another member of my priestly order. Even discussion among yourselves could have unexpected consequences." He took a deep breath and walked through the remnants of the dove. "I ask you now, who will enter this covenant with me?"

My stomach did somersaults, and both halves of my backside clenched. Alvaro gave us no indication what this contract would entail, what the ceremony would ask of us. Who agrees to promise before knowing what it is? I turned to my father, hoping for some guidance, but found only more uncertainty.

"I'll stay," said a voice that surprised us all. Isaiah awkwardly stepped forward, still healing from his injuries, and slowly shuffled through the ritual pathway.

Pride covered Father's face at my brother's boldness, and he too walked between the remains. Emboldened, I, along with all of my brothers, lined up and followed after them. Standing on the opposite side of the courtyard, together we waited for whatever event required such harsh penalties.

Alvaro knelt down and picked up the knife. "Niklas, step forward."

Sacrificial lamb! The old goat planned on *sacrificing* me! I took several steps back, and my brothers surrounded me, placing themselves between the madman and me.

The judge glanced down at his knife and realized what we suspected. He sheathed the blade and stuck it back in the saddlebag. In turn, he picked up the ceramic horn. "Harmless," he said, a little too lightly.

The hedge of my brothers relaxed, and I cautiously approached the judge.

A cork plugged the horn, and as he removed it the scent of curry mixed with cinnamon and garlic filled the air. "You will be safe," his assurance quiet and sympathetic. "I promise."

My head gave a noncommittal twitch.

Alvaro began. "Elohim!" he shouted, and suddenly his voice boomed unnaturally deep, like the last rumbling of far-off thunder. "You who created the Earth and all the heavens, the stewards of your creation beseech thee, come and give us your blessing!"

At the last word, the ground beneath our home shook, pottery tumbling over and smashing on the ground.

"Baal's fat hindquarter!" Abin shouted over the ram braying

loudly in the corner.

I dropped to one knee, trying to steady myself. Then the earth stood still.

"Adonai!" the judge's voice bellowed again. "You humbled the Pharaoh of Egypt with plague after plague! You command the Angel of Death himself. Come and grant us your protection!"

The entire courtyard went pitch black. Not the mere dark of the dead of night, but utter, inescapable nothingness enveloped everything. Shuffling and murmurs floated from my family's direction, but I was too afraid even to try to move toward them.

"Yahweh," the judge's voice spoke softly into the void, "your people, your children, ask you to come and grace us with your presence."

Light returned to the courtyard, and a cool wind stroked my cheek.

"Sovereign Lord, we ask you to bless this anointing." Alvaro dipped his finger into the horn, took it out, and placed it on my forehead.

After the earthquake and blacking out of the sun, my expectations of what came next were fairly high—maybe a tornado combined with a lightning storm. Instead, the climax of the ceremony consisted of scented oil sliding down my forehead and dripping into my eye.

Then everything around me froze. My family stood together like a garden of statues, rigid, not even breathing. The goat in the corner looked as if it had been stuffed. Only Alvaro and I remained moving.

The old geezer glanced around the courtyard, more bored than intrigued. "Apparently, we need a moment to be alone."

Shock covered my face, and my eyes went wide in disbelief, looking to the ambivalent judge for answers.

He shrugged. "You do this long enough, and eventually you just stop asking questions and go with it."

Oil tickled my cheek as it ran down my face. I rubbed it off and asked, "What did you do to me?"

Before answering, Alvaro located a stool against the north wall and sat down, beckoning me to draw near. "You have been chosen to be a part of something much larger than any one person. For centuries, Yahweh has selected specific individuals to champion the causes of our nation."

"Judges," I said, blood suddenly surging through my veins. "Like you."

The judge nodded wearily. "Judges are one way He's acted, but we are by no means the first. Study the history of our ancestors and you see all kinds of people appointed to various tasks. Nomads become the father of nations; murderers become freedom fighters," he gestured toward himself. "Peasants become judges."

My eyes went wide. "So you're saying I'm a—"

"You're not a judge," Alvaro cut me off. "The time of judges has reached its conclusion. The final sentence will be written when I take my last breath. No, you will be something else entirely."

"Something else?"

He paused with his head to the side, listening to the unheard voice. "For now, you will be Israel's protector."

Thoughts of glory immediately flourished in my mind. I had hoped to be drafted into Alvaro's army, his movement, but this was so much better. I would be the hero.

"So I'm going to fight the Philistines?" I asked eagerly.

"Defeating the Philistines will be part of the role, yes."

"All right," I said, flexing my fingers, "and I'll get, what, something similar to the supernatural strength of Samson?" The guy once collapsed a whole building with his bare hands.

The judge looked up into the sky before answering. "No."

Huh. "Then what, a few hundred brave warriors to fight beside me?"

He again checked the heavens. "Apparently that's not happening either." He tilted his neck, listening. "At least, not for a while."

I paused, unease growing in my stomach. "How am I going to fight them then?"

The judge opened his palms apologetically. "That I don't know. Personally, I would recommend getting some practice in with a sword, but that's not the hard part of your mission."

"Single-handedly defeating the sworn enemies of our people isn't the difficult part?"

"No," he answered. "Unfortunately, those who would bring ruin to our nation don't exist solely outside our borders. A traitor among our people threatens to tear down Israel. Your primary mission right now is to find him and stop him."

It took several seconds for me to process everything wrong with what he just said. "You want me to find one traitor out of *literally tens of thousands of Israelites,* and then thwart his villainous plot to destroy our nation?"

The judge rested his back against the wall, nodding. "I'm told schemes are sort of your specialty."

I blinked several times. "But can't your boss" —I flicked my nose upward—"you know, just tell us who the traitor is and get it over with?"

"He certainly could," Alvaro said amicably, "but for some reason, He enjoys having us help in these sort of things. Lord, literally, only knows why."

One last question poked at my brain. "And if I fail?"

For the first time, the old man's eyes didn't show irritation, belittlement, or disgust. All that remained was tired sympathy. "Israel will be gravely wounded."

"Oh," I said simply.

"Bethlehem will be destroyed," he continued with the dire prophecy, "and..."

I blinked at him, knowing only one thing could be worse than my hometown being destroyed. The only question was if it would be one of them or all of them.

"...your whole family will either be slaughtered or enslaved." I swallowed hard. All of them.

Chapter 4

The old geezer's words hung in front of my face like a dark specter. Terror replaced any excitement left in my body, and it took sustained effort not to throw up the last remnants of my lunch. If I failed this assignment, my entire family would pay the price? How was that fair? I turned solemnly toward the men who remained in their frozen state. My goofy father, always ready to tackle any problem with a lame joke. My brothers, simultaneously my best friends and my biggest rivals. I shuddered, refusing even to think about what might become of my mom and my sisters.

Whenever I daydreamed of being the hero, it always centered on the glory and the fame. Sure, there was risk, but I controlled the fantasy, always finding the opportunity to courageously snatch victory from the jaws of certain defeat. Now my family's very lives depended on my success. I didn't want the responsibility. I'd just screw it up.

"Take it back," I pleaded.

The judge met my eyes. "The anointing?"

"Yes. Take it back. Give the job to someone else, someone with more experience, more" —I struggled to find the right words—" anything. There has to be someone more capable. This is ridiculous! I'm fifteen."

The old goat literally laughed in my face. "I know the feeling. I

37

got picked at eight. In truth, my mother made the deal for me when I was conceived, so in a way, you could say I've been stuck with this since birth."

"So, you get it. This is a bad idea. Just give the mission to someone else."

He shook his head. "That wouldn't work. It's kind of a permanent thing. The only way to remove it comes complete with a set of personal burial clothes."

I stared blankly ahead. Talk about a harsh severance package. Alvaro stood up and offered me his seat. I lumbered toward it and sank down—defeated. How in the world, or at least the country, was I supposed to find one traitor? Currently, I was spending more time with sheep than people, and somehow I doubted the conspirator intended to just reveal himself one day: "Tada! I'm the big baddie you're looking for."

Without some kind of assistance, there's no way this would work. I glanced up at the judge, and a thought began blooming in my mind.

"You could help," I said, my words spilling out faster. "You said you're also anointed or whatever. Plus, you have all kinds of experience. Together we have a shot to figure this out."

The old man rubbed his crooked nose. "He's just as bad as the Gibeath brat," he muttered. "I'm retired." It took a moment to realize he wasn't talking to me. He eventually answered my request directly. "This is your assignment, your role. It's your task alone. Trust me, I wouldn't be any help."

"So that's it?" I asked, dumbfounded. "You're just going to offer me no assistance with the fate of my hometown and my whole family at stake?"

He bit his lip, and his eyebrows furled in confusion. "Follow the music," he said absentmindedly. "It will help."

"*Follow the music?*" I repeated. "What does that mean?"

Alvaro shrugged his shoulders. "I have no idea, but I assume you'll understand soon enough." He took a deep breath before looking at the sun. "But I must leave before they get here."

"Before who gets here?" I stood up in frustration. "Come on! Now you're just being intentionally vague."

"I really am," he agreed with a broad smile before his face became more serious. "But remember your covenant; do not discuss this with anyone except for either myself or someone else in my order." He glanced down at the dismembered pieces of the bird. "Remember the consequences if you do."

Then he clapped his hands. Time resumed for everyone else in the courtyard.

My family snapped back to life, shocked at how the judge and I had moved from our original spots while they were frozen. Alvaro made his way over to his ram and quickly re-saddled it.

"What happened?" Sham asked.

"What needed to happen," Alvaro replied. "Jesse, thank you for your hospitality. I needn't stress the importance of keeping quiet about this event."

And without another word, piece of advice, or tiny, minuscule hint of what I should plan on doing next, he left.

My family shared my disbelief, but without the small burden of knowing that if I failed in my obscure, cryptic, essentially impossible mission of uncovering one traitor in our entire kingdom, the best case scenario was they would all get a quick death.

Forget this. The old man was going to give me more answers, whether he liked it or not.

Clenching my teeth, I dashed out the door and down the Bethlehem's main road after the judge. Scanning the side streets, I saw the hindquarter of his ram turning a corner.

Then I heard it.

A melodic, piercing chord of a harp erupted right behind me, stopping my pursuit mid stride. The note lingered on the air for several moments, and I whipped my head back to find its source but found the alley empty. Where in the world did that come from? Whatever—a much more pressing mystery drove me, and I continued my pursuit of the enigmatic judge.

"Let go of me!" a man's voice pleaded loudly in the opposite direction. "You will not enter the city!"

Bloody mercy, the Philistines? Were they attacking?

Every fiber in my body wanted to chase down the judge and force him to explain what he had done to me. Yet the cry for help reverberated in my ears, poking my conscience. What value was answers if they required me to abandon the city?

"Burn it all!" I spun around and sprinted after the voice, which soon combined with several other voices in a heated exchange.

I passed under the city's north gate, searching for the distressed man, when an arm snatched out and grabbed hold of my shoulder. The sudden redirection of my momentum sent me tumbling to the ground. Tensing up for an attack, I found five men, each holding a long knife, standing over me and scowling through their thick, untrimmed beards.

"In a hurry to rescue this pathetic excuse for a guard?" the one wearing a white cap asked, his accent distinctly Israelite. "We found this titan of a sentry sleeping on duty." His compatriots laughed, and he motioned for me to get back up.

Rising warily to my feet, I noticed the town guard from earlier slouched against the wall, abashed.

"Who are you?" I growled.

"Wardens of our king's army," the man in the white cap said.

My head tilted slightly. "Israel doesn't have an army." We barely had a king.

"We do now," he responded, pointing to the green armband each man wore, "and we have come in search of more recruits. As of this morning, our nation is at war."

Chapter 5

"We're not discussing it!" Father said, emphasizing each word with a wave of his hand.

"If we could just talk—" I began before he cut me off again.

"Enough, we've already gone over this. You have work to do, I have work to do, we put your sister Dara to work, and she can't even talk yet. She thinks separating the shaft from the wheat is a game." He pointed to the door. "Go back to the town square and get another bucket of water for your mother."

My knuckles went white as my fingers pressed against the shepherd staff. The town square was the last place I wanted to go.

I stomped out of the house, slamming the staff into the ground with every step. Again, my father had refused to discuss anything about Alvaro's ceremony, adding a fresh brown log to the fortress of crap that made up my current life.

You know those days when fate graciously decides to bestow on you every horrible, possible event into one unruly mess? Welcome to my last three weeks.

I wake up every morning to see my family, only to immediately remember that they're all as good as dead if I don't somehow find a random traitor among tens of thousands of people without so much as a hint of where to start looking.

What little energy not wasted on that super-fun responsibility went to worrying about my brothers Sham, Abin, and Eliab, all who had been drafted into our "king's" new army. Any feelings of glorious battles quickly evaporated after the first injured soldier came back to Bethlehem missing a leg. Now every time I pictured my brothers returning home, it included them minus a limb or being carried on a stretcher with a burial cloth covering their body.

Oh, and there was a good chance I was going insane—like Grandpa after he had a stroke and started talking to our housecat as if it was his uncle Adam nuts.

As I approached the town square, the soft plucking of the harp strings drifted through the narrow roads of Bethlehem. After weeks of hearing its melody, I no longer checked to locate its exact source, nor asked if anyone else heard its music. It became quickly apparent that only I could hear the harp. The whole situation oscillated between mildly annoying and categorically creepy.

Since the night with Alvaro, at least once a day the melody began. My only small solace was the judge's advice to "follow the music," but heaven forbid he tell me what that actually meant. The music would last for anywhere from a few seconds to an hour, but it always eventually subsided—until today. The music began during my first water run at dawn. Six hours and eight return trips later, the blasted melody continued. Never had its notes been this distracting or intrusive.

A growl escaped my lips as I entered the town square, where the cherry on top for this lousy day waited for me.

A captured Philistine assassin sat with his legs out, bound tightly to the olive tree in the center of the village. He stared at me, smirking.

My hands tightened around the shepherd staff. Several creative ways to remove his smile crossed my mind. Most involved something sharper than the blunt piece of wood in my hands.

I passed him on my trip to the well. All the while the harp's melody played louder. The prisoner's dark eyes tracked me.

Two days ago, he and a trio of other bandits snuck into Bethlehem under the cover of night. One of the town guards saw them, and we eventually captured him, but not before they murdered five of our men and we put down all three of his accomplices.

Forty hours vulnerable to the elements had left his body worn, his skin blistered and peeling, his eyes bloodshot and crusty. His face was unshaven, and on his cheek there was a distinct clover-shaped burn mark, almost as if he had been branded. Yet my attention was drawn to his arms. We had taken no chances with his escape, tying the heavy flax rope so tight that his skin had begun to chafe; the first signs of lime green infection showed around his bindings.

He called out from behind me, through a grated, dry voice. "First time seeing a real man, huh?"

My back tensed. *Keep walking; it's not worth it.*

"Come untie me, runt, and I promise to let you live after my people burn this godforsaken gutter village to ash."

I slammed the staff harder against the ground, but I refused to give him the satisfaction of a response.

"At least your family would have one surviving heir!"

An image flashed through my mind—the corpses of my three oldest brothers scattered across a smoky battlefield. I turned and stalked toward him, teeth bared as all my frustrations over the last three weeks boiled to the surface.

"Ha, finally wizened up have—"

My staff swung like a scythe right into the diseased wound. His voice cried out in agony, and I ground the wood deeper into his bicep.

Words failed to convey the heat of my anger, so I simply left him there whimpering to himself. The harp strummed again, louder and twanging harshly, but I ignored it. It could play for the rest of my life because I'd cut off my ears off before I gave that beast another second of my time.

Yet if this continued, cutting off my ears may be the best scenario. Too much was at stake. The answers I needed wouldn't be found in Bethlehem, and the only one who could give them to me was Alvaro. I needed to find the judge.

It wasn't until I walked into the courtyard of our home that I realized I had forgotten the water. I cursed underneath my breath and was debating whether to head back when my goody-two-shoes brother Oz popped out of the house. The war had temporarily stalled my parents' plans to send him to my uncle for carpentry.

"Niklas," he said, "Dad just sent me to grab you. He wants you, Isaiah, and me to get the sheep out to pasture."

I opened my mouth to argue but stopped short of saying anything. Instead, a sly smile crossed my mouth. "Sure, just let me go grab my stuff."

***

Oz called back to me from the front of the herd. "Another flock must have come through here already. There's not nearly enough grass for our group to graze."

I feigned surprise, already knowing full well we wouldn't have been able to use this spot for pasture. Two days ago another shepherd from town had mentioned his flock had already been here this week.

I relayed the message to Isaiah at the rear of our group. His shoulders sank, looking like a chastened puppy. He still limped from the assault from my botched attempt at the swords, and this news would require us to travel at least another four miles before heading home.

Since the war began, Mother insisted shepherding required no less than three of us in the field at a time. "As long as King Erik finds it prudent to send half of my sons off to an asinine war, I'm sure as Pharaoh's overfed bottom going to protect the others."

At first, we thought it a case of oversensitive mothering—the closest front of the war campaign was fifteen miles away—but after hearing the accounts of the Philistine's night raid and attending our guards' funerals, we complied without protest.

Erik, or King Erik as he was now being called, was still a mystery to most of our tribe. A few years ago, he started gathering men to repel larger Philistine invasions, and according to my father, he had several victories under his belt. Yet to call him a king seemed like a bit of an over-statement. Three years ago, Dad had taken a few of us to his "fortress." It consisted of a large farm house with most of his followers living in tents around the perimeter. A war leader, maybe, but when I thought of a king, my mind pictured castles with fortified walls, not farmland with sheep for fences.

Isaiah and I waded to the front of the herd to discuss how we wanted to proceed next.

Oz stood on top of a bluff, surveying the fields below. "We have two options: take the path east and travel through the hill country, or head north and cross through the plains."

For my plan to work, it was now or never. "We should head north. It'll be further, but the terrain will be a lot easier for Isaiah to travel."

My brother sniffed the air. "The humidity's rising. If we're about to be caught by a storm, the hills will offer better protection."

Oz was right about the weather, but my goal lay to the north, fifteen miles north more accurately, to Ramah, the village where Alvaro lived. My plan was to slip away and leave my brothers once we were closer, just before we double backed to head home.

I swept my hands toward the sky. "There aren't any clouds yet, so worst case if a storm does hit, we'll already be heading back to town."

It took a moment, but my brother nodded. "Let's go north, but we'd best do it quickly."

***

Thunder cracked, and another sheep bolted from the herd.

Rain assaulted us from every angle, making it impossible to see how far the ewe had run off. I waved a beleaguered hand toward my brothers, gesturing that I would pursue the fleeing member of our flock. Using my forearms as feeble eye coverings, I ventured into the dark, gray field in search of the runaway, knowing I would never hear the end of this tangled fiasco.

An hour and a half later, the lost member of our flock trailed next to me, and the storm had finally started to wane. Water still drizzled on top of us, but at least the sheep had calmed down. My brothers had corralled the flock under the protection of a massive sycamore tree.

Exhausted and battered, I glared at Oz. "Don't even say—"

A ray of bright white lightning illuminated the branches of the tree. Thunder boomed directly above us, followed by a loud crack. A thick tree limb fell, clipping my brother Oz's shoulder and then pinning his leg to the ground.

"Baal's fat hindquarter!" he shouted in pain.

The startled sheep scattered from the cover of the sycamore, and both Isaiah and I rushed to our brother. The branch weighed a ton, but we managed to lift it up enough to pull a still cursing Oz from its clutches.

The gash on his leg ran from his upper thigh down to his kneecap. I fought a grimace when I realized the wound was deep enough to see the bone. We could bandage it, but he needed medical attention as soon as possible, because either due to bleeding out or infection, the wound could kill him. His eyes rose to mine, a hint of humor in them despite the dire situation.

I stood to quickly retrieve the flight risk members of the herd so we could leave to get him medical treatment but paused as his gaze stayed on me. "Just say it."

A weary smile peeked out across Oz's lips. "Told you so."

Then he passed out.

Chapter 6

The journey to the closest village, Nob, took five hours, giving the guilt of critically injuring two of my brothers within the same month plenty of time to really pummel my conscience. The trip was miserable for everyone. We bandaged Oz's leg in a ripped-off section of my cloak, and Isaiah and I carried his often unconscious body over our shoulders. Every five minutes required me to leave them at the front of the flock to spur on the rest of the herd, an exhausting, one-man game of leapfrog.

Two of Nob's town guards met us at their gate, but instead of coming to help, they gripped their weapons tighter and eyed us warily. The war had everyone on edge, suspicious.

"We need to find a town healer," Isaiah told them through pained breaths and then explained the situation. The trek had clearly pushed his own lingering wounds beyond any definition of healthy.

The older guard shook his white frosted beard, a little more sympathetic. "All of our healers were drafted for the war campaign."

"What about Matthias?" the younger guard asked.

"Huh?" his partner said, biting his lower lip. "Matthias is our head priest," he explained, "and he stores the village's healing ointments. If nothing else, he may be able to give you something for the pain."

A priest? I grated my teeth. Burn it all. I would almost rather go

47

find some Philistines for medical treatment.

Don't get me wrong. I have nothing against God personally. I believe in Him. He's certainly done some pretty epic stuff in our nation's history—the plagues in Egypt, the parting of an ocean, He even did this one trick where fire rained down from heaven. However, He also has dished out some pretty harsh punishments for those who got in His way. He once sent a brood of venomous snakes against our people simply because they complained about the lack of variety in their lunches. So I made sure to attend the religious festivals, drop off a sacrifice, and otherwise stay out of His way. Live and let live, so to speak.

But the people He chose to be His priests, yikes. Are you an uptight, self-righteous, pompous blowhard? Then do I have a job for you. Seeking a priest's help always included a long-winded homily about how your own errors brought you to the point of desperation. Mind you, my own dumb choices had gotten us into this spot, but that's just coincidence. We could have been helping an old lady cross the street and still gotten chastised.

Yet our options were limited, so we'd have to hope for an abbreviated lecture before receiving the medicine.

The two guards pointed us in the direction of his ceremonial tent, promising to watch our flock until one of us returned for them.

A block from our destination, a young child's shrill scream rang out, followed by two shorter cries of distress.

The three of us glanced at one another, and Oz jerked his head for me to run ahead. Terror flowed through my blood as I sprinted down the road, imagining a dozen different scenarios—all involving another ruthless surprise attack by the Philistines.

A young girl, seven or eight years old and wearing a faded purple sundress, ran into the street checking for her pursuer, but then foolhardily darted back through the same archway, out of sight. I passed the last alley and came into the courtyard, seeing eight small children running frantically around an older, wide-bellied man, wearing a turquoise priest's robe. He took off after one of the boys and the child screamed in delight, tossing a white cloth to one of his smaller female accomplices, ensuring the game of keep-away stayed alive.

The priest spun around, sweat pouring from his bald head and breathing deep, but grinning ear to ear. "You win," he said, waving his hand limply in defeat. He noticed me in the entrance to the courtyard as the children hollered in victory all around him. "Would you like to take my place for the next game? I think I need a breather."

The original purpose of our visit flooded back into my mind. "My brother...he needs help."

***

Three hours later, I sat cross-legged in the center of the priest Matthias's large tent, exhausted from fencing in our flock for the night. Isaiah and Oz slept soundly in the corner. They both had received treatment from the priest, apparently free of any condescending lectures. I watched the holy man kneeling next to his ten-year-old son, Abiathar, murmuring quiet bedtime prayers.

He didn't fit any of the stereotypes. Mud caked the hems of his robe; blood had dried on his arms from treating Oz, and his white beard contained enough debris to create a small bird's nest. Yahweh required absolute cleanliness during his ceremonies, so most holy men insisted on maintaining absurd hygiene standards wherever they went, as if at any moment, a person may rush into the room, requiring an immediate sacrifice.

Matthias finished the prayers, and cautiously stood up, careful not to wake his now sleeping son. He crossed over to my side of the tent, poured himself an ample portion of wine, and sat down against the pillar next to me, his large belly serving as a personal table for his drink.

"Quite a day you've had," he said with a gentle, tired smile.

I nodded once, rolling my eyes. And here comes the lecture.

"Times are dangerous," the priest continued. "You did well getting your brothers to safety."

You did well? My face scrunched together, confused.

"Had you not pushed through and gotten them here" —his face crinkled up— "well, there's no use worrying about that particular what-if."

I waited a good minute before responding. "The last time I met a priest, he cornered me for two hours to explain how the misfortune of my broken leg was directly caused by—how did he say it—'my insufferable, immature, irreverent, blasphemous, attitude problem.'"

A deep, good-natured chuckle rippled through the old man's body. "I imagine our forefather Job saw misfortune slightly differently."

"Job?"

He waved his hand, dismissing the subject. "A story for another time. Needless to say, the link between our choices and the successes and failures in our lives is not nearly as simple as some of my brethren would have us believe." He gulped down a generous swig from his cup.

I surveyed the rest of his tent, trying to find more clues to figure out our host. He'd divided the space into two sections. The back portion had been set aside for his living arrangements and the front for his priestly duties. Many of the objects were familiar; ceremonial bowls and knives, colorful sacrificial garments, and scrolls littered across a long table. My gaze swept over the pillar he rested against, an intricate etching carved into its wood. I squinted and made out what looked like the stump of a tree engulfed in flames.

Matthias followed my gaze. "A sigil for the Followers of the Voice."

"Which is…?"

"A group of priests founded by Alvaro. He thought it prudent in these…," he paused, searching for the right word, "complicated times to organize men to pray for wisdom directly from the source."

My mind snapped to attention like a pulled back tree branch. "Alvaro!" I shouted, before remembering the three people already asleep in the tent. I quickly held up my hand in apology before continuing in a whisper. "You're in Alvaro's order?"

He raised his eyebrows in amusement. "I am. You've met the old goat, then?"

I bit my bottom lip, torn on what to do. Alvaro had given me permission to discuss the ceremony with others in his brotherhood, and now with two brothers nursing injuries, sneaking off to see the judge wouldn't be happening anytime soon. Yet years of experience told me not to confide in priests. They'd eventually turn everything you revealed to them against you.

Still, this may be the best and only chance I had to figure out how to accomplish this asinine mission. "I met him," I said hesitantly, "briefly."

"Alvaro's a unique one, for sure. He once came to Nob, and I kid you not, spent the first three days singing lullabies to a sick goat. Half the town thought he had finally lost it. The next day, though, he held a ceremony for the city's crops, and that afternoon, rain we had waited two months for came pouring down."

"So he does a lot of ceremonies?" I asked.

"A lot would be a stretch, but they're not particularly rare. Did you see one recently?"

I couldn't help but chuckle. "Yeah, I saw one."

"What kind? A guilt offering? He's been doing a lot of those lately." He brought the cup to his lips to take another deep drink.

Here we go. "He called it an anointing."

The priest coughed down his wine. "What! On whom?"

Our eyes met.

"Me."

Matthias took my statement in, slowly putting his drink down and rising to his feet. He began pacing back and forth. "I had heard Erik and Alvaro were in disagreement, but to have another anointing take place..." His words trailed off.

"Erik?" I asked. "As in King Erik?"

"Yes," the man answered absentmindedly, still in his own thoughts. "Alvaro anointed him king almost ten years ago."

I coughed. "'Anointed him king?'"

The priest returned to his seat, holding up his hand for me to wait while he finished off his drink. "I'll explain everything I can, but first, tell me exactly what happened."

I recounted the events as quickly as I could, Matthias interrupting me every few minutes to clarify specific details.

"And Alvaro said you were to be Israel's protector?"

My head nodded.

He reclined back, intrigued amusement covering his face. "Fascinating."

I spoke through gritted teeth. "Did you miss the part where if I don't uncover the traitor, everyone I love dies?"

The grin vanished from his face. "Apologies, I imagine that burden has been weighing quite heavily on you."

Several creative, expletive-laden affirmations sat on the tip of my tongue, but my exact reply instead was, "It's been on my mind."

The priest took a deep breath. "Did Alvaro give you any specific timeline as to when you needed to find the spy?"

"No."

His head bobbed up and down. "Then I have good news. Yahweh isn't in the habit of distributing hopeless challenges to his people. When you need to find the traitor, it will become clear, and He will give you the means to stop him."

I let that comment sink in. "Really?"

His smile returned. "Really."

An unseen burden disappeared off my shoulders. My family wasn't doomed. I had time.

"Until then," Matthias finished, "you can just sit back and wait."

My lips begun to curl upward when a single note of a harp erupted in the tent. *Oh yeah, that.* "There's one more thing," I began and then told him about the harp and Alvaro's final piece of advice.

"Follow the music," the priest repeated softly. "And you hear it all the time?"

I shook my head, rubbing the back of my neck. "No, it comes and goes." My mind trailed back to this morning with the Philistine.

"What?" Matthias asked.

I hesitated to tell him but grunted when I admitted the necessity. "Bethlehem captured a Philistine a few days ago. We have him bound up in the center of town. Ever since this morning, though, my mind has been drawn back to a wound around his arms." I grimaced. "The bloody harp wouldn't shut up around him."

"Fascinating," the priest muttered again to himself, staring through me for several moments. "My suggestion is to follow Alvaro's advice and see where the music guides you. Yahweh speaks to each of his chosen avatars differently. Apparently, this is His way of communicating with you."

My mouth hung open for a second. "So you're saying" —my head jerked upward uncomfortably—"He's the one sending the music?"

"Indeed."

An image of venomous snakes swarming all over me flashed across my mind. "And if I don't follow it?"

The priest breathed deep. "Then when the time comes to find the traitor, you may not be equipped to stop him."

My response took a long time. I was too angry to even say the words. Finally, I muttered, "You think I should help the Philistine, don't you?"

Matthias nodded.

"You realize if anyone from Bethlehem sees me with him, it could be seen as treason?" I argued.

"They could kill me."

The priest's eyes twinkled, not particularly concerned.

I kicked the ground with my foot, wondering if there was a way to wash anointings off.

Chapter 7

The next morning, Matthias pulled me aside just before we departed for home, his eyebrows furrowed.

"One last thing: do not, under any circumstances, let King Erik discover Alvaro anointed you. His mental stability isn't great at the best of times, but if he hears about what happened, Erik will see it as a threat to his power. He'll kill you."

My mouth hung open for several seconds.

"Keep a low profile and you'll be fine," the priest assured me, before patting the donkey he loaned us for Oz to ride.

Fantastic. I'll just trade in the apprehension about my family's impending death for the joy of waiting for my own impending execution, this new thought being the perfect companion for a long trip home.

The journey was uneventful, but Mother's face turned a new shade of purple when she saw my brother's injury. Ducking out of the sight before she could heave more blame on my shoulders, I took a small bottle from our home cabinet and went to the center of town.

The Philistine remained bound to the tree, but in the twenty-four hours since last seeing him, his condition had deteriorated, severely. The clover-shaped burn mark on his cheeks had grown a pale, almost transparent color, and blue veins could be seen crisscrossing his face from across the courtyard. His lips were cracked and split, and dried blood trailed down into his patchy beard. With his head hung low, his glazed eyes didn't even glance up at me until I knelt down beside him. The lyre's familiar melody rang out.

He slowly blinked at me twice, before he growled, "Kill me."

I took time with my response. "Why?"

A sudden surge of energy rippled through him, and he strained against the thick bindings, crying out as his infected arms rubbed against the rope. "Cowards, every one of you," he shouted, but even such a short sentence burned out his strength, each word growing quieter and hoarser. "Any Philistine would have killed you the second we had a chance."

"I believe you."

Untying the pouch I had taken from the house, my fingers found two items, a sheathed knife and the small corked bottle.

The prisoner's gaze locked onto the knife, and desperate longing filled his eyes. "Do it...please."

I looked over my shoulder, double-checking that the courtyard was still empty. If anyone saw what I was about to do, I'd most likely be charged with treason, so if I was going to go through with this, it had to be now—and it had to be quick.

I unsheathed the knife and placed it against his torso. *This is so idiotic.*

I shoved the blade between the bindings and his left arm, prying the rope away from his body. His screams of agony exploded in my ears, while the rank odor from the festering wound assaulted my nostrils. I tilted my head away and quickly uncorked the bottle, pouring a small amount of the medicinal numbing ointment onto the infection. His howling abruptly shifted to a dull, euphoric groan, breathing deeply. His eyes rolled back into his head.

I removed the blade and stood back up, again checking to make sure no one saw me.

A full minute later, the prisoner finally looked up at me. "Why?"

Still unaware of the answer myself, I turned and left him there.

Two days later, the Israeli army came and took him away. Neither of us got our answer, but as I walked home, new sets of melodic notes pierced the air, finality in their sound as they drifted off, leaving me in peace.

I glanced up at the sky. "Fine," I said aloud, "let's see where this goes."

***

"Pharaoh's ugly stepsister!" I shouted.

Have I mentioned how much I hate sheep?

After spending three hours shoveling endless manure out of their pen, how did they thank me? By biting my bloody finger! They already took a toe; how many more appendages do they need?

Gladys, the usually benign culprit, bleated loudly. I knew what she wanted. A nursing mother ate twice as much as typical ewe.

"I hear you, I hear you," I said, dismissively waving my hand at her.

And the unholy beast bit me again!

"I'm going to turn you into a stew!" I shouted, lashing my bleeding hand out at the animal. Gladys held her ground and bleated louder.

"What do you wan—" I began, before realizing something very important was missing from this scene. Where was her new baby? Sheep were notorious for sticking together, especially at such a young age. I surveyed the whole herd, without seeing any trace of it. They hadn't left the pen for the day, so there was nowhere else for him to be.

I ran both of my hands through my wet, matted hair, and then I saw them. A quarter mile beyond the fence and atop a hill, a large lion bounded away with a freshly caught lamb between its jaws.

Several emotions bombarded me at once, substantial fear being chief among them. How close must the lion have gotten to steal away the lamb? My eyes quickly swept over the rest of the fenced in pasture, making sure the beast wasn't traveling with a larger pride.

Then the lyre's strumming started, its notes clear and bright, distinctly coming from the hilltop.

My eyes went wide. "Nope!" My attention turned to the blue sky. "Like, we need to come up with a whole new word to explain how much of a no this is. It's a bloody lion!"

The harp continued playing against my pleas, merrier, louder.

"I'm not getting killed for a sheep!" A small, helpless, terrified baby lamb.

The melody strummed on.

The priest's advice echoed in my head. If I refused to follow the music, I wouldn't be ready when the time came to protect my family. There are times when a person knows he's about to try something that may end with more trouble than the payoff's worth. There are times when he knows he's about to do something just plain stupid. And then there are times when he finds himself about to attempt something so foolhardy, so incredibly asinine, that years later he looks back and wonders how he still has all his limbs attached.

My decision making of the next twenty minutes constituted the last one.

Hurdling the pasture fence, I sprinted through the fields with my shepherd staff over my shoulder, a mixture of terror and adrenaline pumping through my veins.

I wish I could say I had a plan, at least one of my typical schemes to separate the young lamb from the lion. I wish I could say I had applicable experience with overgrown felines, some rare insight into how they operate. I wish I could say I had any semblance of a notion of what I intended to do if I managed to catch the lion.

Nope.

Every rational thought screamed for me to turn back. What chance did I have of catching a lion? Would the lamb even be alive when I reached them? At least go back to town and get a group to come with me. It's the youngest, the weakest, the least significant part of the herd.

A picture of the lamb, defenseless against an unrelenting predator, clawed at my heart, sending a fresh wave of adrenaline through my veins.

Mounting the hill I first saw them on, I searched the landscape. Below me, a granite outcropping rose high into the air. At the base of the rock fixture, the lion waited with his back to me, his next meal cowering at his feet.

"Let. Him. Go!" I shouted down at the lion.

The beast turned his shaggy black mane toward me, studying me as a curious oddity.

The insanity of my decision to pursue the creature came crashing down upon my shoulders. The lion's lips started trembling in anger, and then the most soul-crushing roar filled the space between us.

"Let him go," I repeated, with slightly less authority.

As if to mock me, the lion slowly turned and grasped the young lamb between his jaws, and then returned to staring me down.

This was not going particularly well.

I descended the hill, both hands clasped to my staff. The beast made no move to retreat or advance, but with every step closer his deep growl grew steadily louder.

I stopped four feet in front of them, getting a good look at my adversary. His body was covered in the wide remnants of old wounds, but it was one of his eyes that caused me to step back. A long scar traced his right socket, exactly like an adversary I had seen just weeks ago. This was the same lion the Philistines had tried to feed me to. Freedom had been good to him. His face was no longer gaunt from malnourishment, thick muscle covered his legs, and his ankle no longer showed the discoloration of injury. Yet it was the same lion who had probably spent years in captivity under the care of inhumane men. I swallowed hard. Men, who from his perspective, looked a lot like the shepherd dumb enough to confront him over his current meal choice.

He stared at me with a mixture of displeasure and uncertainty.

If I showed any hesitation now, he'd see me as prey. I fortified my determination and stepped toward him. The beast stepped back. I stepped forward. The lion spun and ran.

Primal instinct overrode any rational thought. My staff whipped out like a bat, driving the head of the wood into the lion's hindquarter. At impact, the sound of a harsh cracking split the air, and a powerful vibration throughout the wood forced my fingers apart, the staff tumbling from my hands...

...but the lamb also fell from the lion's mouth. He scrambled toward me, diving awkwardly between my legs.

The predator turned, and for the first time I saw no fear, uncertainty, or hesitation in his eyes—pure rage gazed up at me.

Then five hundred pounds of muscle and claw barreled after me.

Best plan ever.

I had no time to run, to think, or even brace myself. He pounced, and I fell onto my back. Two thick sets of claws landed inches above my face, his scarred muzzle breathing heavy above my skull.

Panting, I gazed up. Fur-coated death glared back at me. He slammed his left paw onto my shoulder, and searing pain tore into my flesh as his claws dug deep.

My mind exploded with the all-consuming burning, and in desperation, I chanced something I hadn't done since I was a kid. I prayed.

It wasn't a poetic prayer. It wasn't long-winded or complicated. There was no time for stringing words together.

"Help!"

One word. One desperate plea. One last, impossible wish.

The impossible flowed into my limbs. With unreal strength, my arms broke free from the lion's weight. I flung one hand up into his mouth, grabbing a thick, three-inch fang, which bought me precious seconds before he could swallow me whole. My free arm lashed out across the ground, my fingers finding a large rock, and with one swipe I smashed it into the skull of the beast.

The scarred animal flew off of me with the speed of a runaway cart, its claws tearing fresh skin from my shoulder as they were ripped away. My fingers held fast to the fang, and it snapped out of the beast's mouth. The lion tumbled side over side several times before he stopped a few yards away.

The alien strength vanished as quickly as it came, and my eyes closed for a long time.

Chapter 8

Pain. I gasped, sucking in air through clenched teeth. My shoulder felt like it was on fire, and for a while, all I did was take quick, shallow breaths.

Eventually, the agony became less all-consuming, and I forced my eyes open. High above, a full moon hung in the night sky. Next to me, a young lamb pressed its firm, moist nose into my cheek.

The battle with the lion flooded back into my mind. The beast's three-inch fang rested against my hand, and after significant effort, I was able to crane my neck enough to locate the animal's corpse sprawled out a dozen feet away.

Conflicting thoughts jockeyed for my attention. Given almost any other circumstance, slaying a four-hundred-pound king of the jungle qualified as the most exciting, personally satisfying accomplishment of my life.

However, the excruciating fire burning in my shoulder tempered my joy. Glancing at the wound, I took stock of the injury. It at least explained the pain. Four long, deep claw marks were dug into my skin. Even disoriented, I understood how dangerous wounds from an animal became if left untreated. More than one person from our village had lost a limb from simply being bitten by a rodent. This injury was several dozen miles beyond a love bite from a scared mouse.

My eyelids started to droop, and my body made a strong case for simply lying down and sleeping for the next half century. I snapped my head up. At this point, sleep equated to death. No one knew where I had gone, which meant the likelihood of someone finding me among the rock cliffs were slim. I needed to get to Bethlehem, now.

I fought to stand up, and the whole world shifted, wobbling back and forth like a giant seesaw. The lion's corpse appeared to move in the world's contortions, and I screamed in fright, stumbling and almost flailing back to the dirt.

The dizziness subsided, but between the wound and my fevered state, quick movements were out of the question.

I tucked the beast's tooth into my belt, used my shepherd staff as a crutch, and called hoarsely for the lamb to follow me. After all the trouble I had just gone through to rescue him, the little wool ball was getting back to the flock safe and sound, if only so I could turn the runt into a well-deserved stew.

Together, we set out on our journey, cool sweat dripping down my cheeks as I shuffled along the rocky ground.

My mind wandered to a nagging question. How did I end up delirious and near death in the first place? I stopped in my tracks. The music had sent me after a freaking lion.

My nose turned toward the sky. He and I needed to have a conversation about this anointing situation, soon.

I started my journey again, albeit with a touch more indignation in each step. The granite terrain was uneven, but as long as I kept my footing, everything should be fine —

Dry, frail branches cracked and splintered beneath me, and my leg plunged down into a crevasse.

"Goat feces!" I shouted as the rest of my body fell through the wide hole hiding beneath the sticks, my skull slamming into a slab of unforgiving granite. The steep angle of the rock partnered with gravity, and I awkwardly skidded down the stone ramp. By the time I stopped, my body had slid ten feet below the surface.

The stars still flickered brightly above me, but the *two* moons I saw hanging in the night sky seemed like a bad sign. Either I was hallucinating, or I was seeing double. Neither possibility filled me with warm fuzzies.

Nor did the noise emanating from the pit beneath me. At first, it reminded me of running water, but the occasional hissing noise left me with significant doubts about that theory. Carefully repositioning my body, I saw what waited at the bottom of the slab: not one Israeli viper, not a dozen, but *hundreds* of the black, venomous inbreds.

Pure terror took over, and I started clawing up the rock ramp. My movement had the opposite effect. Without a stable handhold to cling to, I ended up skidding further into the hole.

The snakes took notice. Several of their triangular heads arched up, hissing angrily at me.

My body went rigid, certain any more movement would provoke them.

Fighting through fear, despair, and every other terrifying emotion on the planet, I sorted through my options. One snake bite wouldn't kill me. One thousand bites were an entirely different story. I could attempt to climb out again, but then I risked tumbling further down the hole. I could stay put and hope someone stumbled upon me, but my chances of being discovered were slim when I was above ground. Hidden a dozen feet below the granite brought the odds of rescue down to zero.

The final option was to simply sleep. My head felt like someone was pouring liquid into it, and the arguments against taking a nap no longer seemed relevant.

Maybe if I shut my eyes for a few moments, I'd be able to make better sense of everything…

"Niklas!" cried a familiar, but far-off voice.

I ignored the cry, so close to blissful oblivion.

"Niklas, you foul-smelling halfwit, open your eyes!"

The insult annoyed me enough to glance up. A dark silhouette waited at the top of the ramp, holding out a long, familiar stick. My father's staff.

"Grab hold," the voice commanded.

It appeared whoever was shouting wouldn't allow me to rest until I did what he wanted, so I reached out for the pole.

Moments later, the wood started inching upward, and my body came along for the ride. At the top of the ramp, I found my brother

Abin, panting.

It must have been another hallucination.

"You're still off at war," I muttered, sprawled out on the ground. He shook his head, checking my shoulder. "The King finally gives us a three-day reprieve, and instead of enjoying it with my beautiful wife and a bottle of wine, I spend the first night searching the fields for my knuckleheaded brother." Abin turned his neck, waving an arm back and forth. "I found him!" he called. "Niklas' injured something serious, but he's alive." His eyes ran over my body. "What did this to you? Those look like...claw marks."

A wave of nausea rippled behind my eyes, and my head bobbled loosely back and forth. "Picked a fight with a lion."

His nose scrunched up. "What?"

I decided it'd be easier to explain everything after a quick nap, followed by a longer night's rest, and topped off with a four-month hibernation period. Darkness closed in around me.

A few years—or possibly minutes later, I felt my body being lifted from the ground by what felt like thick, furry tree trunks.

"How'd this happen to him?" asked another familiar voice from above me.

"I have no clue, Eli," replied Abin. "I noticed the lamb and found Niklas trapped in a viper pit. He'd muttered something about a lion before he passed out."

The tree trunks cradling me shuddered softly. "A lion?" He exhaled several long, warm breaths over me.

"Nik's a magnet for trouble, for sure, but this..." Abin trailed off. "He's not insane."

"The judge," Eliab responded, quiet anger lurking beneath the surface. "This is all his fault. He made Niklas believe he's something special, some kind of hero from a fairy tale. He has always been reckless, but now he thinks he's the second coming of Moses." Fear replaced the rage building in his voice. "It's going to get him killed. We have to find a solution, a way to protect him."

"From whom?" Abin asked.

He pulled me closer to his body. His answer came in the form of a whisper. "Himself."

Part Two: The Mad King

One of the hyenas purred, waking Erik from his slumber. His cheek
rested upon Shelby's checkered chest, the alpha female of the pack.

The king blinked several times and slowly raised his head, taking
inventory of the surroundings. He was still in his stark, barren
throne room. Glancing down at his hands, he found dark, crusty
blood beneath his nails. Had he simply been eating rare meat with
the pack, or had he attacked someone again? He shuddered, not sure
which scenario disgusted him more.

Heavy emotions bombarded the king's conscience. Despair. How
much longer could he endure this volatile state? Powerlessness. He
never fooled himself into thinking he was in control of his condition,
but he had convinced himself it was contained. This latest episode
had begun at breakfast. His children had been eating at the table.

But more than anything else, Erik felt all consuming rage for the
man who had done this to him—Alvaro, Israel's vulture-eating
judge. Alvaro claimed to be his confidant, his guide, and then betrayed the king, unleashing this madness upon him. One day soon,
Erik would see the traitor hung from the walls of Gibeath.

Knuckles cracked from a darkened corner in the hall.

Concentrating through the rage, Erik looked up. "Alexander," he
addressed his counselor, his voice raspy. "How long have I

been...gone?"

A short, almost perfectly round man waddled out into the light, his regal green robes clean and tidy as always. In one hand he held a rolled up scroll and in the other a feather-tipped pen. "Three hours, Your Excellency," he replied simply, as if he had just answered how long the king had napped, as opposed to how long a bout of insanity had lasted.

Erik rubbed his eyes wearily. "This cannot continue."

"Agreed," the rotund counselor said. "Our healers have come up with a new theory to help with your condition."

Erik sighed. "I'm sure they have."

Over the last year, on their recommendation he had fasted, feasted, and drunk until he couldn't see straight, all in an attempt to stem the progress of his madness. All had failed. "What would they have me do now?" Erik sneered. "Shave off every hair on my body and howl at the moon, in hopes of becoming one with its purity?"

The counselor's knuckles cracked again. "They have suggested music may soothe your spirit."

The king growled. Music? The harp is where all his troubles began. Did he dare risk attempting anything that might exacerbate the problem? He shook his head and clenched his jaw. He couldn't keep his sickness a secret forever. He needed a solution, regardless of the risks.

"Fine," Erik said through a feral growl, fighting against being dragged into another episode. "Bring me a musician."

Chapter 9

"Eliab sold me into slavery!" My hands flew up in the air. "Sulking seems like a fairly reasonable response."

Deborah sat next to me, coating her large hammer with another layer of sheep oil to keep it from rusting. She raised an eyebrow pointedly. "He didn't sell you into slavery. He got you a paid, indentured servant position on Michael's farm."

"Indentured servant is a fancy way to say slave," I asserted, warming my palms on the bonfire blazing in front of us. Its light danced merrily upon the cheeks of the thirty soldiers circled around it, all of whom were enjoying their last night before returning to the war.

The festive mood clashed with my surly, bitter thoughts.

Abin suddenly plopped down next to me, a clay goblet in one hand. He threw his free arm around my neck, careful to avoid the bandages mom had used to wrap my injured shoulder. "He's still pouting?"

Deborah nodded. "I've tried my best, but he's pretty much determined to host his own life-as-I-know-it-is-over party."

My brother leaned forward. "Did you remind him of how cute Michael's daughters are?"

The blacksmith's daughter barked a laugh. "I somehow never thought to mention it." She stood up, straightening out her coral printed dress. "But I told father I'd help him start on a new project tomorrow, so I'll leave him in your capable hands." She stopped, growing more serious. "Be careful when you return to the battlefield, okay?"

"Don't worry about me," Abin promised. "I'm deathly allergic to doing anything heroic."

Deborah snorted, amused. "Oh, the valiant courage of our warriors."

She walked away, and my brother turned his attention to me. "It's not the end of the world. Show Father you're smart enough not to go chasing after anymore carnivorous beasts, and you'll be back to your budding carpentry career in no time."

My sandal kicked the ground. "It's ridiculous! If it wasn't for the harp—"

Abin raised his hand, cutting me off. "You heard Dad, we're not talking about that stuff. Whatever"—he bit his lip, searching for a word—"strangeness happened with the judge, it's no excuse for what you did. Hopefully living under the discipline of someone not related to you will give you a bit of perspective. Behave for a few months and then ask to come home." He winked at me. "Plus, Michael's daughters really are cute."

My ire started to subside. Abin was probably right. Dad had been beside himself when Eliab told him what I had done, but he wasn't the sort to carry a grievance for long. It'd take time, but eventually he'd let me come back. Especially once Eliab wasn't there to whisper in his ear how much of a ne'er-do-well I was becoming. The new employment was all his idea.

From the far side of the fire, a man called out over the celebration. "Another round of barley beer for our brave soldiers."

Abin clasped me on the back. "Now that sounds like a good idea. Be a good sport and get me another drink."

I glared at him. "I'm injured. Get it yourself."

He waggled the cup in front of me. "I'll share it with you."

My eyes opened wide, and I quickly jumped to my feet, beginning my quest to refill the goblet. Halfway through the crowd, a hand clasped my wounded shoulder. I grimaced, as searing pain flew from the tender scars all the way down to my toes.

"Pardon me, lad," he apologized the moment he saw the bandages. He was an out-of-town Benjaminite soldier who had arrived with my brothers. "But please, we'd love another song."

Oh, yeah, I may have forgotten to mention I sing.

It's manly.

The ladies like it.

Stop judging me.

Sighing, I agreed. "I can do one more." Unfortunately, most of the women had already left for the night, meaning no new admirers would be gained from my final performance.

"That's the spirit," he said, and then the soldier pushed a friend off a nearby crate, creating a small stage for me to stand on.

"Any requests?" I asked as I set the goblet down and hopped up.

The man stared into the fire searching for inspiration, but it was one of his compatriots that came up with an answer.

"Samson's Revenge!"

A favorite of all the men all across our country. It had everything a soldier could want: girls, guts, and glory.

The original man who requested a song whistled loudly, and the voices from the crowds immediately died down. I stomped my foot to a steady beat. The audience started clapping along, and my voice carried into the night.

"Come listen, brothers, to a tale,
of power, might, and glory,
About a hero of world renown,
and his unlikely story.

His parents named him Samson,
after a most peculiar birth —
Angels came and told his mother,
of the boy's specific worth.

Blessed with the strength of ten men strong,
He'd battle any foe.
His only weakness, his only flaw,
Was how his hair would grow.

A full retelling of his triumphs,
would take all night and morrow,
but thousands of our enemy,
died bloody and in sorrow.

Then one day he saw her beauty,
basking in the sun,
Delilah, fair and sensual,
Samson's fall had now begun.

Each morning she would nettle him,
'Tell me the secret of your fame,'
And thrice he dodged her inquiry,
But next would come his shame.

'If my hair is cut,' he told her,
'It will strip me of my strength,
But worry not, my sweetest flower,
No man shall touch its length.'

True words indeed he spoke to her,
'No man' would strip his hair,
But while he slept she took a knife,
and left him bald and bare.

That very night the Philistines
attacked him in his bed,
He roused to tear them limb from limb,
but found a wretched dread.

Now nothing more than one of us,
they seized him without fear,
gouged out his eyes, and stole his pride,
and shackled him with jeers.

The acclaimed became a mockery,

They'd trot him out for fun,
'Look how the Mighty Samson
is something to be shunned.'

For months they scorned him openly,
and reveled in their prize,
but missed what was in front of them,
with their inebriated eyes.

His hair had once again grown long,
and though he was now blind,
His arms regained their mighty strength,
with one thought on his mind.

He pled with God for just one chance
to fight again for us,
And placed his hands upon the walls,
and with everything he thrust.

The building fell, and all would die,
in one noble sacrifice,
killing more Philistines in death,
than ever in his life."

The clapping had stopped for the final verse, and I held the last note of the song. For a handful of moments, only the crackling of the fire filled the courtyard.

"For Israel," cried a man hidden behind the crowd.

"For Israel!" echoed everyone else, and the merry-making of the group resumed in full force.

Stepping down from the crate, I found Abin holding out his cup filled to the brim.

"For a job well done," he explained. "Plus, I imagine the alcohol takes the edge off the injury."

By the time the festivities ended, Abin had finished two more glasses and needed my shoulder to help walk straight.

"Just promise not to tell Mom how much I drank," he said as we entered the courtyard to the house. "And drink water before going to bed. Lots of water."

I had taken another two steps before he pulled hard on my shirt. "Burn it all," he swore quietly. "Mom or Dad's still up."

Lantern lights flickered softly in the common room of the house, and the faint hushes of whispers carried into the open patio.

We silently moved closer to the door frame, but the first words we caught stopped us cold.

"The Mad King will kill him!" my father spat out.

Knuckles cracked.

"Careful," an unknown man warned. "Whispered into the wrong ears, the combination of *mad* and *king* will get you hanged for treason."

"Tell him," Father replied, his voice rising, "we still will not permit our son, our *underage* son, to serve under a man who reportedly spends more time hunting down traitors among his chambermaids than he does running our country."

"I could send enough men here to take him by force," the stranger replied.

A metallic sound gently rang out in the room. "Sir," my mother said, "that would require you to leave here alive."

Abin and I looked back at each other, both of our eyes wide as the moon. Mom could be scary, sure, but I'm pretty sure she just threatened to actually kill a man. Who was inside?

My brother nodded at the door frame, and I returned the gesture. He held up three fingers, and one by one counted down. At zero, we rushed into the common room, expecting to find swords drawn, blood only moments away from being spilled.

Instead, we found our parents sitting crossed legged on the floor, across from the most rotund man I had ever seen. He too reclined on a pillow, but he appeared more like an oversize children's ball, his height as expansive as his width. He wore a forest green robe, clean brown pants, and a purple and gold head cap. Grey hair had begun to sprinkle his thick black beard, but even hidden beneath the beard's protection, his double chin was clearly outlined.

In one hand he held a cup of tea and in the other a feathered quill. He cracked the knuckles of his writing hand. "Good evening," he said, without the slightest indication in his voice that he could care at all how our evening progressed. "Niklas, and your brother Abin, I believe. Your parents and I were just having a discussion about you. Why don't you two join us?"

I checked with my father, who appeared unsure of how to proceed. He opened his hand slowly for us to sit down beside him. Next to him, Mom's appearance alternated between nervous and furious. In her hands, she clutched two long bread knives so tightly that her knuckles were ghost white.

"Very good," the wide-bellied man continued. "I imagine your attendance will expedite the discussion. I am Alexander, son of Simeon, King Erik's chief counselor."

Neither my brother nor I responded with any kind of greeting.

He continued. "Niklas, you have a unique opportunity to serve your country. Our great leader, King Erik, has been afflicted by a most worrisome illness. The war with the Philistines has taxed him, and he is currently battling a sickness of the mind. Our best medics have found no lasting solutions, and the attacks are getting worse.

"However, some of our healers have suggested an alternative solution to calm our afflicted ruler. Music. I've been traveling with the contingent of soldiers resting here in Bethlehem, and by happenstance overheard your performance earlier. While it's doubtful the need for tavern songs will arise, others from this town gushed that you are versed in all manner of sonnets. Your talent may be the key to alleviating the burden on our king."

"We already gave you our answer," my father stated, visibly holding back his anger. "Our underage son will not be going with you."

Alexander cracked each finger on his left hand individually. "You know our laws. No man, even the king, has the right to conscript another parent's son before the age of sixteen. I cannot force you to accept my offer."

Mother closed her eyes and breathed a deep, long breath of relief.

"But," Alexander continued, "three of your sons already serve at the king's pleasure. War is such a fickle, merciless risk our soldiers endure. At any moment, their lives can be snatched away, especially those assigned to the front lines."

Mom lunged forward. "You devil!" Dad barely managed to grab her shawl and pull her back before her blade reached his throat. Most of me wished he had allowed her to gut the pudge ball. This was blackmail.

"I assure you," the counselor replied evenly, unfazed by the outburst, "I am no devil. Only a man who prefers numbers over emotional arguments. In this agreement, you are assured the safety of three of your sons for the use of another. The math favors making the deal. Plus," he paused, searching for the right word, "as…capricious as our king may be, I give you my word: his presence is less dangerous than that of the battlefield."

A weight fell upon my chest. Turning to my brother, an unreadable expression on his face, I realized both the threat and the opportunity that Alexander's offer posed to my family. Since my brothers were conscripted into the war, our whole family had lived with unspoken fear. Would we survive this war whole? Already, several other households from Bethlehem had lost sons to the conflict.

If I took this offer, Abin, Sham, even Eliab, would be safe.

Yet the terror in my father's voice made it clear that if I served the king, my own safety was far from assured. Even during Alvaro's ceremony, where the judge had threatened to cut us into literal pieces, Dad hadn't been this unnerved.

Abin shifted uncomfortably. "Niklas, you—"

A wave of my hand cut him off. A question burned in my mind. "What happens to my family if the king doesn't appreciate my voice?"

Alexander contemplated the question. "I can promise your brothers' protection if you accept the offer. As for your own safety, well, it would behoove you to give the performance of your life."

Translation: If Erik didn't appreciate my voice, at least one of my parents' children would return home in flat, wooden box. We had reached the heart of the matter—risk my safety for the guaranteed protection of my three brothers.

My mother set down the knives and crawled next to me. "Sweetie, you don't have to do this. Yahweh will protect your brothers."

I looked up, past the ceiling toward the starry night, and a genuine grin of disbelief touched my lips. Deep down, I agreed with her.

He had provided a way to keep our family safe, to protect my family as Alvaro had promised.

Winking at my mom to mask the raging uncertainty in my decision, I turned to the counselor. "I'll do it."

Chapter 10

Elaborate limestone pillars decorated the front of King Erik's expansive home. It had been rebuilt since Father had taken my brothers and me here years ago—no longer a simple farmhouse but now truly a residence fit for a king. The palace was built like a layered square cake, stood three stories tall, and was constructed from rich, crimson cedar-wood. On the top floor, twelve types of gemstones wrapped around the building: the black onyx of the tribe of Joseph, the purple amethyst of Levi, the red jasper of Reuben, the green emerald of my own tribe of Judah, along with precious stones representing the last eight tribes making up Israel. Its significance seemed clear, a diadem to crown Erik's palace.

I stood outside its large colonnade, rewrapping the cords of my slingshot around my arm for the fifth time in the past ten minutes. Each time I repeated the process, my hands shook more. The last words from my brothers had haunted me since Alexander, and I left for the royal estate.

"Do not upset the king," Sham had warned. "I saw him throw a lieutenant off a cliff simply for coughing during one of his speeches. If ever there was a situation not to be you, Niklas, now is that time."

Abin echoed our brother. "No schemes, no plots, no midnight hijinks. Sing your songs when asked and then stay quiet and out of sight."

They spent my last morning at home randomly dropping in on me, offering piecemeal advice on how to survive my new position.

"Figs, he loves figs. Find him some."

"He appreciates warriors; play up the story with the lion. Don't forget to take that tooth!"

Only Eliab refused to offer any council. We agreed it best to hide the deal struck with Alexander from the rest of my family. Not just for fear of hurting their pride, but also to avoid sowing resentment among the other soldiers if anyone else found out about their protection.

The morning I left, my eldest brother argued for an hour with my parents, trying to convince them this was simply another one of my hair-brained schemes. "He's too impulsive, too glory hungry, too immature. This assignment is going to end with him dead."

The ungrateful, arrogant know-it-all. The next time I made a deal to protect the lives of our family, I'd make sure to leave him out of it.

If I lived long enough to see a next time.

I began anew rewrapping the cords around my arm.

Alexander waited outside the entrance to the palace, reviewing a number of documents that had been handed to him upon reaching Erik's hometown and our new capital, Gibeath.

The high counselor sniffed the air in disgust. "I leave for two weeks and every food store and tax levy is off five percent."

The door to the main manor burst open, and two guards dragged a newly beaten man over their shoulders. Both of the victim's eyes were swollen shut, and deep lacerations ran down the sides of his bloodied face.

Another soldier followed them out, waving to Alexander. "The king only has one more guest before he will be ready to see you and the new musician. Come along." The man disappeared back into the castle, and the counselor rolled up the scroll he was reading and gestured for me to follow him.

The beaten man passed me, his head hung low, and suddenly the confidence in my singing plummeted. "Shouldn't we wait for a less..." I swung my head back to the broken man. "...emotional time before the introductions?"

Knuckles cracked. "It appears the king is in one of his moods—

the very type you were enlisted to soothe."

I swallowed hard. "What did that man do?"

"I do not know for certain," Alexander said, unconcerned. "Maybe he spied for the enemy, or he simply looked at one of the king's daughters crossly. It's hard to tell these days without sitting through the trial. But come along. I promise you, testing his patience will not further your cause."

He turned his back to me and stalked into the palace, the matter settled.

Crap. Mountains of oxen-smelling crap.

Between my brothers' warnings and the very real case study I had just witnessed, what were the odds of surviving if I didn't please the king? One million to zero?

Yet making him wait served no purpose but pushing those odds into the negative column, so I reluctantly followed after Alexander.

Never before had I been in a structure this massive. The ceiling rose at least fifteen feet into the air, and long hallways ran to the right, left, and straight ahead. Windowless, muted darkness filled the corridors, and the torchlight left the halls feeling cold despite the midday sun coming in from the entrance. Alexander stood ten feet straight ahead, his foot tapping impatiently as he waited for me to catch up.

I hurried forward.

He took one step toward the next door and then halted. "Also, a word of warning: do not look the hyenas in the eyes. They see it as a challenge."

Hy-what? I froze, gawking. Could I outrun the entirety of this insanity?

"Chief Counselor Alexander son of Simeon!" announced a young page on the other side of the door. "And the musician, Niklas, son of Jesse."

"Enter," commanded a deep but weary voice.

My hopes for escape evaporated, and I trailed after Alexander. He veered off to the right halfway into the grand hall. At the far end of the chamber, the king sat upon a raised, ivory white, wooden throne. He was tall, probably larger in height than even Eliab, with a freshly shaven head encircled by a bronze crown. His beard was thick but clean, and he wore a faded purple robe over simple shepherd clothes. He was a strong looking man, kingly even, except for his sunken, empty eyes.

At the base of his throne, three spotted hyenas, larger than any wolf I had ever encountered, lay curled up next to each other, bored. Even inattentive, they terrified the elderly man cowering several feet in front of them.

A knuckle cracked once. The counselor kept his eyes fixed ahead, but one hand pointed to a spot beside him. I quickly took it.

"You were saying," King Erik said, lifting a hand toward the man.

"Your Highness," the elderly gentlemen replied through chattering teeth. "I swear by the God of our forefathers Abraham, Isaac, and Jacob, I did not curse my neighbor's flock. His herd was hit with some unknown pestilence, a tragedy to be sure, but not one of my making."

Erik rubbed his eyebrows. "Do you know much about hyenas?"

"What?" the man squeaked.

"They're fascinating creatures. They live within a hierarchy they all follow. Each one has a unique position, starting with the alpha leader, typically a female, all the way down to the runt of the pack. Each member honors the ones above it." He reached down and scratched behind the ears of the thickest beast. "Do you know where I rank in their eyes?"

"No, sire," the prisoner said.

"I am the alpha. They respect me, they listen to me, they obey me, and in return for their loyalty, I provide for them and protect them. The system works because they are faithful."

"I am faithful, Your Highness, I swear—"

"Enough!" shouted the king, rising to his feet. The hyenas became alert, growling softly. "We found the Philistine idols in your home, along with the remains of a burnt offering." He pulled out a small ring from his robe. "Among the charred remnants of the ritual, we discovered the ashen signet ring of your neighbor! You used foreign magic to advance your dark agenda, you craven hypocrite! In the middle of a war with the accursed Philistines, my own people are praying to their gods!"

The captured man's face went ghost white. "Have mercy, sire," he pleaded, his tone desperate. "My neighbor kept pushing the boundary lines further into my property. I needed a way to stop him."

Suddenly, Erik's whole demeanor calmed. "I have reached my judgment. Simon, son of Jonah, you are hereby convicted of witch-craft."

"No!"

The king grabbed the man by his collar and held him inches from his face, and then threw his body toward the nearest guards. "Take him to the back. My *faithful* pack has not eaten yet today."

"Please! Give me a chance to defend myself!" the man cried out.

A soldier struck him in the stomach, and his pleas were replaced by wheezing. They dragged him back to a room behind the throne, the three hyenas eagerly following after them. A moment later, the guards returned to the hall. The door to the back room was so thick barely anything could be heard, but we all knew what was happening.

My lunch started pushing its way up my throat. I covered my mouth and bent over, forcing the bile back down.

The king kept his eyes closed for a good minute, muttering aggressively to himself before he finally turned his haunted gaze toward me. "Well, musician," he said, flippantly flicking his wrist, "sing me a song."

Chapter 11

So that was utterly terrifying.

Oh, and I also didn't get fed to hyenas. Hooray.

The first song I sang King Erik, "The Harrows of the Red Sea," pleased him well enough to gesture for another. By the time I finished the final note of the second melody, he was fast asleep, slumped over in his throne.

Alexander seemed pleased by my performances, or more accurately, he found no fault in them, and he arranged for me to stay in the servants' quarters. An hour after lying down, my mind still buzzed, so I crept out for some air and now found myself alone, standing upon the second-floor terrace of the palace.

The temporary relief of surviving my first audience with the king was quickly replaced by a bleak realization: Erik was worse than anything I had expected. His servants talked about him in whispers, claiming his persona could change from a benevolent ruler to a merciless executioner over the slightest perceived offense. You tread carefully in his service, or he'd soon be using your bones as chew toys for his pets.

Not known for subtlety, I feared how long my tenure as the musician could last. "Second chances" seemed like a dirty word in his court, so if displeasing him was inevitable, I could save everyone some time and get sized for my casket now.

My best bet was to follow my brothers' advice, keep my head low, perform when told, and avoid the king at all cost.

"You sing well."

My body jerked in surprise, and I cried out. I turned my head and found the alpha hyena, the Mad King eight feet behind me. Wearing only his simple shepherd clothes and a dark wool blanket to shield him from the cold, he seemed less a royal despot and more a weary, middle-aged farmer.

"Thank you," my voice squeaked. Then the shock of whom I was speaking to hit me like an empty bucket. "Thank you, Your Highness. I'm sorry, I forgot to—"

A faint smile crossed his lips at my distress, and the king raised his hands for me to stop talking. He approached and took a place next to me, surveying the rolling hills. "I come up here often when I can't sleep. I find comfort in seeing our nation at rest."

"Do you want me to sing you another set of songs?" I asked hesitantly.

He chuckled, his throaty laugh booming against the quiet of the night. "There is no need. The few hours of rest I just enjoyed are the best I've experienced in well over a year. My mind is clear. I wish to savor it." He paused. "Maybe it will keep the Mad King at bay."

Yeah, nothing good came from talking about that subject. I froze, trying to keep my face from betraying any reaction to his comment.

"Fear not," Erik continued, "I am well aware you had no part in sowing those accusations, nor do I claim they are without some merit. They're the cost of many hard, unpopular, but ultimately necessary decisions combined with other...infirmities." He pulled the blanket tighter around his shoulders. "What terrors he must do who wears the crown."

The muffled sound of bones crunching as the spotted beasts turned a man into kibble rang in my ears. I shuddered. Terrors indeed.

"Do you think my verdict was unfair to the man you saw in my court today?

Second-guessing the king? Again with the conversations that will end with me dead. I paused for a moment, weighing my words. "They really found the remnants of a curse in his hearth?"

Erik nodded.

"And you believe curses actually do something?"

A haunted look appeared in Erik's eyes. "Oh yes, I believe in the power of curses and blessings. It's no small thing to plead with any deity for or against another man."

My shoulders rolled and fidgeted. "So the curse succeeded?"

"Whether it succeeded or not, I do not know, but for even attempting to place a dark shadow on a neighbor's life, well, that type of diseased thinking must be purged from any nation." He closed his eyes.

His reasoning was brutal. For most of my life, I hadn't put much thought into the idea of curses, considering them a tale to tell around a campfire, not something to be taken seriously. But after the anointing, which was kind of a blessing—at least when it wasn't sending me after ravenous beasts—I could no longer deny outright the possibility of the supernatural.

"I'm not sure what I'd have done," I answered honestly.

"Either way, the matter has been settled." He opened his eyes and smiled at me. "Alexander tells me you are a son of Jesse, from Bethlehem, correct?"

I nodded.

"And he has seven sons, if I am not mistaken."

"Eight, Your Highness."

He barked a laugh. "I am mistaken. Not many would be so quick to correct me."

My mouth went wide. "Sire, I did not mean—"

"Fear not," the king repeated. "You spoke truth. I'm not so mad I'd hold that against you. Still, I imagine with the war, not many of your brothers are left to help your father manage the farm or the herds."

"No sire, but they'll find a way to make do."

Erik nodded and took a deep breath of the midnight air. "I'm sure your father would, but he won't have to on my account. Would I be correct in assuming Alexander made some kind of deal with your family to get you into my service?"

I bit my lower lip. "He did."

"And, I also imagine, that vague but palpable threats were made against the safety of your brothers already in my service if you did not agree to it?"

Betraying Alexander's deal to the king seemed dangerous on pretty much every level, but if Erik found out I had lied, I might as well feed myself to his spotted hounds right now. "Yes."

The king waited in silence for several minutes before he continued. "Your family needs you, and so do I. Both sides will be left wanting somewhat. I'll permit you to return home and help your family manage your land, but at least once per week you will spend a day in my court, keeping my demons at bay, so to speak. Does that seem fair?"

His question prompted conflicting emotions. Utter terror of his violent mood swings still ranked at the top, but speaking to him now, he seemed like an entirely different person than the monster from this afternoon, more like one tormented by the burden of ruling than the tormentor of a powerless people. If my songs helped him navigate that narrow path, maybe it was worth the risk of helping him.

I nodded in agreement.

"Good. I am already in your debt, Niklas, son of Jesse. It brings me a measure of comfort, in some small way, to pay it back."

Being alone with the king, even knowing I was on his good side, still made me uneasy, and I shifted uncomfortably. "With your leave, I'd like to go to bed, sire."

"Sleep well," the king said, keeping his attention fixed on the surrounding countryside.

I took two steps away before his voice stopped me.

"Niklas, one last thing."

"Yes, Your Highness."

Erik craned his neck around to lock gazes with me, a touch of sorrow in his eyes. "Take extra care not to disappoint me during one of my episodes. I would mourn having needlessly disposed of such a promising young man because he failed to navigate my moods."

I swallowed hard, the exact nature of my situation becoming clear. No matter how peaceful Erik may seem, the Mad King would always lurk nearby, waiting beneath the surface. Tread lightly or get turned into a hyena snack-stick. I clasped my hands together to keep them from shaking. "I'll try, Your Highness."

"Merely trying will end poorly for you. Do," he commanded and turned away.

Message received. My life depended on it.

Part Three: The Giant

"You're small," growled a deep, resonant voice from the marble throne. The chair sat beneath a pavilion and atop a five-step platform. A massive man reclined in it, one leg dangling over the armrest. "I doubt you're even worth the time. My brother should have just killed you and saved us both the hassle."

The twenty-something-year-old man kneeling at the foot of the steps squeaked and dropped his head lower, pressing it against the earth. "Please, I've...," he began. "I've...I've come to join you."

"Yes, yes, I know, another Israeli rat trying to escape a sinking ship," the monstrous man replied. "Whether you're worthy of us is another matter. Do you know who I am?"

The Israelite's head bounced up and down. "Everyone does. You're Goliath, the legendary champion."

Goliath scratched his upper thigh. "Tell me about my legend."

The young man's fingers started fidgeting along the ground. "They say you're a demigod, son of the war goddess Astarte."

"Indeed," the giant replied, waving his hand around the pavilion. "They built this temple for me and my mother. Every day, they bring me fresh offerings of food, gold, and entertainment. Can you guess my favorite form of worship?"

"No, sir."

"Battle," Goliath answered and stood up, excitement burning in his in his eyes. "The thrill of spilling another man's blood. Today, you and I will worship together."

The prostrate man's chin bolted up, horror shining in his eyes. "But I came to join you."

"A flea may wish to join a household, but what does it offer besides draining a family's blood? Fight me. Prove you're worth more than a blood-sucking insect."

The deserter's eyes went wide. "I could never hope to win against a god."

"Of course you won't win," Goliath said, spitting on the ground. "But if you can force me to draw my sword, I will allow you to join our country." He pointed to an equipment rack in the corner of the tent. His voice became hard. "Take a weapon or die on your knees."

Scampering up at the threat, the Israelite headed toward the rack. A dozen different types of blades and blunted weapons rested upon it: axes, war hammers, daggers, and polearms. His gaze swept nervously over all of them.

"Hurry!" barked Goliath.

The young man jumped and a moment later reached out for a long, wooden spear. He carried it awkwardly in front of his body and came back to the center of the tent.

The giant's eyebrows arched. "An interesting choice. It will give you distance, which could help, but it's far too heavy for you." He rolled his shoulders and then picked up a sheathed blade resting against a pillar. It was almost as long as the spear, at least six inches wide, and had a golden inlaid handle. "Come now," he said, "let us bring an offering to my mother."

Unsure of himself, the young man froze, but then in a burst of aggression plunged the spear at Goliath's torso. The thrust was painfully slow, as if going through water.

The giant grunted, easily slapped aside the attack, and grabbed hold of the spear, ruthlessly tearing it from the Israelite's possession. He swung the butt of the weapon into the young man's jaw, knocking him unconscious with one strike.

"Get my brother in here!" bellowed the giant. "We have another useless deserter to string up." He tossed the spear on the ground but held fast to his sword. For over a year he had carried it, and not once had he drawn it from its sheath for battle. *Soon*, he told himself. Soon he would find the opportunity to draw it, a sacrifice worthy of its power. He just needed the right adversary.

Chapter 12

One year later

Wading out of the river, I slipped on a stone covered in moss and nearly face-planted into the ice-cold water. The four furry legs dangling around my shoulders jerked in fright. Tiny, the same undersized lamb I had rescued from the lion, bleated directly into my ear.

"Always with the complaints," I grumbled to the fluff ball. "Well then, gain weight so you can cross by yourself."

Setting her down at the top of the river bank, I double-checked to make sure none of the other sheep had refused to cross. Content everyone had successfully completed the needlessly complicated task, I decided to rest a moment before continuing on. Reclining on the prickly grass, I laid down my staff and took off the lyre strapped to my back.

The instrument provided a constant reminder of how dangerous my life had become. As mundane as the career of a shepherd could be, it at least had a longer life expectancy than my role as court musician. King Erik's wrath always lurked nearby, as if at the edge of my peripheral vision.

My songs kept his madness at bay, and he had been true to his word, allowing me to spend most days at home with my family. In his right mind, Erik was a good and just ruler. Yet the mental sickness built up in my absence, which meant every time I returned to his court, a more unstable, manic, and paranoid king awaited me. I shivered. God help me and everyone else in the kingdom if my music ever failed to soothe him during an episode.

I lifted up the instrument from the grass. Alexander had recommended I learn it to aid in my duties as musician. Wanting any advantage in pleasing the king, I practiced regularly and worked it into my routine.

Gently plucking a couple of strings, I tried to recreate the melody of the unseen harp. At least once a week I'd still hear its music, but it had yet to send me on any more suicide missions, now mostly content to send me on tasks of the "helping an old woman cross the road" variety.

The sun beat down upon the fields, tempting me to sneak a nap (deathstalker scorpions wouldn't be out at this early morning), but I had gained a modicum of maturity over the past year and instead rose to my feet, whistling for the sheep to begin moving.

"Hold up!" cried a voice from the other side of the stream. Isaiah stood along its banks, waving his hands.

I leaned into my shepherd staff. "What's wrong?"

"Father wants me to take the herd out today. He has another assignment for you." He hiked up his robe and crossed the river.

"Do you know what he's got in mind?" I asked, clenching my jaw. The last time Dad recalled me back from shepherding duty, he stuck me with filling latrines at the outskirts of town.

"Nope," he answered, "but he didn't have the shovels out."

The job turned out to be less demeaning than feared. Father explained how Eli, Abin, and Sham had been stationed at Elah for the last forty days, and he wanted me to bring them and their commanding officers fresh food. My epic career as a delivery boy was about to begin. The bards would sing tales of my role in the war for years to come.

After picking up a loaded wicker-pack from Mom, and swearing to her no less than twenty-three times I would be careful, I left from the west gate of Bethlehem. Elah lay fifteen miles west of Bethlehem, which meant I had a full day's walk ahead of me.

Setting out on my journey, a grin split my face. In the king's court, I regularly overheard updates about the war with the Philistines, but I had yet to see either army close up. The fringe benefit of this assignment meant I'd finally get a firsthand look at what our soldiers were up against.

My first encounter with the enemy happened a bit faster than anticipated. I was still about two miles east of Elah when I crested over a small bluff. At that height, it was impossible to miss the five shirtless Philistines sprinting across fields to the north. My lungs constricted. Marauders?

They weren't headed toward me, but instead would soon intercept an old man who was hunched over and wrapped in a faded and frayed cloak, slowly shuffling down a wagon trail. The unlucky traveler had yet to recognize the threat, and outnumbered as he was, they'd tear him apart.

I swallowed hard, deciding what I should do. I could probably reach the soon-to-be victim before the Philistines caught up to him, but two unarmed men against five trained soldiers was only slightly less suicidal than the current situation. Getting myself killed in a desperate attempt to be brave served no purpose.

Every sane, rational, and life-preserving thought argued for avoiding the conflict and going to search for help, yet I found my feet almost moving on their own, running full speed toward the wanderer.

Thirty feet away, it became clear why the traveler hadn't noticed the incoming enemy. The hapless man was praying. He wore a gray *tallit*, a prayer shawl, and what I had thought were loose threads hanging from the edges of it were in fact knotted *tzitzit*, religious counting tassels.

"Sir!" I called out.

He gently raised his hand toward me, signaling for me to wait. He was mumbling, "...with all your heart, and with all your soul, and with all your strength."

I reached the man mere seconds before the Philistines, calling out loudly. "Grandpa, I hate to interrupt your little pow-wow with the guy upstairs, but we're about to be overrun by Philistines. A little less prayer and a bit more situational awareness is probably appropriate."

His neck turned slightly toward me, but the shawl hid his face. "I would disagree with that thought," he responded, unnervingly calm despite my warning of impending doom.

The bare-chested warriors reached us before the man, and I could settle our disagreement. They stopped a dozen feet in front of us. Each of the Philistines carried an identical weapon, a blade I knew well. They were the same make of swords I had discovered in the back of the Philistines' cart over a year ago.

"This is our lucky day," said the oldest soldier, a grizzled warrior in his forties. The rest of the men weren't much older than me, and one of them may have even been a little younger. "Here I thought we had only stumbled upon one decrepit Israelite vermin, and by the time we get here, a second whelp crawls out of his hole."

I moved closer to the cloaked man, holding my oaken staff up. "Our countrymen are all around us," I threatened, trying to keep my teeth from chattering. "They could be here any moment."

The seasoned Philistine barked a laugh. "Doubtful. We were sent to chase down any stray Israeli deserters. You've been fleeing like mice from a drowning ship for weeks. We've already gutted four of your comrades without seeing so much as a single scout."

The five soldiers began spreading out around us, and I couldn't keep track of them all. My fists clenched in fear around my staff. This would be over quick.

The shawled man rolled his shoulders. "I offer each of you now a chance to join our nation, to become one of the people of Yahweh. He invites all to come and freely call upon His name, no matter the number or extent of their past wrongs."

Come again? My eyes went wide at the audacity of his statement, and I turned to him in shock. How far off the reservation was this guy?

The sentiment was shared by the Philistines. "Join you?" their leader asked, amusement dancing in his eyes. "Did you hear that boys? Their little god will accept us. Should we take the offer and become one with the cretins just before our nation wipes them off the map?" His men laughed and moved a bit closer. "Sorry Grandpa, we're going to have to pass on the invitation." The Philistine raised his blade and moved within five feet us, close enough for a killing strike.

91

"Fair enough," my hunched-over companion replied.

A sharp *whoosh* whipped out from beside me, and before I could even comprehend what had happened, the enemy leader cried out in agony, and a thick, bloody gash appeared across his sword arm, the blade falling upon the path.

Gleaming in the light, a three-foot long sword was now pointed squarely at the injured Philistine's chest. It had a long, black hilt, and the color of the blade was hued with a red tint. Its owner, my pious companion, stood up straight, and now fully upright was a good head taller than me. His free hand removed the tallit, letting it gently float to the ground. Beneath it resided not the elderly grandfather we had suspected, but a young man, maybe two years older than myself, with light brown, wavy hair. He wore a bound-leather breastplate, and his iron shoulder guards were shaped like two wide, black feathers.

He turned his gaze to me and flicked his nose at the warrior furthest to our right. "Would you mind handling the youngest fighter while I see to the other four?"

I gawked in disbelief, both due to the sudden change in the situation and the unexpectedness of his request.

"The smallest one," he repeated through a small smile, again nodding his nose toward the youngest Philistine to my right.

"Kill them!" yelled the wounded enemy commander, and the other four soldiers rushed in.

The religious wanderer moved forward, placing himself in front of three of the armed Philistines, leaving me to fight the smallest opponent. My adversary's eyes turned into large circles when he realized he had to fight me by himself, and his sword shook like a divining rod as he lifted it up to meet me.

Equally as insecure, I moved my staff into a defensive stance, and for a second, we simply stared at one another, the harsh sounds of blades ringing against each other to our left.

"Rondic!" bellowed their leader, and my opponent flinched. "Finish him quick and help us with this one!"

The order spurred Rondic to action, and he raised his blade above his head and then drove it down toward my skull. Terror surged through my limbs as I watched the weapon plunge toward me, and I instinctively intercepted it with my oaken staff. The sword slammed hard into the wood, but the staff held off the attack.

The boy-soldier pulled back the blade and swung again, this time aiming at my side. Again, I parried the blade with my staff. His third attack was a thrust, which I side-stepped by ducking to my right. He had overextended himself with the attack, and I used the opportunity to swing my wooden pole and smack him across the back, sending him tumbling to the ground. His shoulder landed on his blade, and he cried out in pain as the sharp metal tore into his skin.

Clutching his wound, Rondic knelt with his back to me, defenseless.

What was I supposed to do now? My hope had been to catch a glimpse of a battle, not participate in one. I swallowed hard, and my eyes swept back in search of guidance from my mysterious companion. I expected him still to be engaged with his own opponents, but instead found him standing among four motionless bodies lying on the earthen path.

My mouth hung open. How long had it been since the fight began? Fifteen seconds? He dispatched four men in less time than it would take me to cut four fingernails?

The victor turned toward me. He took a spot on my right and pointed his red blade at the still gasping young warrior. "I offer one last time. You are not too far gone. Surrender and our people and our God will accept you."

He still intended to give him the option of defecting to our side? Part of me wanted to feel indignation at his offer; less than a minute ago the little punk had attempted to divide my body into two proportionate halves. Yet the anger wouldn't come. Kneeling in front of me, I didn't see a bloodthirsty, merciless, Philistine, but a young, scared boy, far from home and involved in something far more frightful than he had imagined in his daydreams. I saw myself.

"Why?" asked the defeated boy quietly.

My companion ran a hand through his tan hair and surveyed the field. "Yahweh built this world for all of us. Eventually, we'll have to find some way to get along in it."

Rondic took several deep breaths. "And you promise I'll be safe?"

"On my life," said the wanderer.

The boy thought for a moment but then dropped his sword, his chin bobbing up and down. "Okay."

The unusual man held out his hand, and the Philistine took it. "I'm Damon."

"Rondic," said the warrior.

"It's my distinct pleasure to meet you," replied Damon. He stooped down and picked up his tallit from the ground, dusting off the dirt. Then he turned back to Rondic. "I'm going to have to tie you up, just until we get you back to our base. However, I promise you will not be harmed. We'll need you to answer a few questions, and you'll be watched for a time, but eventually you'll be free."

Rondic weighed the statement but nodded his head nervously. "Okay," he repeated and placed his hands behind his back.

"How do you plan to tie him up?" I asked.

Damon's gaze swept toward me. "I don't suppose you have any rope on you?"

My first thought was no, but then I remembered the pack that I carried from my mother. Peeking inside, I found the cheese she had sent packaged in a wool cloth and wrapped in twine. Undoing the knot, I handed him the cord. "We got lucky," I said.

He smiled and took it, and then went to Rondic to bind his hands. Finishing, he patted our new prisoner on the back and came back to me. "I owe you a debt of gratitude. I had been expecting only a pack of two or three roaming warriors. Had you decided not to help me, they very well may have been too much for me."

I gave a skeptical glance toward the remains of the four men he had defeated. "You seemed to handle yourself fairly well without any help."

Damon barked a laugh. "Yahweh is good at His job. He provides what is needed." He motioned to Rondic. "Cords for prudent binding and a new compatriot to fight beside. As I said to our new countryman, I'm Damon."

"Niklas," I said and held out my hand.

He clasped it and used his free hand to point toward Elah. "Would I be right in assuming you were heading to the front?"

"Yes," I answered, "I have some supplies for my older brothers in the army."

"Then we shall be our own mini-caravan," Damon said merrily. "It's only another mile and a half to where we're camped. We should be there within the hour."

We set off on the journey, but before we had walked fifty feet, Damon let out a small gasp of pain.

Rondic and I both noticed his hand on his side, blood seeping through his fingers.

"You're injured!" I said, going to take a look at the wound. His leather armor had a gash on its right side and red blood caked its edges.

The wander held up his free hand. "It's more a flesh wound than anything else, though it seems to be a touch deeper than I had originally hoped. I may need a bit of assistance making it back to our camp."

Staring in admiration of his strength, I offered him my shoulder. He gratefully accepted, and we began our travel anew, though at a slower pace.

Our eclectic band of a Philistine-foe-turned-Israelite-convert, a pious war hero, and a singing shepherd eventually made it to the outskirts of our camp. Two sentries noticed us approaching and held up their spears warily.

"Announce yourselves from there," called one of the guards.

Damon raised his hand. "It's just me, gentlemen," he said, "and a couple of my new friends."

Both guards squinted when they heard his voice. One of them moved toward us and cursed when he recognized the young warrior. "Prince Damon? Your father's been searching all over for you!"

My neck craned to the injured man. "*Prince* Damon?"

A sly grin crossed his lips, like a child after his mother caught him swiping a dollop of honey. "Did I forget to mention that tidbit?"

Chapter 13

"Yes," I exclaimed, "that nugget of information was definitely left out of the introductions."

The prince shrugged his shoulders and then let out a small grunt when the motion stretched his wound. "Didn't seem relevant at the time."

Prince Damon, King Erik's oldest son, was a borderline legend in Israel. The story went, two years ago, he and his page singlehandedly challenged and defeated an outpost of twenty Philistines. His exploit seemed to grow more fantastical with each retelling. The last time I heard it told around a campfire, the storyteller had insisted the prince had slain the twenty Philistine commanders with nothing but a wooden spoon he had found lying on the ground. The bit with the spoon still seemed a stretch, but after seeing the prince fight up close, maybe the story had more basis in reality than I had originally thought.

I assumed that eventually we'd run into each other in Erik's court, but when I asked about him to the other servants, they informed me that since the war with the Philistines had broken out, he had only returned to the capital a handful of times, and always when I was back home.

Rondic's surprise, however, dwarfed my own. Our captive's pupils looked like they were seconds from popping out of his eye sockets. "We tried to kill the prince," he said quietly, his teeth beginning to chatter. "They're going to slaughter me."

"No," Damon stated emphatically, "that's not going to happen. I promised on my life you would be safe, and you would find a home among our people. You'll be fine."

The captive boy's stance relaxed slightly, but his fingers still fidgeted nervously.

My shock had yet to wear off. "What was a prince doing wandering the plains by himself? You could have been killed."

"I wanted some time alone to pray," he answered simply, before raising his eyebrows in amusement. "If the opportunity arose to put a stop to the band of Philistines terrorizing our rear flank, all the better." He paused. "Plus, I have found that with my father, it seems to be easier to ask forgiveness than permission for these matters."

I slowly shook my head. "You're insane."

The sentries reached us, and the taller of the two addressed Damon. "The king has ordered whoever found you to bring you straight to him. We need you to come with us, Your Grace."

"The obligations of royalty never cease," the prince said with a sigh. "Now you know why I didn't mention it." He placed a hand on our prisoner. "This is Rondic. He has surrendered to our forces, and I have accepted his request to swear allegiance to our nation. Take him to General Behaj to gain any information about the Philistines forces, but under no circumstance are you to use any harsher form of interrogation on him. From now on, he should be treated like any other Israelite. Do I make myself clear?"

"Yes, sir," replied the shorter guard, before taking Rondic deeper into the camp.

"Well," Damon said to me, "this is where we part ways. Again, I am in your debt. I'll do what I can to settle the ledger."

"It was nothing," I replied. "You did all the heavy lifting."

He grinned at the comment and nodded toward the sky. "That's His job actually. If you're searching for your brothers, they'll probably be on the front lines straight north of here."

"Thanks," I said, and then passed the prince off my shoulder to the first guard.

The two of them headed west into the camp, while I turned toward the north to return to my original mission — delivering supplies to my brothers.

With most of our men stationed on the front lines, the camp appeared eerily deserted. Hundreds of thigh-high tents dotted the landscape, along with thousands of bedrolls. Smells of stale bread and dried meats hung in the air, and smoking fire pits left the entire encampment in a cloud of gray haze that diluted the mid-day sun. It felt like walking through a dreary, pupil-burning dream.

I kept heading north and eventually reached the main contingent of Israel's army. Our numbers, probably five thousand men strong, were impressive.

Our armaments, however, were another story entirely. None of our troops had swords, or spears, or shields, or — I don't know, *any* kind of actual military equipment. Instead they carried different types of metal tools. Many, like my brother Eli, brought axes. Others had long knives, and some even held wheat scythes from their fields.

Thanks to Eliab's hulking form, my brothers were easy to find. They stood together with the bulk of the army which was lined up three men deep along the top edge of the valley's east cliff.

"Abin!" I shouted.

He turned and smiled broadly. "Niklas! My favorite brother!"

My other two siblings turned around as well, though both of them gave me a much more level greeting.

Eliab frowned. "What are you doing here?"

"Who cares?" Abin interjected, and he wrapped his arms around me, the smell of wine thick on his breath. "Niklas can sing for us!" He announced enthusiastically to the surrounding troops.

I untangled myself from Abin's embrace and raised my eyebrows at Sham. "How long has he been drinking?"

"The whole time," my brother answered. "Forty straight days."

Abin hiccupped. "Who knew war would be so much fun?" He noticed my backpack. "Oh, what do you have there?"

Ducking out of his grasp, I unhooked the straps and gave the fresh bread to Eliab. "From Mom. I also have some cheese to deliver to your captain."

Eliab looked warily at the wicker pack. We had barely shared five words since I entered the king's service. "Fine, you'll find him at the command tents to the north. His name is Carmi. Drop it off and head home."

"No," Abin said in a drawn-out yawn. "At least let him see the show before he leaves."

"The show?" I asked.

"The demigod himself is about to make his daily —"

"Enough," Eli cut him off. "Niklas, deliver the cheese and go home. This is no time—"

A trumpet call burst through the air from the valley.

"Too late," Abin said with a smile. He grabbed my shoulder and pushed me through the throng of soldiers.

Reaching the edge of the valley's cliff, I saw a mass of Philistine warriors standing atop an opposing hill. It was hard to make out too much of their forces, but it was easy to tell they had gathered at least as many soldiers as we had. Combine that with the weapon advantage they commanded, and the outcome of imminent and complete defeat seemed clear.

Two men walked into the valley between our armies. One appeared to be a page about my age, carrying a gold-plated, round shield large enough to cover half his body. Yet it was the soldier standing next to him who captivated everyone's attention.

Adjectives like *big* or *massive* failed to do the warrior justice. He stood at least three feet taller than his attendant, with arms thick enough to make tree trunks envious and shoulders wide enough to carry a packhorse upon. From head to toe, he was covered in golden armor; his helmet, chainmail, and leggings all sparkling like the sun. In his right hand he carried a spear as long as he was tall, and on his back, he wore a sword nearly five feet long. A very familiar, gold-inlaid handle marked the weapon.

Mother of mercy. It was the same one I had tried to steal a year ago.

The pair stalked forward into the center of the valley, and the giant took off his helmet. "Hear me, fabled warriors of Israel!" He shouted, raising his arms above his head. "For generations, we Philistines have heard stories of your legendary triumphs over Egypt. However, for weeks I have asked for a champion to face me in single combat. Surely I, one man, cannot compare to the terrifying army of the Pharaoh you conquered. So again today, I challenge any of your so-called warriors to a winner-take-all duel. If I win, your people will become our slaves. If your champion wins, we will become your slaves." He glanced back at his own troops and made a needlessly inappropriate gesture. "Today, I defy each of you. I defy your nation. I defy your pathetic god! Face me or die in shame!"

His speech finished, he pulled out his massive sword and held it over his head. The Philistine army erupted in shouts and laughter. As their voices echoed throughout the floor of the valley, our own military shrunk back.

Somewhere, deep down, I knew that best chance of living a long life meant avoiding such a warrior, but that logical voice seemed to be trying to speak through a thick wall. Have you ever encountered someone, and thirty seconds after meeting them wanted to punch them in the nose, stuff sand down their undergarments, and write dirty names on their face while they lie there unconscious? Multiply that by ten, and it pretty much described how I felt about this bloated pig.

"How long has this been happening?" I asked my brother.

Abin brought a flask to his lips. "Forty days," he said before taking a long drink. He flicked his head for us to make our way back to our brothers.

We waded through the depressed troops, their shoulders hunched over, their eyes bleak.

By the time we returned to our family, my mind raced with questions. "Why hasn't someone challenged him?"

The question brought a smile to Sham's face. "It's not for lack of incentive. The king has promised his eldest daughter in marriage to the man who slays the beast."

"And no one's taken the offer?"

"Oh, our wives would love that," Abin said, frowning as he turned his now empty flask upside down. "Coming home from war with a medal of bravery and a new bride. Talk about living dangerously! I'd rather the brute just kill me then and there and get it over with."

"More importantly," Sham continued, "you saw their champion. It'd be like trying to slay a mountain with a pickaxe. The task is a death sentence."

"But still, he's just a man," I argued. "Put the right end of spear in him, and he'll die just as—"

"Niklas," Eli interrupted me. "Take the cheese to our captain and go home."

My hands flew up in aggravation. "This is ridiculous! Someone has to fight that thug. He's a bully. One punch to the face and they always back down."

"Enough!" my oldest brother commanded, placing one of his massive hands on my shoulder. "Will you never grow up? We are at war; people are going to die, and still you insist on plotting and scheming. Go home before you get someone killed!" He pushed me away and turned his back to all of us.

Abin opened his jaw as if to challenge Eliab's decision, but then shrugged and mouthed, *See you later.*

I wanted to pull my hair out. This whole situation was ridiculous: my brothers' cowardice, our soldiers' refusal to accept the challenge, all of it. This wasn't about me. This was about the overgrown man-child openly mocking our nation.

And then the sweetest sound I had heard in months emanated from the valley floor. I heard the harp.

Apparently, *Someone Else* agreed with me.

I stalking off, my mind ran through scheme after scheme. The harp was telling me there was some way I could help. Maybe I could convince one of the warriors to bury the backwater bully. Since stringing my first words together, I've practically perfected the art of convincing a person to do what I wanted. Yet for this to work, it required a better access point.

I needed the king.

Chapter 14

Bickering captains and generals filled the king's command pavilion, giving me the chance to slip in unnoticed. Erik sat on a wooden seat in the center of arguments, staring forward with sunken, hazy eyes. He had a cupbearer on his right and a young woman fanning him on his left, but the king paid neither of them any attention. His focus lay squarely on his son Damon, the devout warrior from earlier, prostrate at the king's feet. He still wore his prayer shawl, but his armor had been stripped off, and fresh white bandages were wrapped around his torso.

"Please, Father," the prince pleaded, his forehead touching the ground. "Give me permission to challenge Goliath in battle. Let me fight for our kingdom, our people, our God. Yahweh saved me once already today. He will do so again."

One of the generals closer to Erik nodded. "Your Highness, there is wisdom in your son's words. Give him a day or two to recover, and he could be our solution. He is a proven warrior, and with a little luck, he could slay their champion and end this conflict."

The king's lip slowly curled up in malice, glaring at the commander. "'Luck?' You would counsel me to chance my eldest son's life on 'luck'?" He flung his hand up and knocked away the wine chalice, its metallic ring clanging along the ground. "Remind me about our *luck* over the past year? Where was our *luck* when the locusts took our crops? How strong was our *luck* when we lost a tenth of our army in the battle at Midan? Our nation hangs by the barest of threads, and you would send my son to battle an undefeated Philistine butcher? Before the war, that savage had already gutted over one hundred of our people! He will not come near my son!"

The general held his head low and took a step back. "I meant no disrespect, my king."

"Yet it was freely given," Erik spat. "If we weren't in the middle of a godforsaken war, I'd spend a whole month testing your own luck against the Philistines in battle."

"Father," Damon said in a hushed voice, raising his chin. "Please, guard your words. We are not God-forsaken. We simply need —"

"Do not test me," the king said, fresh color rising in his cheeks. "Just because I do not wish some uncircumcised barbarian killing my firstborn son does not mean I won't end you myself. Your stunt from this afternoon will be punished, and my answer is no."

Damon, realizing his cause was lost, curtly nodded and backed away.

For a moment, the tent was silent, but soon Alexander's massive girth emerged from a corner. "Your Highness, you show great prudence in not risking the death of our future king on such a dangerous mission. However, we must send someone to fight the Philistine. Every night, we lose more of our troops to desertion. Soon we won't have enough men to hold off the enemy even with the high ground."

Erik scoffed. "Have I not given enough incentive? Is the promise of my daughter so lightly regarded that not one of my men would fight to have her hand in marriage? Even my generals cower in fear."

The men in the room said nothing, each keeping their eyes locked anywhere but on the king.

A compulsive urge to strangle every person present not named Damon nearly sent me on a rampage. We had thousands of men, a few built as large as my brother Eliab; how could they all be missing the stones to accept this challenge? Damon had called him Goliath — even his name made me want to trek into the valley and punch him in the face.

Finally, a commander, far older than any other in the room, spoke. "We can't risk this fight on simply any soldier who volunteers. Whoever we send must have experience, some previous labor to inspire confidence in his chances. We need a hero of old."

The king leaned back in his chair. "Heroes are extinct. All we have left are the shadows of their myths."

Pressing against one of the pavilion's tent poles, I tried to push through my anger, reflecting on the old man's words. We needed someone with a past accomplishment of heroism, a past feat to inspire confidence in his chances. A horrible thought took root in my mind. *A young, audacious lion-slayer might qualify?* Of course, he'd have to be an idiot of legendary proportion to volunteer to fight a literal giant.

My mind went into overdrive, running through all the reasons why someone else would be a better pick. One, I was only sixteen. Two, outside of this afternoon's misadventure, my three-year-old sister Yeva and I shared the exact same amount of battle experience. Three, in the last ten seconds since contemplating fighting the man-beast, I'm pretty sure I wet myself a little.

Yet in the face of all those valid, reasonable, life-preserving arguments, my feet started taking me toward Erik. If Alexander was right about the numbers—and insufferable as he could be, the rotund counselor knew his math—if someone didn't step up soon, we'd be slaughtered. My family would be slaughtered. Someone needed to stand up to the monster.

"I'll do it," I croaked.

Every head whipped toward me.

I knelt down before the king, fighting unsuccessfully to ignore the insanity I was volunteering for. "I'll fight the Philistine."

A chorus of quiet snickers sprinkled the tent.

Alexander approached me, his measured, calm voice betrayed by his frozen glare. "Bard, your skills have not been requested. You will take your leave."

I bit my lip, more than a little unsettled about refusing an order from the human toad. Debating Alexander was like arguing with an abacus: you could apply all the emotional arguments you wanted, but if the numbers didn't add up on the slides, he just stared back at you, cold and uncaring.

Beyond that, the chief chronicler's presence was simply unnerving. He never got outwardly upset, but disdain waited behind his eyes. People who challenged him soon either left the capital or ended up gone—like found two months later in the bottom of a trench, gone. If I pushed him too hard, he could have me erased just as easily as a troublesome line in his accounting scrolls.

Yet there was no other way.

Meeting the counselor's gaze, I held my ground. "I can kill him." Squaring my shoulders, I turned to the king. "I will kill him."

A merciless smile split Erik's face. "How? By singing him to sleep and slitting his throat as he rests? He would snap you in two and use your skull as a bowl for fruit."

Another round of laughter burst from the commanders.

I pulled out the lion's tooth I carried as a memento of my victory. "Your Highness, last year, a lion came and took one my father's lambs from our flock. Something came over me, a power, and I hunted them down and killed the beast with one strike." As I spoke, a truth I had avoided for over a year poured out of my mouth. "Yahweh delivered me from the lion. He will help me conquer this uncircumcised inbred."

This time no one laughed.

King Erik arched an eyebrow suspiciously. "Is this true? You killed a lion?"

Damon took a step closer to his father and me. "You're Niklas from Bethlehem?" he asked.

I nodded.

"I've heard stories of a young shepherd who killed a beast, Father." He paused, idly stroking the tassels on his shawl. "I believe he's telling the truth."

Holding his palms together, the king put them under his chin, studying me. Serving in his court for the last year, I had watched him deal with everything from foreign dignitaries to the destitute, but never had I seen this look upon his face. The memory of his hyenas flooded into my mind, and I averted my eyes, keenly aware of how quickly my imprudence could end with me as one of their midday snacks.

Erik closed his eyes and tilted his head, as if listening to something, and then his facial expression softened. "Fine," he agreed, shocking even me. "Niklas will be our champion."

The entire tent erupted in protests.

"Sire, this is madness, the stakes are too high!"

"Our nation will be enslaved!"

"Please, Your Highness, listen to reason."

Only the prince remained silent, watching me with a steady gaze.

"Silence!" The king's voice boomed over the noise. "The next man to question my decision will take his place as champion."

Apparently, no one else wanted the job.

Rising from his seat, Erik stood over me. "Damon, take the boy and prepare him for the duel. He'll need armor, so modify mine and let him wear it into battle." He turned to me and placed his hand on my shoulder. "As for you, Niklas, lion-slayer of Bethlehem, divining the favor of Yahweh is a fool's errand or a desperate man's hope. This is a time of desperation." His voice dropped to a whisper, and he turned away. "God be with us all."

Damon patted me on the back. "Let's go."

The commanders parted as we walked out, an ominous hush covering all of them as they stared at me in disbelief. I'm pretty sure I shared their expression. The passion of the moment faded, and the reality of my decision sank in. A sixteen-year-old shepherd would face a monster.

We walked away from the pavilion, and the prince directed us down through a row of taller tents. The moment we passed the last canvas shelter, two tall, identical men came out of the tent's shadow. The twins had raven black hair, cut no longer than a fingernail, with long, sinewy limbs, which they used to roughly grab my shoulders and lock me in place.

"Hey!" I shouted in confusion, struggling against their hold. My protests halted the moment Damon drew a knife and pressed it firmly against my throat.

"I'll give you one chance," he said quietly, "but if you lie to me, I swear, you'll die here and now."

He moved in closer and his blade stung my skin. "Have you sold us out to the Philistines?"

Chapter 15

"What?" I gasped, bewildered by the ludicrousness of his accusation.

Even that slight movement of my throat caused his blade to break skin, and a trail of warm blood trickled down my neck. The prince's face contorted, showing an entirely different persona than the pious, almost too-humble man I had encountered earlier. Had the king's mania been passed down to his son?

Damon's pupils darted back and forth over my face, searching for some kind of tell in my reaction. I'm pretty sure all he found was a stupefied boy, seconds away from screaming like a five-year-old girl.

Then, with the same abruptness of his assault, he moved away from me and held up a hand to the twins still holding me. "Let him go," he said, and immediately they released me. "He's not working for them. You can take your leave."

The two men nodded. As they walked away, I noticed the twins also wore identical belts, heavy flax with several black feathers sewn into their bindings. My eyes went wide at the revelation of who my captors were.

"They're Seraphim," I said in astonishment.

"Yes," Damon answered matter-of-factly, distracted by other thoughts.

My heart raced faster. The Seraphim were almost as legendary as judges, serving as covert assassins within Israel's military. The details about them changed depending on who you asked, but one fact was agreed upon: they always left black feathers at the scene of their targets.

Another thought struck me. "Your armor," I said, pointing a finger at him. "The black shoulder guards shaped like feathers. You're one of them, too."

Damon locked eyes with me, and he bobbed his head once.

That at least explained how he had taken care of the marauders earlier. The Seraphim were supposedly trained in the most brutal, effective methods of combat. Yet it still didn't answer the more immediate, personally insulting question.

I brought my hand up to the wound he had left on my neck. "Why would you think I was working with the bloody Philistines?"

Damon glanced down. "I am sorry for the accusation, but it's the only thing that made sense. Why else would you volunteer to fight the monster unless you were working with them?"

"Who in the silent underworld is 'them'? The Philistines?" I asked, growing more defiant now that a blade wasn't half an inch away from ending my life.

The prince shook his head and clenched his teeth, inhaling sharply through them. "I don't know yet, they're like a shadow," he finally admitted. "But for the last year, someone has been working against our nation from the inside. It's never anything major, nothing I could trace back to one person, but a battle will go south at exactly the worst possible moment, or a small but crucial supply shipment will be intercepted."

The judge's mission flittered to the forefront of my mind. "You think there's a traitor," I said a bit too softly.

"Something's off," he said. "And then this latest engagement with the Philistines happened. Honestly, they have enough forces to drive us halfway to Gibeath, but all they've done is send out their champion every day, challenging us to this ridiculous contest. Why would they risk the entire war on such a risky roll of the dice?"

I started fitting the pieces together. "You think it's a setup."

"That's why I wanted to be the one to fight, at least then I could guarantee someone wouldn't intentionally sabotage the battle. But then today, you mysteriously show up as I'm being attacked by the marauders, and the next thing I know, you've convinced my father to let you fight for our country. It would be the perfect chance to drive the final dagger into our nation."

I ran both of my palms over my scalp slowly. Super, not only did I wiggle myself into fighting a giant, a specimen who probably belonged in the mythical beast section of history, but the battle was likely rigged against me from the get-go.

Fan-freaking-tastic.

"Have you told your father about your suspicions?" I asked.

Damon shook his head again. "He wouldn't believe me unless I had proof. He's convinced all the setbacks have been a result of his advisors' collective incompetence."

Biting my tongue, I tried to find some silver lining, some plan of action that didn't result in me walking feet first into a trap. My head rose in a thought as I recalled Damon's identical comrades. "Could another member of the Seraphim take my place?"

The prince's face fell. "Our order's existence depends on us remaining in the shadows. Part of our vows requires us to swear an oath of secrecy. We do not participate in open combat."

My brow furrowed in confusion. "But you offered to fight Goliath twenty minutes ago."

"As the son of the king," he answered, "not as a Seraphim agent."

It seemed like a technicality, and my admiration for Damon grew a little knowing he at least tried to exploit it. Still, that option was off the table. "And if I try to back out of the fight because it's a trap?"

"Without proof," Damon said quietly, 'my father would have you executed for either desertion or outright treason."

I rubbed my eyes. Death-by-hyena seemed only slightly less enjoyable than suicide-by-giant.

"Let's get you the armor," the prince said, motioning to his right. "I don't know how long we have before the battle."

I shuffled after him, not because I had much interest in the plan, but because at that moment, I had no idea what else to do.

Twenty minutes later, we stood along the riverbed, and the attendant quickly began outfitting me with the bronze armor of the king. The task turned out to be nothing more than salt in an already festering wound.

The fancy metal left me feeling like a toddler during his first week of walking, stomping around bowlegged and off center, always a moment away from face-planting into the sand of the riverbank outside the king's tent.

"Not like that," Damon chided me, tightening the shoulder guards. "You need to follow through on each action. The joints aren't designed to change direction midstride."

"Then how do you expect me to dodge attacks?" My arm lashed out at him. "You moved around well enough in your armor today, what's the trick?"

"It's a process," he admitted, "but once you get the hang of it, it'll feel like a second skin. It just takes time."

"Perfect," I said dismissively, "something I possess in abundance. We have, what, a couple of hours before the match? I'm sure that's plenty of time to master the finer points of both swordplay and armor training. Maybe I'll squeeze in an afternoon nap."

The metal arm pieces clanked against one another as I tried to draw Erik's sword. I got it halfway out before I lost my balance and ended up flailing upon the dirt.

The prince extended his hand and helped me to my feet. He smiled, but it was apparent he too was becoming increasingly uncomfortable with my chances. "Maybe there's a way we can delay the fight. At least until you get a hang of the basics."

"Out of the question" came a precise voice from behind us. Alexander waddled out of the trees. "The enemy champion has agreed to fight you. The battle will commence in thirty minutes."

"Thirty minutes?" I repeated, choking on the words.

"Finish your"—he shook his head in disbelief—"preparations and proceed to the edge of the valley." Then he spun on his heels and left.

My legs gave way as the situation's harsh reality crashed down on my shoulders, and I fell back to the ground. Lying on the wet sand face up, cold and hopeless terror assaulted my thoughts. Some kinds of fear drive you to fight; others urge you to flee. Yet the insurmountable, horrifying task in front of me stripped away any notion of survival, paralyzing me.

"I'm going to die," I whispered.

Damon didn't reach out help me up again, but instead unbuckled his sheath and sat down next to me with his legs crossed. "Everyone does," he stated, "eventually. Yet none of us know if our final breath will happen today."

Scoffing, I raised a hand raised to wipe my face. "There's some pretty good evidence for betting against myself." I paused, too tired to dance around the truth. "I'm scared."

The river burbled and popped next to us, and I probably took a hundred deep breaths before Damon finally responded.

He placed a hand on my kneecap. "Have faith."

I inhaled sharply. The flippant—and quite frankly utterly useless answer—sent hot anger through my blood, and I used the passion to push myself up. "Seriously, faith? Despite the massive manure-storm I'm about to face, your solution is to simply let some make-believe emotion help me feel better!" I shook my head in disgust. "Thanks, but I'm going to pass on that revolutionary idea."

The prince stared forward, unfazed by my contempt at his suggestion. "Have you ever heard about my battle against the Philistine outpost?"

"What?" I asked, confused by his change of subject. "I mean, yeah, every Israelite has heard of it, but what does that have to do with me?"

"Because," he began, a smile growing on his face, "much like your current predicament, it was the most terrifying, idiotic, and reckless choice I could have made at the time. For weeks prior to my impulsive adventure, our army had gathered across from the Philistines, and much like today, we were too afraid to march against them.

"Day after day I prayed and fasted, begging God to come down and fight for us like He did in the stories—sending fire from heaven, opening the ground and swallowing them whole, anything. I figured if I just believed enough, He had to honor my request. Yet nothing happened, and in truth, every day we lost more troops to skirmishes. Then one morning, I was walking with my armor bearer, and we stumbled upon the Philistine outpost. There were twenty enemy soldiers camped on that hill, and I stared up to heaven and demanded answers. 'Why haven't you done something about them?'"

Damon glanced at his hands. "I never got a verbal answer, but a sense of peace came over me, calmly asking me the exact same question, what was *I* going to do about it? I started recalling all the stories of Him rescuing our people against impossible odds, so I turned to my attendant and asked him what he thought about picking a fight."

Admiration filled my cheeks. "And you defeated them," I said.

"We did," he agreed, but then shook his head. "But not immediately. First, we had to climb the mountain. It took the better part of an hour, and it wasn't long before the enemy soldiers began heckling us, saying we were rats crawling out of our holes. What hope of survival did the two of us have against ten-to-one odds? By the time we reached the summit, I had run through dozens of horrifying scenarios, all ending with our carcasses broken and laid to waste on the battlefield."

I knew the feeling. "How'd you overcome the fear?"

"Overcome it?" he asked, chuckling. "Not likely. Most of me wanted to find one of those holes they kept talking about."

"So why didn't you turn back?"

"When we reached the summit, I had a theory. What if faith meant believing in what you can't yet see and acting accordingly? What if the reward of faith meant eventually seeing what you believe? So we fought."

"And then you won," I said, quieter.

He nodded. "Then we won."

The reasons for volunteering to fight slowly bubbled back to the forefront of my mind. The Philistines being only one battle away from crushing our nation. The melody from the harp. The desire to lay the smug, overgrown inbred on his backside. My resolve hardened.

"Let's do this," I said, straightening my back and struggling to my feet. My mind began working out the plan of action. I only saw this working one way. "I need your help with something."

"Anything," he promised, rising with me.

I pulled at the armor. "We need to get me out of this bronze death trap before the battle."

The prince coughed and stopped moving. "You want to fight without armor? You're not serious."

"Deadly," I replied. "If I'm going to die, I'd rather do it in something more comfortable." I grinned. "Though death is definitely not Option A."

Reluctantly, he assisted me in stripping off the bronze plates. Rolling my neck, I sighed in relief. "Much better. No, keep the sword, too. I'd be as liable to stab myself in the heat of battle. I'm only taking things I know how to use."

"Which are...?"

Kneeling down next to the stream, I plunged my hands deep into the muddy riverbank. In a matter of moments, my fingers discovered what they sought: five smooth stones, half the size of my palm.

I stuffed them into my pouch, double-checked the sling wrapped around my wrist, and gestured to him. "Pass me my staff, would you."

Damon handed me the wood, staring at me like I had an arrow sticking out of my ear. "You're going to duel the monster of Gath, the bloodthirsty desolator of our people, with a stick and a bag of pebbles."

"It's my favorite stick," I said in mock offense. "Besides, when you fought the Philistines, did you defeat them purely through superior sword skill?"

"No," he scoffed, "but I still used a sword."

"Because you knew *how* to use one," I replied, holding up my sling and staff. "This is what I know. The big guy upstairs will have to make do."

The prince rubbed his eyes. "Niklas, there is a fine line between confident faith and complete insanity."

"When deciding to fight a literal giant, that difference seems mostly semantic."

Damon weighed my words. Finally, he let out a sigh and laughed. "Fair enough, Niklas, lion-slayer of Bethlehem, we'll do it your way."

Together we strode to the battlefront. Well, the prince had a stride, each of his steps containing an equal measure of grace, power, and a quiet confidence. I was proud my knees didn't visibly knock together from the terror of this idiotic scheme.

Most of our troops recognized Damon and gave him nods of respect as we passed, giving our journey a touch of dramatic flair. At the edge of our forces, Erik waited with his commanders. We approached, and Alexander stepped toward me, his eyes filled with indignation. He opened his mouth to speak, but I already knew what was coming.

"I am not backing out, toad man," I said dismissively. His eyes bulged at the insult, and smug satisfaction swelled within me. If today was my last day breathing, at least I had the opportunity to tell the overfed fool off. "The armor just chafed."

The high counselor, along with every other captain and general, gawked at me. King Erik, however, watched me with a steady gaze. "You're confident you will win?"

I considered the question. "I'm confident I am supposed to be out on the battlefield."

He studied me quietly for a moment and then opened his hand toward the valley. "Then go."

I bowed and started the descent into the valley. Reaching its floor, I looked up to the skies. "All right, this is your show," I said to the one who had orchestrated all of this. "It's time you did your part."

Nothing happened.

"Seriously," I said, my voice cracking. "I have no idea what I'm supposed to do next."

Nothing.

"Really?"

Nothing.

"Boy!" called Goliath from across the valley. "Look at me, boy!"

I blinked several times.

I was so incredibly dead.

Chapter 16

When it comes to foul language, my vocabulary is quite extensive, yet none of my words did justice to the amount of feces I had just walked into. Every sane bone in my body wanted to sprint back up the hill and disappear into the deepest, darkest hole I could find.

This grand scheme had revolved around God doing his god-thing. Another bout of supernatural strength like during my fight against the lion. Raining hail the size of fists upon the battlefield, a horde of locusts viciously terrorizing the enemy champion, or maybe an outbreak of debilitating boils. At this point, I'd settle for a bad rash of acne. I had been so confident Yahweh would go all Jericho on him, reducing the barbarian to ash. Instead, here I stood at the bottom of the valley, very much alone.

The Philistine warrior waited in the center of the field, waving aggressively at me. "I said get over here!"

I bit my lip, glancing at the sky. Why had He set this whole thing up only to leave me hanging in the wind? What was worth this level of sacrifice? Rubbing my eyes, I turned my head around. Thousands of soldiers waited at my back, and even from a distance, their fear was evident in the way they huddled together. As a whole, we'd forgotten how to stand up for ourselves.

Okay, so maybe we were outclassed and outnumbered, and had failed to recruit an actual giant to our roster, but did that give us the excuse to simply lie down and forfeit the match? Someone needed to remind our troops we could still fight, regardless of how desperate the circumstances. I swallowed hard. If my battle inspired our people to get back up, regardless if I lived or died, maybe it'd be worth it.

I strode out to meet the Philistine champion.

The Philistine sneered as I approached. "What trickery is this? Erik promised that he finally found a warrior to challenge my skill, but instead of a soldier, he brings me a boy. Did he hope sending a child to beg for mercy would save his craven scalp?"

Clasping tightly to my staff, I glared up at him—all the way up at him. Sweet Lord, the man was huge. "I'm not here to beg."

"Then what?" Goliath questioned, and he dropped down and placed his hands on his knees. "Does Erik offer you as a pet for me? I suppose that's appropriate. Israelites are little more than mangy dogs." He rose back to full height and addressed his forces. "What do you think, men of Philistia?" he bellowed. "I found a stray puppy! Should I keep him, or do you think he has fleas?"

His army burst into laughter, shouting obscenity after obscenity about the various ways to dispose of me.

I steadied myself. "I'm not here to beg, and I'd rather kiss your mother than be your slave, which honestly is saying something, because judging by your hideous mug, I'd wager she's quite the ugly beast."

The Philistine's shoulders tensed, and he slowly turned back to face me. "Watch your tongue, mongrel. I do not require it to give our reply to your king. Our response to this...insult"—he spat on the ground—"can be engraved into your corpse just as easily."

"Erik isn't interested in your response," I said, taking a step forward, "since you'll be dead by the time I leave this valley. I'm here to face you in combat."

Goliath's head jerked back. "What!?" He began laughing. "You? I think not. My blades and spears have ended the lives of hundreds of your kin. I'd not sully its steel against you, a mere child, in this battle of men. My people, real warriors, would consider me a coward." Dark red color filled his cheeks. "I've changed my mind. I'll let you live long enough to inform Erik that this insult will cost him the lives of all his troops. Forget the offer of slavery. We'll leave your rotting, pathetic bodies for the crows."

The Philistine champion pulled a flask off his belt and took a long swig. He finished, realized I was still there, and swung his arm out. "Go!" Then he gathered up his spear and shield and began stalking back to his troops.

Goliath's outright rejection hit me like a kick to the stomach. He didn't even consider me an adversary worth killing. How could I ever face the king, Damon, or my family?

I shook my head. Forget that. I have a talent for making people want to murder me—ask any of my brothers.

"You're like a sheep!" I called out to him.

He stopped but refused to turn around. "What?"

"*Sheep*," I said, elongating the word. "They're pathetic animals; cowardly, defenseless, insolent. They're dumber than dirt, and they crap everywhere." I paused. "They're just like the Philistines, and you're the chief, bloody ewe!"

He shuddered, his armor grating against itself, and he pivoted slowly, murder in his eyes. "You're dead," he whispered.

Well kudos to me—for the first time in recent memory, one of my plans actually worked. I managed to set eight feet of pure muscle and mayhem on a murderous rampage. I really need new hobbies. Dropping my staff, I quickly began unwinding the slingshot wrapped around my arm.

"Have your people told you of my past victories?" he asked, drawing the sword from behind his back. The blasted thing was nearly as tall as me. "Our king gave this to me as a reward for killing my one hundredth Israelite soldier. I remember the Israeli dog well. I severed both the head and an arm from his body in one strike. That was with a sword half this size."

My wrist started twitching. That merry visual alone made me want to dash away screaming, but now wasn't the time to show fear. I needed him upset, unbalanced. "Glad to know it's not simply compensating for something else."

He brushed off my comment, admiring the weapon. "I haven't used this blade in battle yet. I had hoped to christen it with a victory worth its effort." He glared at our troops. "I see now no one in your pitiful country could ever offer such a challenge."

I pulled out one of the stones from my pouch.

"They say I can't be killed," Goliath continued, cracking his neck as he closed the distance between us.

"I imagine your people say dumb stuff pretty regularly." My sling began to spin over my head.

He approached, purpose in his steps. "They say I'm the son of Astarte, the goddess of war herself."

"Now you're a deity?" I asked, raising my eyebrows, the leather sling whirling faster. "That's going to be awfully hard on her temple attendance when me and our God kick your oversized butt then."

"Your God cannot save you in this fight," he said, a body length from me.

His last statement brought us to the crux of the matter. Maybe he was right; maybe God would rather support the biggest, baddest guy on the block, or just avoid the matter entirely. But maybe not. Maybe He'd rather stand next to someone who'd risked it all to protect those he loved than someone merely devoted to wanton destruction.

The distinct notes of a harp strumming played over the valley, and a snarky grin peeked out of the corner of my lips. *Go team.*

"You obviously haven't read about my God," I said, and then turned my attention back to the sky. "Together."

I loosed the sling.

The stone flew straight into the giant's face, slamming right beneath the nose guard of his helmet. His neck snapped back, and for a moment he stood limp, as if merely dazed. Then his body crashed forehead first to the earth.

The entire valley was silent. Neither side moved. Neither side believed what they saw. In all fairness, I struggled to believe it, and the giant's corpse was casting a shadow on my feet.

I survived the battle. The smile on my face grew. No—I won the battle!

Next to the man-slayer lay his precious sword. Kneeling down, I grabbed the golden hilt. When I killed the lion, I kept a memento. Killing a giant seemed worthy of one, too. It took all my strength just to lift the blade into the air, but then with one swipe I brought it down, separating the giant's head from his body. It rolled next to my feet, and I bent down and lifted it by his sweaty hair.

Mentally, physically, and emotionally exhausted, my breath came fast and hard, but I lifted my gaze. Thousands of Philistine warriors glared down at me, a mere shepherd boy, who had just dismembered their legendary hero, a near deity in their eyes. The sword fell from my hand. I believe they meant to kill me.

Spinning toward the Israelite camp, for the first time ever, my people pleasantly surprised me. As one unit, our troops surged down the walls of the valley, fury in their eyes and pure energy in their shouts of war. Today, we took the fight to the Philistines.

Chapter 17

The flap of the tent opened, and a young page stuck his head in. "Excuse me," he said apologetically, "but King Erik requests your presence."

I rubbed the sleep from my eyes. "I'll be right out."

The boy watched me, his pupils wide with a mixture of excitement and caution. "They say you killed a demigod today. They're calling you 'The God Slayer.'"

"Demigod?" I scoffed. "Not likely. The man was more flatulent blowhard than deity. I still have his stink on me."

The page didn't press the point, smiling and disappearing back outside. The king had given me a private tent after the duel. My eyes swept over the room. Goliath's sword and spear lay in the corner. It took two men just to bring them back to our camp. The giant's head remained outside. He smelled bad enough alive.

The afternoon had faded into night during my nap, leaving me with no idea of how much time had passed while I slept. I rolled off the mat and massaged my temples, still processing exactly what had transpired. Demigod or no, an untrained shepherd had just slain one of the fiercest warriors in recent history. It strained belief...or at least challenged it.

I touched my forehead, remembering the anointing oil. Alvaro had christened me Israel's protector. Matthias had promised God would give me the strength to accomplish the task. *This is what they meant.* Part of me wondered if the victory over the giant completed my mission, but then I shook my head. There was still the matter of the traitor lurking among our own people to uncover before I could rest. Who knew a dab of oil could affect so much change?

I shook my head. Making Erik wait too long could prove more dangerous than facing the monster. I left the tent and meant to go straight to our command center, but then doubled back to grab the remains of the Philistine.

The current atmosphere around our encampment contrasted sharply with the solemn mood twelve hours prior. Together, men sang ballads of triumph and glory. Feasts of ox shank and lamb mutton roasted over fires, and the smell of fermented beverage wafted from every direction.

For the most part, my journey was unimpeded, but every so often a soldier noticed what I carried, and a cry of thanks to "The Hero of Elah" would erupt from our troops. The title seemed slightly less pretentious than god-slayer.

At the king's tent, the captains and generals carried on with the same merrymaking as the soldiers outside. Their cheeks rosy from wine, they pointed to the map in the center of the pavilion, back-slapping each other about how far our troops had advanced.

"Our boys drove them back to the gates of Gath *and* Ekron!"

"Oh, it's better than that; we littered the road between there and Elah with at least five hundred of their soldiers. The next time they leave the protection of their walls, the cowards will have to worry about tripping over their own soldiers' carcasses."

One man was not caught up in the mood. Alexander's beady eyes showed no mirth. I wondered if the man actually had a beating heart or if accounting ink flowed through his veins. He noticed my entrance and gestured toward Erik.

The commanders embraced my shoulders as I approached the king.

Sure, now they supported me, the temperamental old goats.

King Erik sat cross-legged on the ground next to the map. His goblet half empty and resting between his thighs, it was the first time in months I had seen him wear a genuine smile. "Niklas!" he cried as

I approached. "My bard *and* my champion, well done!" He smacked the ground next to him. "Come, sit with me."

While I followed his order, he snapped his fingers and summoned his cupbearer to bring me a chalice of my own.

Before drinking, I presented the hairy remains of the Philistine warrior to Erik. "A tribute for you."

The king barked a laugh. "A fitting gift indeed. I accept it gratefully." Erik took a long draught of his goblet. "It's quite the feat you accomplished today."

"It was my distinct pleasure to quiet that windbag, my king." I sipped from my cup, and then remembered a thought that had been bothering me. "May I ask you a question?"

"Tonight, you may ask me anything you want."

"Why me?"

Erik's brow furrowed in confusion.

"Why did you allow me to challenge the Philistine champion? I'm not your strongest warrior. I'm not even a soldier. Yet you still allowed me to fight with the risk of our whole nation being enslaved."

The king's head bobbed up and down, and he rocked back on his hips. "Now that is a good question. Have you ever heard how I became king?"

I shook my head.

"It wasn't by choice, or at least my choice. My father had sent me out to find three lost donkeys. Someone else found the donkeys. I found a crown."

Now I was confused. "What?"

"In our search for the livestock, my servants and I came across a seer named Alvaro. He assured us our animals had already been found, and then he invited us to stay the night with him. In the morning, we awoke expecting breakfast. Instead, he dumped a flask of sticky oil on my head."

That was a familiar story. I almost blurted out Alvaro had done the exact same thing to me, but I held my tongue. His warning about the repercussions of discussing the ceremony still haunted me.

The king never noticed my unease and continued. "He told me I was chosen and sent me on my way. What he failed to mention was what I was chosen for. A week later, the seer gathered all the tribes of Israel together and announced I would be the first king of Israel."

Erik's eyes darkened. "Honestly, I wanted none of it, but the old man had more sway than I ever imagined. He promised that I would be changed into the king I needed to be, and that I would know how to lead my people. I needed only to do as I saw fit and it would work out.

"For a while, he was right. Every decision I made turned out wonderfully, and if ever I was in doubt, I'd hear things, music, that would direct my choices. We won battle after battle, and our nation was on the verge of peace." He paused, his eyes focusing elsewhere. "And then Alvaro abandoned me."

"What happened?" I asked.

"War with the Philistines." He stared at the map. "Our men were there, Gilgal, and the Philistines had amassed over ten thousand warriors to slaughter us. We tried to wait for Alvaro's blessing before we went into battle, but he never showed. So I attacked—I did what I felt was right—and we won, just in time for Alvaro to stab me in the back.

The king slowly shook his head. "He took away whatever charm he had granted me and replaced it with the madness. Instead of hearing the melody of a soothing harp, I hear insidious voices of doubt or grating, ear-splitting noises."

"Alvaro did this to you?" I asked, an uncomfortable, silent doubt growing in my mind. Would he betray me as well one day?

The king finished off his goblet. "Yes. And for the last year and a half, I have suffered its torments, not knowing how to lead the country, not being able to concentrate for more than a handful of moments, until today. When you came before me offering to slay the Philistine, I heard the music again and knew the right way forward. So I sent you."

He grabbed me by my shoulder. "But now for your reward. My daughter's hand in marriage!"

Marriage? Wine went down the wrong tube, sending me into a coughing fit. "Come again?"

"That was the prize for the man who triumphed over their giant."

A whole new kind of terror arose in my stomach. In all the insanity, I had completely ignored that part of the deal.

"Your Highness," Alexander said, coming forward. "The boy is not yet considered a man. It would cause significant tensions should he marry your eldest daughter."

Never before had I been so thrilled to see the human toad.

"Agh," the king said in disgust, "do you ever bring me good news, Alex, or do you simply find pleasure in crushing the dreams of others? Fine, the boy will not marry my daughter, but his family is exempt from paying taxes."

Alexander's cheeks sagged at the mention of one less tax line for him to control. "As you command," he said, slinking back into the corner.

"What will you do now, Niklas?" the king asked.

I hesitated, thinking. "Honestly, I just want to go home."

"A more than fair request," Erik replied, motioning toward the exit. "You have my permission, O Hero of Elah. Go with my blessing."

I bowed to the king and left the tent.

In all the excitement, I had yet to check on my brothers. From all reports, we had barely lost any men in our pursuit of the Philistines, but still, some of our soldiers must have been injured.

My fears were unwarranted. As I approached our tribesmen's camp, Abin's loud voice carried over the night.

"To my brother, Niklas!" he shouted.

"Aye!" echoed a chorus of soldiers.

I rounded the tents and discovered Abin standing atop a wagon, flask in hand. He caught sight of me and burst into a fresh smile. "Niklas, the god-slayer himself!" He bounded off the cart and threw both his arms around me. "You little rascal, the set you have on you."

Sham came up behind him. "First a lion, now a giant; what do you plan on fighting next Nik, an archangel?"

Laughing, I shook my head. "I'd like to conquer a pillow, for a good week at least."

I slung an arm around each of their necks, and together we walked toward the campfire. Eli sat next to it on a stump, studying its flames. His neck slowly turned to watch me, a blank expression on his face. Then, without any comment, he rose to his feet and stalked toward us.

I stopped midstride, grimacing. He had given me a direct order to go home, and my stunt had explicitly ignored his wishes. Yes, I had won, but I still couldn't tell him about the music. From his perspective, it must have seemed like I gambled the fate of our whole nation on dumb luck. With my father being absent, my brother would be well within his rights as acting head of household to punish me on the spot.

Clenching my eyes tight and inhaling sharply, I waited for whatever discipline he deemed appropriate.

Instead, the Bear of Bethlehem wrapped me in a bear-sized hug, lifting me several feet off the ground. "You did it!" he exclaimed, pressing me deep against his body. "You stopped them."

After rattling me in the air several more times, he finally set my feet back on the earth. I looked up at him, surprised by his approval. "You're not mad?"

His unshaven face scrunched up. "Mad? When I realized it was you heading down to the meet their champion, I almost marched out and killed you myself." He barked a throaty laugh, motioning me to follow him back to the fire. "The Philistines had us dead to rights. I never expected any of us to leave this valley alive, which is why I wanted you as far away from the battle as possible, but then you go and win. Sweet Lord, you killed a man who made me look like a beanpole—seems like sour wine to hold that against you."

Abin reappeared with fresh glasses of ale and took a seat by the fire. "To the sons of Jesse!" he bellowed.

The soldiers around us enthusiastically echoed the cheer. Flanked by my family, the world felt right, whole. The celebration continued through the night, and by the time the sun peeked over the horizon, only I remained awake. My feet shuffled through our camp, searching for a soft spot to curl up, and—if the Hero of Elah had his way—pass out for the next three weeks.

With my eyes only half open, I walked straight into Alexander's expansive girth he called a stomach.

"Watch your step, boy," the counselor sneered.

"Yeah, yeah," I replied, too tired to be scared of the man. I tried to walk around him, but one of his sausage-link-like arms snapped out, grabbing my wrist.

"We need to talk," he said.

"In the morning then," I said, attempting to pull my hand free, "or the afternoon, I guess. I'm exhausted."

"The king would have his response now."

"A response to what?" I said but stopped trying to break free from his grasp. "The king gave me permission to return home."

"And now he changed his mind?" the counselor replied in mock shock. "How very unlike him. He sent me to offer you a new, permanent position in his court."

"What kind of position?" I asked, wary of what came next.

Alexander shrugged. "He hasn't decided. He could want you to be his performing monkey, for all I know. His Highness seems to be under the unfortunate belief that you're some kind of good luck, and he wishes to keep you close."

"And if I respectfully deny his offer?"

The rotund man's beady eyes narrowed. "You've spent enough time with him to know how the king repays those he believes slighted him." He cracked his knuckles. "Blood relatives are often the focus of his displeasure."

Translation: my entire family would land squarely in the king's bow sights.

"And if I accept?" I asked.

"His Highness has informed me that all of your brothers will be exempt from fighting in any future conflicts."

After seeing a close-up view of what war actually looked like, the thought of keeping my brothers from its dangers was appealing.

The only small pothole in this grand plan was it required me to leave the safety of Bethlehem and live full-time with a capricious, manic king. What happened when my 'luck' failed?

Yet I would never be able to live with myself if something happened to any of my siblings when it had been in my power to keep them out of harm's way.

Swallowing hard, I nodded wearily. "I'll do it. Just give me a few days to let my family know what's happened."

"No," the counselor replied curtly, "the king wants you with him during this crucial junction of the war. I will send news to your father through the appropriate channels."

My shoulders sank, longingly gazing at the tent my brothers slept in.

Little did any of us know, the next time we all saw each other, Bethlehem would be in flames.

Part Four: The Voices in the Dark

It was half past midnight when the Israelite shuffled beneath the doorframe of the small, darkened house; his shoulders hunched over.

The man inside the home bolted up from a floor cushion when he saw his younger brother's silhouette. "What happened at the trial?"

The visitor shook his head slowly, dead eyes staring into the house.

"But your son was just singing a song," the older brother protested, "surely that didn't warrant..." He couldn't even force his mouth to form the word *execution*.

The two siblings remained silent; the cool, dead night draped over their thoughts.

Finally, the grieving father looked up and barred his teeth. "King Erik must die."

Chapter 18

I stalked my prey, careful not to disrupt the surrounding environment. One wrong move, one false step, and any chance of capturing my prize disappeared faster than the morning mist. The mission was undeniably tricky, as always they traveled in a pack, cloistered together, creating a nearly impenetrable wall. Isolating my target would take every ounce of wit I possessed.

The five girls halted to survey a bouquet of followers, and my sandals kicked up dust as I skidded into a side alley, hoping the princess didn't notice me.

I wasn't following Merab, the eldest princess Erik had originally offered to me in marriage. Merab was almost ten years older than I was, and in truth looked a bit like a stork, tall, with thin legs holding up an even more elongated neck.

No, his daughter Michal, the raven-haired beauty, was the one I sought. Only a year older than me at seventeen, her body curved where her sister's straightened. She seemed smart, alert, and her eyes hinted at a little mischief.

The problem was the herd of women that literally traveled with her everywhere—the dining hall, the gardens, the temple. Talking to a girl took enough courage one on one; trying to have a conversation with them en masse—I shook my head. I'd rather chance a fight with another giant.

Still, while I saw no fruit coming from a direct conversation, there were other avenues to make myself known. The scheme was simple. By now, everyone within my now permanent home, the growing capital of Gibeath, knew who the Hero of Elah was. At least once a day, some villager would approach me, expressing their gratitude for slaying the Philistine champion. All I needed to do was come across such a patron in the presence of Michal. Nothing displays a man's success like an independent admirer.

Bored with the flowers, the female flock moved on deeper into the city. Following after them, I watched for the right kind of individual. A woman would serve best. They always seemed more generous with praise than their male counterparts. Maybe a grandmother type.

Michal and her friends stopped again, this time admiring trinkets from a market booth, and my best chance presented itself—an old woman hunched over in a shawl, walking with an uneven gait. I directed my steps to intersect with her path.

A moment before colliding, I stopped and gently placed my hands up. "Sorry, ma'am."

The old crone glanced up and tilted her head. "It's all right," she began, before recognizing my face. "It's you!" she said, pointing with a bony finger.

Perfect.

"You buffoon!"

Huh?

Her hand started shaking, and her voice peaked in the air. "A year ago, you came shooting around a corner and knocked me over like a sack of grain. My dress tore, the wheat I had spent all day gathering blew off into the wind, and I spent the next five days with a canteen of cool water pressed to my rear. It looked like I wet myself every time I stood up."

It took a moment, but then it dawned on me. The old lady I had accidently pushed over during the chase in Lachish. She must have come to the capital with the other refugees.

The woman glanced from side to side, attracting the attention of everyone on the road. "This boy," she stated to the curious crowd, "this boy is an idiot! He has zero respect for his elders."

People snickered as her threats continued over my apologies. "I ought to leave your backside as sore as you left mine, you uppity runt."

Out of the corner of my eye, I watched Michal cover her smile as she whispered to her friends. They cackled together at my predicament, and then left me at the mercies of the embittered hag.

Ten minutes later, I finally untangled myself from her verbal abuse, disheartened and indignant. I might be the most famous person in all of Israel, yet somehow I stumble across the one woman determined to leave me battered and bruised.

My plan more than ruined, I decided to seek out Damon. He had promised to show me around the city, but first, he had some princely functions to attend. I went back to the castle and began asking around, eventually finding out he had left to inspect a new shipment of swords. After our last victory over the Phili-swine, our envoys finally gained enough courage to order blades from Egypt.

The prince came strolling up from the south entrance, his prayer shawl shading his head from the midday sun. "Good afternoon!"

"Maybe for you," I said.

Patting me on the back, he smiled. "What happened?"

My eyes stayed on the ground. "Have you ever liked a girl?"

A deep belly laugh emanated from him. "Yes, that has been known to happen from time to time."

My gaze peeked up. "Then why aren't you married? You're royalty. You're likely the most eligible bachelor in Israel."

Damon shook his head. "Apparently, marrying as a prince comes with complications. My father was already married when they made him king, so he didn't have to deal with any of the complexities. But he's determined to find me the 'perfect' future queen. At this point, I'm starting to believe that by perfect he actually means *nonexistent*."

It was my turn to chuckle. "I never knew princes had it so tough."

He smirked, but then winced and pulled his hand up to his forehead. A fresh scar dripped blood.

"That's new," I commented.

"Indeed," he said. "A reminder from my training to keep my blade up at all times."

Seraphim training, no doubt. I'd been serving the king full time for a month, regularly spending time with the prince, but Damon never talked about their activities. "What kind of training?"

"The kind you better learn fast from," he responded, coy as ever.

I walked in front of him and turned. "Come on, can't you give me some kind of hint about what you're learning? Everything I've heard about the Seraphim is said in hushed whispers. Do they really teach you how to fight for three days straight?"

"Oh yes," Damon said, his voice rising in a grandiose fashion, "and we learn to hide within the darkness of our own shadow and scale castle walls without ropes." His grin returned. "In truth, we train, and then we train some more, and after that, a bit more training."

"No missions?" I asked, a bit disappointed.

"They come on occasion, but I haven't gone on any official assignments yet."

My nose cursed up. "We met while you were hunting a pack of Philistine marauders."

"No," he replied, a smile tugging at his lips. "I was out praying. Any encounter with the enemy was simply fortunate happenstance. Seraphim missions are on a whole other level."

"You killed twenty Philistines by yourself," I asserted.

"First off, my armor-bearer was with me," he said, correcting my statement. "And second, a single victory hardly makes me invincible. I still have a lot to learn."

He and I both. Since my battle with Goliath, a lingering burden pressed upon my conscience. As proud as I was about my victory over the loudmouth, the truth was it had been as much luck as anything else. I couldn't deny the heavenly air support I had received, but continuing to bank on divine favor to pull me out of the fire left me feeling helpless, exposed.

I doubted my encounters with the Philistines had finished, so what happened if the next time I fought them, the music refused to lend its assistance? Training was my only option, and if you're going to do it, you might as well take lessons from the best.

"Could you teach me to fight?" I asked.

He pulled off his shawl and ran his fingers through his hair, sighing. "You're a bit young yet. Give it a couple of years, and we can work something out."

His comment frustrated me on multiple fronts. First, at eighteen, he was only two years my senior, so age seemed inconsequential. Second, being the youngest of eight boys, the "when you're older" excuse never sat well with me.

"I was old enough to fight the giant."

The prince tilted his head. "That was a special case, just like me against the Philistines. You had help."

"You think so?"

"I know so."

I smelled a challenge. "I'll fight you, right now."

Damon sniffed the air. "Really? Like sparring?"

"Yeah, just to prove the point." After watching Damon systematically dismantle the four Philistine marauders on our first meeting, I had no delusions I would actually win, but it would at least prove I was worth training.

He weighed the idea. "Maybe it'll be good for you."

I pumped my fist. "So where do we want to do this?"

"The barracks have a sporting ground we can use," he said. "I'll meet you there in an hour."

I raised my right arm, displaying the sling wrapped around my skin. "I have everything I need right here. Why wait?"

Damon arched his eyebrows. "Eager, are we?" He patted me on the back. "Fine, let's get this over with."

Several men were sparring with staffs when we arrived at the barracks' courtyard. We waited for them to take a rest, and then the prince asked if we could step in for a quick match.

We started on opposite sides of the open square, thirty paces apart.

I unwrapped my sling and pulled out a stone. "What weapon are you going to use?"

He shrugged. "Don't need one."

"Now who's the overconfident one? You know I killed a giant with this thing."

"Yeah," Damon agreed, "but, like I said, it was a special case. I doubt Yahweh will pick a side in this fight."

My eyes narrowed. "I'll try not to aim for your face."

"Whatever you say." He bent down and stretched his legs. "We'll begin on three."

"One," he said, still holding his feet.

"Two." The prince straightened back up.

"Three!"

I loaded my sling and darted toward my friend. Even from our starting positions, I could have hit him, but the less distance there was between us, the less time he had to react. Intending to strike him in a knee cap, I stayed low to the ground.

He waited to move until there was probably fifteen feet between us. Then he leaned to the left before launching himself to the right. Gauging his direction, I unleashed the stone to impact where he should have run, but then he snapped back, shifting to the left. My projectile sailed a foot wide, and before I could even reach for another stone, his foot was lodged behind my right ankle. He pushed hard, and I tumbled to the ground. Within another breath, his knee pressed down on my throat.

"Yield?" he asked.

He translated my choking gasps as *yield* and released his knee.

The soldiers watching clapped and chuckled, and then their commander ordered them to resume their training.

Once air regularly found its way into my lungs, Damon held out his hand.

Humiliated but in awe, I accepted it.

"That was amazing," I said. "How did you move so fast?"

"Training."

"And you're still not considered good enough to go on missions?"

He shook his head.

I failed to even touch Damon, and still the Seraphim considered him too green to even send on an assignment. How much did I still have to learn? I felt like a five-year-old child, thinking he was finally strong enough to arm-wrestle his father.

"How do you join?" I asked.

The prince's face went pale. "Trust me, you don't want a part of this. Not yet anyway."

My eyes hardened, and I repeated my question. "How do you join?"

"It's not about joining," he explained, suddenly looking around the barracks. "You get accepted."

"Then how do I get an invitation?"

"You—" he began before getting cut off.

"You ask," said a grizzled soldier off to the side, sitting on a stool. He wore a leather tunic with three black feathers embroidered into each of the shoulder pads.

The prince reached for my shoulder. "Please, don't do this now, not yet."

"Ask who?" I said, brushing off Damon.

"Any of us," the soldier replied, touching the set of feathers on his tunic.

"Then I'm asking. So I'm accepted?"

"Oh no," the man answered, standing up and flexing his palm. He was missing a finger on each hand. "Asking gets you invited. Acceptance comes if you survive."

That last sentence had a comforting ring to it.

"Survive what?"

The veteran soldier shook his head, a knowing grin on his lips.

The feeling of powerlessness still fresh in my mind, I found myself reflecting on how easily my battle with Goliath could have had a very different ending. At my current level of strength, I couldn't guarantee my own safety, let alone protect anyone else. I needed to get stronger. I needed training.

"I'll do it," I said, fortifying my voice, "whatever it takes."

Chapter 19

We followed the veteran warrior out of the city and toward western hills. The terrain was covered with granite rock and broken earth, useless to farmers and herders alike, leaving the area barren of any signs of civilization.

"Now remember," Damon said, using the journey to give me advice, "whatever happens, there's always a way out, there's always some wrinkle you can use. It's simply a matter —"

"You know the rules," the old soldier warned. "He passes or fails on his own. They bend for no man, even royalty."

So we traveled deeper into the wildness in silence, accompanied by nothing but the sound of our sandals kicking up loose rock and dirt.

Caves of different sizes soon indented the hills, some bigger than houses, others no larger than an oven hearth. Occasionally, a shadow would move within one, but I never caught a glimpse of the creatures hiding inside the caverns.

We crested one of the larger cliffs and found ourselves staring down into a vast, abandoned limestone quarry. Dozens of mining shafts burrowed deep into the earth, and at the center of the excavation site, two men stood in conversation. The larger of the duo's head was shaved, showing several thick scars carved into his scalp. He wore leather body armor and a cloak sewn together with black feathers, hundreds of them. The other man was younger, maybe twenty-five, and clearly the subordinate.

Our guide started down the cliff toward the bald man. The leader's gaze slid over us, but then returned its attention to the conversation. "Then tomorrow night we strike the village to the west of Eglog."

"West?" his comrade asked, nervously stroking the black feathers sewn into his pant leggings.

"Yes," Black Cloak said. "The time is ripe to show the Philistines we can strike anywhere in their nation, regardless how deep they hide within their territory. From tomorrow on, they will all enjoy the nightmares of that which moves in the night."

The young man nodded. "Do we leave survivors?"

"Do the Philistines?" the commander asked. "No, we kill them all, man, woman, and child."

"Child?" I repeated, shifting uncomfortably.

His gazed again returned to me, and this time, his eyes lingered, narrowing to slits. "You take issue with cleansing this village?" His hands went to the hilts of the two long, curved knives at his belt.

I swallowed hard but pressed on. "I take issue with murdering children."

The man smiled, showing several teeth as black as soot. "It's not the current children who are the problem. It's what they will become." His head cocked to its side. "Have you ever met a war orphan?"

I nodded, thinking of several children in our village.

"Tell me," he asked, eerily amused by the subject, "did they seem like the overly forgiving type? Ready to leave their loss behind them and move on with their lives?"

He answered for me. "No, they remember what was stolen from them, and more importantly, *who* took it from them. It haunts them, year after year, until one day they're no longer children. They become the monster for some other child's nightmare." He turned to his comrade. "You have your orders. Go."

"Yes, Gabril," the young soldier said. He bowed his head and then ran full sprint up the east side cliff.

Part of me wanted to chase after the man and somehow intercept the order. My stomach twisted in disgust at what these men intended to do, but though I sought an adequate counterargument, my mind couldn't find fault with their reasoning. Was that the only choice: living with the murder of entire villages on your conscience, or letting our enemies' children live long enough to rise up and avenge them?

"As for our bleeding-heart philosopher," Gabril said, his full attention on me. "There is only one reason why Ezekiel and Damon would bring you here because there's only one way you leave this pit outside of a coffin: acceptance into the Seraphim." He paused. "Yet we typically don't take applicants so young." His head tilted toward Ezekiel, expecting an answer.

The soldier jerked his nose toward Damon. "He inquired about initiation to a member of the Seraphim. By rights he was given the opportunity. Plus, if I'm not mistaken, he is not your typical boy. This is Niklas, the acclaimed Hero of Elah."

Lips curled up on Gabril's face. "The god-slayer himself."

"Goliath was no god," I said evenly.

"On that," the Seraphim's commander replied, "we most certainly agree." He took a moment of silence and then continued. "Do you have any other feats we should be aware of?"

Thinking for a moment, I pulled out the lion's tooth from under my shift. "I killed a lion over a year ago."

Gabril's eyebrows rose. "A giant- *and* a lion-slayer? You are a rare find." The commander shook his head in amused sarcasm before he turned on his heels, the black feather cloak whirling behind him. "Very well, you shall be given the right of initiation. While we have no gods or lions for you to fight, I believe we have the perfect test."

Damon and I traded nervous glances, but we followed after him.

He led us down one of the mine shafts, and the smell of damp rock and thick moss saturated the torch-lit tunnel. "Have you heard how the Seraphim came to be?"

"No."

"Before our people took this territory, our nation wandered in the desert for forty years, our men too afraid to purge their land from its current inhabitants. Eventually, a new generation came up with the gall to take what was theirs. During one of the battles, it's said that an angel tore down the walls of an entire city, clearing us a path to cleanse the region. Afterward, our people found black wings covering the battlefield. On that day, a group of men swore never again to hide in fear and took upon themselves the mantle of clearing the path for all our people. The Seraphim were born."

The commander turned a corner and led us to an open cavern where several other men sat around a table playing dice. They nodded their heads in respect as Gabril approached, but he waved his hand for them to continue with their game.

"However, we found that the cowardice of our ancestors still tainted our blood, so we needed a way to sort the courageous from the craven. Thus the crucible was born—a test to prove the merit of any who wished to join our order."

He pointed to a barred metal door, and one of the gaming soldier's face went white before he slowly nodded his head. He moved to the gate and held out a set of keys.

Gabril continued. "Each trial is different, depending on the circumstances of the candidate, but the process is always the same, survive and be welcomed into our brotherhood, die and be proved unworthy." A cruel smile crossed his lips as he pointed toward the door. "Your trial waits on the other side of that gate."

Damon stood next to us, but his face gave me no indication of what was in store if I passed through the metal bars. I approached it slowly, my mind racing with the possibilities about what awaited me. A captured enemy soldier? A deranged lunatic too unsafe to live in normal society?

Reaching the gate, I turned my head. "Do I get a weapon?"

Gabril grasped both his knives. "Only the ones you brought with you."

Curse it all. I checked my pouch. Three throwing stones remained.

The Seraphim soldier guarding the door gently turned the key and swung the gate out, placing himself behind it.

I took a step inside, the outside torchlight only covered half of the room, making it difficult to see. I swept my eyes over the granite space twice, before I noticed a dark mass wrapped in its own shadows, pressed into the far corner. I squinted but couldn't figure out what crouched against the walls. A large man beneath a bundle of heavy blankets?

Clanging metal met metal as they shut the door behind.

The brown mountain grunted, rising to all fours, and the five-hundred-pound Syrian bear came into the light.

Chapter 20

Of course it's a bear. Why would I have expected anything less?

Also, I definitely did not shriek—my coughs are just very pitchy.

While my stomach began a robust routine of jumping jacks, I tried to take note of my surroundings. The cavern was a medium-sized square, maybe twenty feet across, but considering I shared its limited space with half a ton of claw and fur, it felt like they had locked us together in a chicken coop.

Syrian bears inhabited the mountains to the north of Bethlehem. Occasionally, one or two would wander down from the hills and try to pick off a sheep, but I'd never heard of one attacking a human. For the most part, it was a live-and-let-live kind of relationship.

Somehow, given the circumstances, I doubted this particular animal would share that philosophy.

Lifting its muzzle, it sniffed the air several times before it grunted. It shifted a light brown paw toward me.

I glanced back to the metal door, where Gabril, Damon, and Ezekiel watched through iron grates, each with differing levels of anticipation. The commander raised his hand toward the beast as if offering me a beverage.

For a moment, I thought of pleading my case to Gabril, begging for some other trial, but even with such a short introduction, I recognized that he would never change his mind. I needed to spend what precious seconds I had left finding some kind of advantage.

The bear took another two steps forward, cutting the space between us in half. Back-stepping to the metal bars, I kicked something hard—a half-decomposed rabbit skull. *Perfect.* At least I didn't have to wonder if this was one of those vegetarian bears.

"We captured him salvaging among the remains of a village," Gabril said. "He maimed three of our men before we found a way to get him in chains. This should be child's play for you, though. I heard the Philistine champion killed hundreds."

Part of me was tempted to waste a stone just to shut the commander up, but my thoughts quickly returned to the matter at hand—namely not becoming an afternoon snack for my cuddly new bunk buddy.

Again, the beast smelled the air, and then it took several more steps forward.

Lunging to my right, the bear swiped its front paw in frustration. His claws missed me by a wide margin. A long, low rumble shook his jaws, a growl lasting for a good ten seconds. For the third time, he sniffed the air and then slowly turned toward me.

Realizing I had a clean shot at his head, I immediately unwrapped my sling and set a stone. The leather spun, and I unleashed a projectile. It struck true, hitting the bear right between the eyes, complemented by the sound of a harsh crack.

And it accomplished nothing but ticking it off.

The vibrations of his roar reached my lungs, and he lashed out with his paws, one after another in my direction. Again I dove, trying to get back to my original position, but an extended paw blocked my path and forced me instead to scramble back to a corner.

Pressed against the wall, I realized there might not be enough space to attempt another dodge. All the beast had to do was charge, and I'd be finished.

Yet instead of using the opportunity, the bear smelled the air again, its snout swinging violently back and forth. Why didn't he end it?

Then Damon's advice came back to me: this wasn't a hopeless case, they had given me an advantage to exploit. I noticed the wrinkle. The torch light struck the animal's face, and I realized it hadn't been squinting. It was blind.

Still, how exactly do you kill a bear, blind or not?

I calmed my chaotic thoughts and forced myself to take several long, even breaths. Very quiet breaths. I imagined this crucible was meant to be completed with a blade, but I never carried those kinds of weapons. I needed to use what I had. What would kill a bear? My eyes popped open. The same sort of thing that would kill a golden-maned feline.

During my battle with the lion, I had used the rock to strike its jaw, and the blow had killed it in one swoop. The major differences here were that the bear's skull appeared larger, I had no rock large enough to repeat the task, and I didn't feel any supernatural mojo flowing through my limbs.

I did, however, have two smooth, flat stones left in my pouch. I pulled them out and laid them on top of the knuckles on my right hand. I quickly secured them by tightly wrapping the leather of my sling around them and my fingers, and pounded my makeshift glove against the wall. It would have to do.

The bear, meanwhile, used the sound to locate me and started lumbering forward.

All I could to do now was hope that I was right about my second assumption: that the crack I heard from my first shot had been from fracturing the beast's skull bone, and I just needed to finish the job. There would only be one shot at this, because if it didn't work, I'd be too close to duck away. His blindness would become irrelevant, and I would become dead.

Pressing my feet against the corner, I set myself. The bear took another tentative step forward, and I lunged toward him.

My prey heard the approach and reared up on its hind legs, towering over me. Its snout bent down, and I took my shot, winding up my shoulder and throwing everything into the punch.

My stone-fortified fist connected, breaking through the bone and into soft tissue beneath it.

Without another movement, the beast's body went limp, and the Syrian bear plummeted forward, all of its weight crashing down upon me, pinning us both to the hard ground. I was being bear-hugged. Literally.

The gate swung open, and Damon rushed to my side. "Give me your hands!" He grabbed hold of them and slowly dragged my body out from under the bear blanket.

He let go, and I lay limp, staring up at the ceiling, utterly spent. Ignoring the rapid-fire questions of concern from the prince, my mind floated from thought to thought, every so often landing on a common theme. First a lion, then a giant, and now a bear. I may have a problem with my brain not working right.

Eventually, I returned to the present, pushing myself up with my elbows and nodding to the prince. "I'm fine."

Gabril stood over me, a newfound respect in his posture. "The tales of your victories seem to be more than mere fabrication or ignorant luck. You fought well," he said, offering me his hand. "I stand mistaken."

Part of me wanted to tell the commander exactly where I thought he should stand, but I held my tongue. Regardless of if I appreciated him on a personal level, he held the keys to my acceptance into the Seraphim.

"So I'm in?" I asked.

"If you choose to be," the commander said. "Though I should warn you that the trials will only get more difficult from here."

Arching a skeptical eyebrow, I took his hand and got back to my feet. "Do you have any more bears caged within these caverns? No? Then I'll somehow manage."

He barked a laugh and turned away. "Oh, there are things far more terrifying than beasts and giants, my new comrade. Far more terrifying. You'll begin tomorrow. You'd best get some sleep."

For once, I agreed with him. Damon and I headed toward the exit.

As we climbed out of the quarry, a question blossomed in my mind. "Damon, what did your crucible entail?"

My friend took his time answering before he mumbled something under his breath.

"I didn't catch that."

He hung his head a little lower. "They made me wash their undergarments for a week."

I froze, first dumbfounded and then pissed. "They force me to fight a bloody bear with a slingshot, and you get away with doing a few loads of laundry?"

"I'm a prince," Damon said, shrugging his shoulders. "Maybe they wanted to make sure I'd follow orders."

"Unbelievable," I said, marching onward.

Un-bloody-believable.

Chapter 21

Two years later

The night wind scraped against my face. It had been two hours since the last ray of sunlight had faded over the horizon, and now I lay in wait just outside the edge of the slaver's camp. So far, the plan was running smoothly. The hired thugs were huddled tightly around their bonfire, terrified and thoroughly inebriated.

I was almost there. If tonight went well, I'd have officially completed my training within the Seraphim.

Gabril had convinced King Erik that an elite Seraphim agent hiding beneath the guise of a mere musician could prove invaluable. He promised the king he'd train me himself, keeping me close enough that I could still make regular appearances at court. By day, I served as the palace's bard. By night, however, the Seraphim commander began forging me into a something far beyond a simple fighter. He intended to create an unyielding weapon.

Our first time out together, he took me to Mount Horeb, handed me a blindfold, and ordered me to scale the flat cliff of the mountain. For survival skills, he made me trek barefoot, back and forth over the Negev desert, ten miles every night for a week. The assignment began with nothing but an empty canteen and a four-inch knife. The commander taught me the art of camouflage by throwing me into a leper colony and making me learn the names of every infected resident. On rare occasions, I still woke up in cold sweats, dreaming of gray scales covering my body.

Yet tonight I stood on the verge of entering in to the most elite fighting force on the continent. I only needed to accomplish one last task.

"Kill the Philistine slaver and anyone else with him in his tent," Gabril had commanded. "He has thrown hundreds of displaced Israeli refugees into bondage. How you do it is entirely up to you, but..." He paused, his voice hardening. "Know we will be watching the whole time."

It had taken the better part of a week, but my plan was solid—if not a touch elaborate—even by my own lofty standards.

First, I needed to ensure his caravan would arrive at a set destination, so I sent a forged buyer's agreement, offering an overly generous offer to purchase slaves in the city of Gezer.

Next, I counted on the human nature of slavers. Knowing where their route would take them, I left two casks of cheap wine on a broken cart in their path. Celebrating their find, the slaver's bodyguards took it along with them, and as soon as camp was made for the night, proceeded to drink away their good fortune. By the time the sun had set, even their sentries could barely walk straight enough to stumble to the outskirts of their tents and relieve themselves.

Which brought me to the final part of the plan: keeping them by their fire. Part of my Seraphim training focused on knowing the psychology of the average person, where to push them, how to manipulate them. One of the first lessons they taught me was that from infancy, humans fear the dark. We have found dozens of ways to mask that fear, but something deep within each of us believes that night is where unknown evil lies in wait, always a moment away from overtaking us. The slightest nudge would drive us back to those primal thoughts.

The push came in the form of ten freshly killed rabbits littered in a circle around their camp. Within an hour of sundown, wolves approached their site—scratching, prowling, howling. The beasts only came for the easy meal and would avoid coming any closer to the camp, but the drunk mercenaries didn't realize that. Instead, they huddled around their fire, not leaving the light of its flame.

Nothing stood between me and their master's tent.

The dark of night at its blackest, I crept among their canvas village, fingers ready at the hilt of my dagger. Gabril had personally trained me to use a fourteen inch, iron-fortified blade. It was the perfect weapon for an assassin, small enough to hide beneath a tunic, but long enough to defend against an enemy's short sword. The Seraphim called it a *dabar*, which loosely translated to messenger. Once I found the Philistine, a clear message would be delivered of what we thought of slavers.

My only hesitation would be if he brought a woman to sleep with. At best, she would be his wife, an accomplice in his trade. At worst, he may have a slave to keep him warm, a victim in her own right. Either way, definite doubts lingered if I had the stomach to murder an unsuspecting woman.

I silently unfastened the cords and ducked into his large tent. In the black of night, it was almost impossible to notice everything under its canvas, but the large body of a man lay in the corner under several thick blankets.

I breathed a silent sigh of relief — no companion lay beside him.

In a matter of moments, I would be a Seraphim.

The weapon slid out of its leather sheath without a sound, and I glided toward the bed. At the same moment my hand covered his mouth, the dabar's blade crossed his throat, and his body barely convulsed before he lost all strength.

The job was done, and a smile curled on my lips. I had completed my training.

Then I saw them.

Two children lay next to their father underneath the blankets. Their forms were so small; I couldn't even tell their gender.

Stumbling back, it felt like someone was surgically ripping a hole in my stomach. Gabril's exact order flew into my mind. "Kill *everyone* with him in his tent." Part of me wanted to throw up. Part of me wanted to cry. Absolutely no part of me wanted anything to do with the weapon in my fingers. The dabar dropped to the ground.

My brain battled against my heart. If I left them alive, they would awake to find their father's murdered corpse sleeping next to them. It would scar them, turn them into monsters. Plus, somehow I knew this had been Gabril's intention all along, a true test of my loyalties, to see if I had the stomach to follow through on his orders.

Yet my hand would not move toward the blade. I couldn't kill; no, I couldn't murder these children any more than I could harm my own little sister. I fell to my knees, uncertain of any way forward.

"It seems you have a problem," a man's hushed voice commented from behind me.

My Seraphim training kicked in, and in one motion I grabbed the dropped blade and dove toward the direction of the voice. The fear was unwarranted. Its owner was bound tightly to the center pole of the tent. Needing to ensure his silence, though, I brought my knife to the edge of his throat.

The man smelled like the wrong side of a donkey. His long tangled braids matched his unkempt facial hair, and he wore nothing but a ragged, cotton tunic. His body was large even for a full-grown man, and he stared back at me without any fear, a small grin playing on his face, despite the blade at his neck.

My mind raced, trying to figure out what to do next. "You didn't cry out before I killed your master."

His smile sharpened. "There is little love lost between a slave and his owner."

"Fair enough," I whispered. "But then why are you here? In his tent?"

He blinked. "He liked to watch me suffer. He found me unique."

"How so?" My eyes darted around the tent, double-checking that no one else resided within it.

"Most slaves are taken by force," he responded. "I gave myself up."

My eyebrows arched.

He sighed quietly. "That story is for another day. Your current problem seems to be quite urgent."

I scoffed. "Says the one tied up."

"By the looks of it, your hands are bound far worse than mine." He turned his gaze to the bed. "I'm not the one sent to murder children in their sleep."

"How did you—?"

"I know how war works," he interrupted, "intimately. Egyptians,

Philistines, Israelites, different names, same humans. Yet you don't seem to want to kill these children."

I paused, uncomfortable, glancing at the two sleeping youths. "No."

"So what will you do?"

I had no answer, no solution that would work. If I let them live, Gabril would find out eventually, and he *would* finish the job. The only difference being I'd join them on their trip to the afterlife. Our men were out there, watching, so there was no chance of sneaking them out myself.

"I could help you," the man said, realizing I didn't have an answer to his question.

My eyes narrowed. "What's to keep you from killing the children of your former master the second I release you?"

"Nothing," he admitted, "but I have a suspicion if I don't help, they're dead anyway. There'd be no benefit in doing it myself."

"Then you'd just try to escape."

"A more probable scenario," the slave said, "but I won't leave without the children. I swear, on my life, to get them to safety." He shrugged his shoulders. "Or die trying."

"And I just have to take you at your word."

He nodded. "If you have a better option, feel free to use it."

I ground my teeth. Every scenario left something to be desired, and most of them left the and me children dead.

Two gentle harp notes played in the tent. Great. Over the past two years, I had heard it less than a handful of times, and *now* is when it decides to start back up again. Did it want me to trust him or leave him here to rot? Blast it all! Why couldn't the guy upstairs have picked a less vague form of communication, like say—I don't know—using actual words, written or verbal, or talking animals? At this point, I'd take pretty much anything.

Running out of time, I pushed my knife deeper against his throat. "If I untie you, and you so much as—"

"Spare the threats," he cut me off quietly. "I already know you're not afraid to kill."

Taking a deep breath, I moved my blade to the cords binding him. *This is so mind-numbingly stupid.*

The cords tumbled to the ground, and he rolled his arms in relief. "Much better."

My blade still at the ready, I locked eyes with him, searching for some sign of betrayal. I found nothing but a weary gaze.

"So do you have a plan?" I asked.

"Fragments of one," he said, and he pointed to a chest in the corner, before slowly crawling to it. "We have to get the children away from here quietly, but they won't come willingly once they realize what's happened." He opened the trunk and began sorting through its contents. "My master kept a bottle of ointment he used to put unruly slaves to sleep." He pulled out a small glass bottle and a rag. "The children will wake up with quite the headache, but they'll be alive."

I analyzed the bottle. If he meant to harm them, there were simpler ways. I nodded. "But how do we get them out of here without either his guards or my allies noticing?"

He swept his eyes to the far side of the tent. "I can carry them both easily enough, but we'd need something to draw everyone's attention elsewhere."

The mercenaries would still be cowering by the campfire, but the Seraphim wouldn't be so easily distracted. I guessed they'd be within a quarter mile of my assignment. We needed something bigger, something brighter.

"Fire," I said softly.

"What?" my unlikely comrade asked.

"I'll set one of the other tents on fire. If you sneak out from the back, its light won't reveal you, and it'll hold everyone's attention. Find cover beneath their horses, and then wait five minutes. By then, those watching me should have left for the rendezvous, and you can steal away. It's not perfect, but it's our best chance."

"Fine," he answered.

"Wait till you see the flame, and then stay in the shadows. If the people I'm with catch you..." I let him fill in the horrors with his own imagination.

"I understand war."

Resolute, and still confident this plan was shoddy by even the most meager of standards, I moved to leave the tent. Just before exiting, I stopped and craned my head around. "I'm Niklas."

I couldn't place the expression on his face, but he replied, "Yashobeam."

"Thank you Yashobeam," I said, "regardless of what happens." With that, I snuck out of the tent.

The next part of the plan went without a hitch. I found an empty tent at the other side of their site, and quickly placed a burning lamp beneath its canvas wall, leaving as the edges of it sizzled. Part of me wanted to double back to the children, but I knew my presence was being watched. Now all I could do was hope the slave kept his word.

By the time I reached the edge of the camp, the tent's blaze had furled high into the air. Shouts of discord rang out behind me, and I disappeared into the night.

A mile away, I reached the extraction point Gabril had given me. He, along with four other members of the Seraphim, waited in silence.

I held up the bloody knife to show him the job had been accomplished and hoped he didn't ask any questions.

His expression unreadable, he stood inches from my face.

Terror gripped my chest. Did he see Yashobeam fleeing with the children? Were they already dead?

The commander brought his fist up to my cheek, and then slowly turned it over, opening his palm to reveal a black feather. "Welcome to the Seraphim."

Chapter 22

A full moon lit the sky, hovering above our campsite at the outskirts of the capital. Kneeling at a table, I ground my back teeth against each other. The next couple of hours promised to leave a painful headache in the morning. Almon, an unusually ugly brute of a man, sat across from me, smirking.

I hate smirkers.

Fine. I hate it when other people smirk.

The Seraphim had an unofficial rite of passage for the newly initiated, one that tested both our strength and our intestinal fortitude. The night began with the new member drinking glasses of wine equal to the difference of feathers owned between him and his opponent, the second newest member of our order. Every time a Seraphim agent completed a successful mission, we were given another feather. Almon had been a busy little cutthroat. Four black plumes hung around his throat, meaning I started with three drinks already in my system. Afterward, together we alternated between a challenge of strength and then downing another glass of wine. This continued until either one of us passed out or conceded defeat.

I finished my third glass of wine and shook my head. "So what's the first challenge?"

Al slammed his massive elbow down on the table. "Arm wrestling."

My shoulders sagged. At least it'd be over quick.

He won handily, and we each drank another glass of wine. Typically, I enjoyed a glass or two a night, but with four already in my system, the room was already beginning to wobble like a seesaw.

Grappling was the next activity, and while I held my own better than in the first challenge, eventually I lost my balance and my big, but dumb, comrade kicked my legs out from under me. My skull smacked against the floor, and Almon's forearm fell on top of my chest.

He bared his yellow teeth and laughed in my face. "They must have lowered the entrance bar after I passed if the Seraphim let you in, singer boy."

Grimacing both from his insult and his breath, I climbed to my feet and gently stroked the back of my head. At least there wasn't any blood.

Almon belched loudly. "Another round!"

The idiot needed to be put in his place, and I almost grabbed the glass they had poured for me, but when I sniffed the air, the tip of my nose tingled. Advice from my father echoed in my mind. "Niklas, when your nose goes numb, it's best to stop drinking. Decisions that leave bruises will follow."

Taking a deep breath to clear my mind, I remembered that the judgment and ability gap would only widen between the two of us if I continued the "game." My best option would be to forfeit and stop the bleeding before literal bleeding began.

"I'm done," I said, weakly waving my hand at the glass. "You win, Almon."

His facial expression morphed several times, shifting from confusion, to disappointment, to all-out rage. "What? We haven't even begun yet!"

Sensing the opportunity for a little payback, I swept my arms out wide, and I bowed my head. "I concede to your prowess and skill."

The anger burned so intensely in his eyes; it wouldn't have been a surprise to see smoke bellow from his ears. I wondered how long he had endured his initiation before he finally passed out in his own fluids. With an ego as large as his, he must have weathered quite the punishment. No wonder he was upset. I had denied him the opportunity to pay the humiliation forward. This was better than winning, and it spared me from waking up with a pounding migraine.

For the next hour, Almon raged about my cowardice, throwing insults in my direction every chance he could. He promised to continue the game without me, finishing glass after glass of wine. To disregard his insults entirely, I grabbed my lyre and plucked at its strings cheerfully, thoroughly enjoying the show.

Finally, he stood up, swaying mightily, and pointed a grimy index finger at me. "You're a disgrace," he said, his head bobbing up and down, "to every *Sarah-pen*."

"What's a Sarah-pen?" asked a female's voice from the other side of the fire.

Every head craned to find its owner. Michal, Erik's raven-haired daughter, waited in a sleeveless, purple summer robe.

Al's posture straightened, and he started stumbling toward her. "Princess, what I meant to say—" And then he tripped over his own feet, face-planting into the ground and groaning incoherently.

Amused, Michal gave him one last glance. "Anyway," she said and proceeded around him and strode toward me, "I'm here with a message for Niklas."

I stood up, doubly thrilled that I hadn't continued drinking. "Yes?"

"Your presence is required at court."

My face scrunched up. "I thought your father and brother were off negotiating a trade deal with Lebanon?"

"They are," the princess said, bored with the explanation. "Alexander needs you."

Yuck. Meetings with Alexander almost always were painful, demeaning, and altogether to be avoided. I grabbed my satchel, combat knife, and lyre. "Let's get this over with."

"I'll go with you," Michal said, "I have business with the court as well."

We left together, leaving a large swath of space between us and the still disorientated Almon, but when I turned right to head toward the king's court, she lightly placed her hand on my shoulder.

"No," she said.

I pointed toward the castle, "But you said I was needed in court."

A spark flashed in her eyes, and a mischievous smile danced across her red lips. "I might have fibbed." She held up her index finger and her thumb an inch apart. "Just a little." She made a left at the corner, and I followed after her. "In truth, I wanted to congratulate you for being accepted into the Seraphim."

My heart beat faster. Over the past two years, my crush on Michal had only grown, but while we occasionally spent time around one another during my duties at court, she never showed any direct interest in me.

"Thanks," I said.

She strolled on in silence for another block. "I've been watching you for a while now."

"Really?" I squeaked. I coughed and repeated in a deeper voice, "Really?"

The princess nodded. "First a musician to the king, then the giant-slayer, and now a full-fledged member of the Seraphim. You're quite the conquering hero. They'll be writing songs about you in no time."

As she spoke, I walked a little taller, and a tingly sensation flooded my body. Michal had been following my exploits. I tried to keep my emotions from running roughshod over my mind. "None of it's that big of a deal," I said.

She winked. "It is to me."

Another wave of euphoria swept over my brain.

The princess turned another corner.

"Where are we going?" I asked.

Her playful smile returned. "Somewhere we can be alone."

For the next five minutes we conversed while we walked, but to be honest, I can't remember a single topic we discussed. My mind had detached from the rest of my body, and it floated somewhere above the city in a cloud of bliss. When she stopped, I came crashing back to Earth.

I blinked several times. "Why are we at the temple?"

"I told you," she said, "to find a place where we could be alone. At this hour of the night, the priests have all gone home. My friends and I come here all the time. Piety is the perfect excuse to get out of the palace." She grabbed my hand and pulled me into the holy structure.

The temple was supported with massive timber poles and covered in heavy, purple fabric. Divided into several large gathering spaces used for group prayer or meditation, scrolls of our ancient texts rested on lecterns in each room. The princess headed straight for the back corner. The light from the small lamp at the building's center barely reached the spot where we finally stopped, leaving us wrapped in shadow.

"There," Michal said, "much better. Sit with me."

Together we sat cross-legged on a prayer rug, and she began lightly tapping my knee. "Everyone says you're the best musician in our land. Would you honor me with a song?"

I glanced around the temple, skeptical. "Here?"

The princess's shadowed form nodded enthusiastically.

Considering all the time I spent performing in front of a temperamental king, not much should have been able to throw me, but singing love songs in a holy shrine while trying to impress a girl was uncomfortably new. Still, I pulled the lyre from my back and sang her "The Sonnet of Jacob and Rachel."

Michal giggled in delight as I finished. "That was marvelous, Niklas." Then I felt her hands on my torso. "Now, I wonder what we should do?" Before I could offer a suggestion, she took matters into her own hands, pressing her lips to mine, and suddenly any other ideas seemed immaterial.

For a while we stayed locked together, blood flying through my body, but then the blasted harp started playing.

No! My mind screamed. *Not now!*

The music played on, crescendoing louder and louder.

I tried to ignore it for a good minute, before finally taking a deep breath and pulling away.

"What's wrong?" asked Michal's soft voice.

"Nothing," I answered quietly, hiding my anger over the music's timing. Tonight was off limits. "I just needed a breath. Okay, let's get back—"

I stopped short of re-engaging the embrace. At the barest edge of my senses, I heard another sound in the temple, voices whispering to one another. The princess pulled close to me and tried to find my lips, but I gently pushed her back. "Wait, someone else is in here."

Her shadowed form stiffened, but then she said quickly, "I hear them, too." She clung tight to my tunic. "Why would someone be here so late?"

My mind raced to answer that exact question. "The same reason we are. They wanted to make sure they'd be alone. Stay here." My hands laced around the hilt of the dabar sheathed beneath my tunic. "I'll be right back."

I relied on the voices to guide me. Crouched down low, my Seraphim training kicked in, and I passed through the temple without a sound, before finally finding the other interlopers. There were two distinctly male voices, and their passion was evident even through whispers.

"He will have this country in ruins before the year is out. We have to act now," the first man argued.

"I've lost as much as you, but we need to give it more time. What you're planning"—the second man paused—"we may not be forgiven for."

The first voice scoffed. "The time for patience and caution has passed. The plan is already in motion." The unmistakable swoosh of a blade leaving its sheath rang in the air. "Within the month, King Erik, Prince Damon, and the whole royal family will be dead."

My face went flush from rage, and for several seconds it took all of my willpower to keep myself from jumping into the room and gutting both of the men. This had to be it, the conspiracy for which Alvaro had anointed me—my family's survival hanging in the balance. Yet now the mission was even more personal. The threat they posed to Damon, my best friend, would not be ignored. The threat they posed to Michal, my...well, whatever she was now—they weren't getting near her either. My new training always at the ready, I could end these two before they even realized what was on them.

However, the Seraphim had taught me something far more worthwhile than simply efficient ways to overpower people. They taught me self-control. As much as I wanted to surgically disconnect the limbs from their bodies, information was crucial. If this was a plot to harm the royal family, most likely it extended far beyond these two spies. One of them needed to still be alive after our encounter for interrogation.

There were several unknown factors in play. At least one of them had a blade, but was the other man armed? How well did they know how to fight? And most importantly, was there another way out of their room beside the exit I crouched at?

The lamplight barely touched their compartment in the tabernacle, and I couldn't tell how thick the exterior pavilion flaps were. My own thoughts had been elsewhere when Michal had pressed me against them.

The safest bet would be to wait until they finished their conversation and follow them back home. Then I could grab one of them alone and take my time getting the information. I grimaced, realizing I wouldn't be able to tell Michal why I had left her by herself in the spooky temple.

Feet shuffled behind me.

Had they brought someone to watch the entrance?

Spinning on my heels, I darted toward the sound. Two silhouettes waited at the front of the temple. My blade up, I crashed down on the larger one and pinned him to the ground, metal to his throat.

His companion, a woman, shrieked to my right.

A woman?

The moonlight showed both their faces. The male I had tackled was probably a year younger than me, more boy than man. His eyes went large, and he choked out words from fright.

His accomplice was a young girl, and she backed up several paces, her hands up. "We're so sorry. We'll never make out here again, we swear."

The boy's head jerked up and down nervously in agreement.

When did the temple become the "it place" for people to get intimate?

I pushed off him in disgust and sprinted back to the plotters. They must have noticed the commotion, but they hadn't left through the front. My only hope was if they couldn't escape through the sides of the canvas. Disregarding my training, I rushed into their room. The far corner of the tent was pulled out, the section vacant.

My heart sank. I had let them escape, and now the entire royal family—along with my own—would pay for my failure.

Chapter 23

Frustration tore apart my intestines. We didn't have time for another dead end, and so far, my latest "unorthodox investigation" had failed to get me any closer to uncovering the traitor. Still, I forced the smile to remain plastered on my face, as I sat with four of Erik's personal attendants.

The five of us sat in a semicircle around the hearth of the modest servants' quarters. We had been celebrating for the better part of three hours, and I had just finished retelling the tale of my fight with Goliath.

The king's fat cupbearer, Bartholomew, clapped several times and hiccupped. He fumbled for his goblet and raised it high. "To Niklas, the Giant-Slayer!"

His three companions echoed his toast. "To Niklas!"

I raised my glass. "To me!"

We all erupted in laughter, and I slapped the back of the servant to my right and stood up. "Who wants more mutton?"

Bartholomew placed a hand on his increasingly protruding belly. "I shouldn't, really," his mouth argued, but his eyes told a different story. "But *shalom*, it's not every day you get to eat from the king's table. Load me up with another plate."

A mousy page, who couldn't have been older than fifteen, raised his hand. "May I have some, as well?"

I nodded and cut off several large slices from the lamb. The other two servants also accepted a fourth helping, and we sat back down. My own plate had barely been touched.

Since the night in the temple, it felt like a mud-brick had taken up residence in my stomach, making it difficult to eat anything.

Three weeks of Seraphim investigations had produced the sum of zero leads. Gabril had dispatched dozens of operatives all over Israel, yet we had not uncovered any actionable information of the plot against King Erik and his family. Oh, we found out the kingdom had little love for their ruler—most people we questioned seemed genuinely delighted when hearing about the possibility of his assassination, at least until the harsher interrogation started—but none had any connections to the conspiracy.

Since the Seraphim operated outside of Israel's official power structure, we weren't shackled by typical codes of conduct. Gabril kept increasing the pressure, torturing prisoners and threatening Israelite merchants, peasants, and elders alike, but it backfired. All we accomplished was alienating the people from our order. Citizens now cringed when they saw one of our black feathers, disdain lurking in their eyes.

We needed a different approach, a new angle to see the problem. The idea had come last night while we wandered the streets of Gibeath. A mother recognized me on the street and pointed me out to her son. "Jacob, that man is Niklas, the hero of our whole nation. When you grow up, I want you to be just like him."

The people didn't see me as another member of the Seraphim. They saw me as a protector, a guardian, someone worth their trust.

So here I was, sharing a month's allotment of meat as appreciation for the servants' work, hoping to discover any lead into an anti-Erik movement.

"You know there's a song about you?" one of the other servants, a court scribe named Matthew, informed me.

My eyebrows arched. "A song?"

He grinned, cutting into the meat. "My wife loves it. 'Niklas slays tens of thousands, giants and warriors alike.'"

"Bah," I laughed. "That's a song?" I turned to his friends. "Tell me he's joking."

161

They all shook their heads.

"It can't be popular!"

"In the right circles, it's almost all that's sung," Bartholomew said, before belching loudly. "I'd just be careful not to sing it in front of the king. A few days ago, Erik executed a whole family he heard singing it."

"A whole family?" I asked, horrified. "For singing a song?"

"I didn't tell you the first part," the scribe said. "'Erik kills by the thousands, though half are his own people.'"

I grimaced, knowing full well how the king would respond to such a verse. "The lyrics do border on treason."

Matthew's face morphed, all humor disappearing. "And executing your own people? What side of the treason border does that fall on?"

I slowly ran my finger along the lip of my cup, uncomfortable with any answer.

The last servant raised his glass. "To our fallen brethren."

We each echoed his sentiment.

"How bad has it gotten?" I asked.

Bartholomew's eyes narrowed. "With the king?"

"Yeah." It had been two years since Erik regularly used me in his court. Alexander never called for me anymore, and I had assumed the mania had finally subsided.

"Bad." The large cupbearer finished off his goblet. "Take a walk sometime among those begging at the city gates. Dozens of our men are lame, and only a fraction are from the war. Most caught the king on a good night."

"A good *night*?"

"He holds his inquisitions while our city sleeps," Bartholomew explained. "He says those who plot against him in the shadows deserve to die in them, and he has a whole squad of black-feathered thugs to play executioner and clean up."

Unease crept up my back like a spider. "Black-feathered thugs" clearly referred to my Seraphim brethren, which meant while Gabril had trained me in the desert, the king had unleashed other members against our own people. It didn't make sense. During the king's worst episodes, he could be harsh, but he wasn't a monster. He always had a reason for what he did.

Didn't he?

"Has anyone spoken to Alexander? The chief counsel may be a bloated goat, but he's always had a way of navigating King Erik's temperament."

Matthew shrugged his shoulders, keeping his eyes down. "If it doesn't cost the treasury money, the lard bottom doesn't take an interest."

That, at least, seemed truthful. "I'll speak to Prince Damon then," I promised. "Erik listens to him. He'll find a way to help. We can end this."

"Oh," Matthew began, tearing into another piece of meat, "it's going to end—"

"Enough," Bartholomew said, locking eyes with him.

An unnatural hush fell over the room. Neither of the other two servants looked up, but it was apparent everyone knew more.

Leaning forward in my chair, I gestured for Matthew to go on. "What were you going to say?"

The scribe slowly broke off his gaze with the cupbearer and lightly smiled. "Nothing, just that one day, of course, it'll end."

Matthew lied right to my face.

Years of trying to sidestep trouble taught me the art of deception. He had almost let something slip, but he thought better of trusting me at the last moment. I slipped my hand behind my back, grasping the knife tucked into my belt. These men had answers that I needed.

Springing up from my stool, I grabbed one of its legs and threw it hard at Bartholomew. It splintered into pieces as it crashed into him and the cupbearer tumbled off the back of his chair. Next, I used my momentum to propel myself into the last servant in the room, a middle-aged mason, and slammed him into the back wall. He crumbled to the ground, which left only the mousy page and Matthew. Pulling out my dabar, I pointed it at the boy and tried to keep my voice calm. "Stay right there, and I promise nothing will happen to you."

My attention turned to Matthew. "So, before Barth interrupted you, it seemed like you had more to say about King Erik's future. Let's explore that a bit."

The scribe's eyes ballooned but then quickly narrowed. "You're one of them," he sneered.

"Me, one of 'them'?" I asked, pointing the blade at my chest. "As in, a defender of our kingdom, yeah, I am." I took several steps toward him.

"No," he replied, "one of Erik's Seraphim dogs. You're worse than his hyenas. They don't realize their master is a tyrant. What's your excuse?"

My head bobbed up and down, and I chuckled before rushing forward and closing the difference between us. I towered over him, using every trick to intimidate him. "How does the saying go, 'Sticks and stones may break my bones, but a Seraphim's knife will leave you holding your liver.' Get talking or not saying words is really going to hurt you."

Matthew lashed out and grabbed my knife hand. At first I thought he was trying to pull it away, but instead he leaned into its edge, pushing it deep against his throat. "Get this over with," he demanded, staring me straight into the eye. "The king murdered my brother for singing *your* song to his son. I guess it's appropriate I'd die by your hand."

The king had murdered his brother?

My hand started trembling, an emotional storm raging in my mind. How far would I go if someone had killed Abin, Sham, or Isaiah? Wouldn't I be plotting and scheming to avenge my family?

Yet if we didn't find the traitor soon, my own brothers' lives were at risk. Alvaro had tied my family's fate to stopping the plot.

Clenching my eyes shut, I shouted in frustration and pushed the scribe hard against the back wall. The impact shook him, and he lost his grip on my arm.

I swept my eyes over the room. All of the servants cowered at my gaze. They were terrified of me.

Slipping the dabar back into its sheath, I shook my head back and forth. I couldn't in good conscience torture them, and if I turned them over to the Seraphim, execution would be a welcome relief after the torture they'd experience. There had to be another way to stop the assassination. It just needed to be uncovered quickly, because we were running out of time.

Calming myself, I looked down to Matthew. "We have to talk through this before–"

My plea ended rather abruptly, as what I can only assume was a chair crashed into the back my skull. When I awoke, the room had been emptied of most of their personal belongings and the servants were gone.

"You bloody moron!" I groaned, cursing my own pathetic mixture of hesitation and incompetence.

Rubbing my throbbing head, I intended to report the lead to the Seraphim, but then noticed a scrap of paper stuck between my foot and my sandal. Bending down, I found a note with a simple message on it.

Meet me at the royal pasture tomorrow at dusk. There's still time to save the king.

Chapter 24

Twelve hours later, the sun dipped below the horizon, and I wove through the capital's alleys toward Erik's personal pasture. The note had left me too wound up to sleep, so my day had been filled with activity, sparring with other soldiers, restringing my lyre, sharpening my dabar. I even stooped to cleaning my room. Who knew my mother's prayer for cleanliness would be answered by the impending destruction of our nation?

I fought to keep my hopes reasonable, but this was the first concrete lead in the conspiracy against the crown. It seemed impossible to overestimate how important tonight could be. I decided to go to the meeting alone for two reasons. First, the fields left almost no place to hide for cover, and I didn't want to scare off the informant by bringing backup. Second, I had serious suspicion that my Seraphim brethren may still be a touch too eager in their hunt for the traitor. I didn't want anyone to get hurt, especially someone who was trying to help us.

Passing beneath the east gate of the city, I swept my gaze over the sheep's pasture. The king had by far the largest flock in the country, with almost seven hundred ewes and dozens of rams. No one else appeared to be in the fields.

Had I simply arrived first, or had the informant gotten cold feet?

Shaking my head, I started wandering around the perimeter of the fenced-in pasture.

At the northeast edge of the field, two feet poked out from around the corner. Sprinting toward it, I discovered the body of the man they were attached to. A dark red spot soaked through the bottom of his tan tunic. It was the corpse of the mousy page from last night's meal in the servants' quarters.

I pressed my hand against my forehead and rubbed it down my face, sorrow and guilt ripping through my heart. His body seemed so much smaller now. The boy had just been trying to do the right thing, and cowards murdered him for it. What kind of low-life would butcher a child to advance their agenda?

Hot fury grew out of my sorrow. Someone would pay for this.

My prey didn't make me wait. From behind me, a man's voice called out. "Give us a moment to explain."

I turned slowly, finding the scribe Matthew and three other unknown men walking up behind me, each carrying an iron sword.

"We didn't want to do it," he explained.

"You didn't want to murder a boy?" I asked, my voice cold and quiet as I pulled out my knife. "You should have stuck with that feeling."

The men raised their blades defensively, and the scribe continued. "He would have ruined everything. Our nation's only hope is to remove Erik from power. He's the real murderer."

My eyes focused on the page's lifeless form. "So Erik murdered the boy?"

He gripped his sword with both hands. "I understand you're upset, but—"

I flung my empty hand up, cutting him off. "No, Goliath, the giant who slayed hundreds of our soldiers made me upset. He was a rabid dog, but at least he fought in the daylight, against men. You slaughtered a boy who was just trying to do right by his country." I brought up my blade, pointing it at him. "*Your* country. We are several miles beyond *upset*."

The men glanced nervously between themselves. Matthew nodded, and they hesitantly fanned out around me. "We want you to join us, Niklas. Someone like you can help build a new kind of nation, not one ruled by a tyrant but ruled by the people. In time, someone like you may be made king himself."

I smiled softly and evaluated the four men's positions. Each stood within my striking distance. They were all novices to combat, meaning this would be over quick. My attention returned to the scribe. "I already have a job, thanks."

"It doesn't have to be this way," Matthew said, finality in his voice.

"Yeah," I said, my eyes hardening, "it really does."

The two men at my sides moved first. They both brought up the swords high above their heads and charged at me. I spun into the one coming from the right, and my dabar found his unprotected neck. Before his body could even crumble, the second man was bringing his blade down upon me, but one side-step later his throat was within reach, and I opened it with my blade. At his comrade's death, the third man ran forward in unbridled rage. For him, I copied the wound they had given the innocent page, burying my knife deep into his torso, and then pushed his deflating body away.

Only Matthew was left.

I gave him credit; even knowing how hopeless he was, he held his ground. "I can't tell you anything."

"No, not can't," I corrected him. "Right now you *won't*. That will change momentarily." The concept of torture always made me uncomfortable, and yesterday that feeling had gotten the better of me. My mistake had cost a boy his life. Tonight my resolve wouldn't falter. I stepped toward him.

He bit his lip, thinking, and then he roared in rage and threw his sword end over end at me. The sudden action caught me off guard, but my reflexes took over, and I ducked safely away from his blade.

Jumping up, I lunged at the now defenseless man, who had used the brief moment to take something from his belt and stuff it in his mouth. My shoulder hit him like a sack of grain, and I pinned him to the ground. He didn't resist but quickly ground his teeth as he looked up at me.

My mind raced to figure out what was happening, and it clicked as soon as I saw him swallow. Poison.

The effects were almost instantaneous. Even in the dark of night, I could see his throat slowly swell. At this rate, he had maybe a minute before he would be dead, and dead men don't give up information, no matter how much you tortured them.

"Tell me about the plot against the king!" I demanded.

His body began convulsing, but his bulging eyes found mine. Matthew's lips struggled to form words. The scribe's throat refused to let out any sound, but a manic smile crossed his lips as he mouthed the words, 'Too late.'

Erik was already dead.

Chapter 25

Two words shattered my whole world. I limply rolled off the scribe, my mouth agape and shoulders low. The lives of everyone I loved had depended on me uncovering the conspiracy before they accomplished their mission. Now all of them would be killed because Alvaro had trusted the wrong guy to protect the kingdom. No, not Alvaro—Yahweh had given me this mission. Shouldn't He have known I would never live up to the challenge? The assignment should have gone to another brother, a more capable sibling. Maybe if He would've picked one of them, my family wouldn't have to...

I couldn't even complete the thought, shaking my head harshly and running through all my decisions since finding out about the conspiracy. What should I have done differently? Did I discover it too late? Should I have been more vigilant in my search for the traitor? The priest Matthias assured me I'd be given the time and information required to complete my task. Had I missed something?

King Erik, Damon, and Michal were already gone. Who would die next? Would it be my brothers on the battlefield, or would my family be wiped out in one fell swoop with the rest of Bethlehem?

Despair sapped any strength left in me, and I brought my knees to my chest, holding myself tightly. *Too late.*

At first, I didn't hear it, my own bitter thoughts drowning out all other possibilities, but then, as if carried by the gentle breeze blowing through the pasture, the melodic notes of the harp touched my ears.

Basking in its music, my body slowly unfurled, and a quiet seed of hope blossomed in my mind. He hadn't abandoned me. Maybe I hadn't failed — not yet at least.

My mind started fitting the pieces together. The castle was on high alert, so a direct attack on the king seemed highly unlikely, which meant they'd come at him sideways. But how?

The traitor's legs spread out at the periphery of my vision. I turned toward him and slowly evaluated his dead body. What kind of man carried poison for no reason? It's useless in a direct confrontation. Poison was good for only one thing.

I tightened my fist in excitement. Matthew had died almost instantly from the toxin, but he had eaten it directly. Mixing it with food should dilute its effectiveness and slow the process, in theory anyway.

And for the first time ever, the music transformed into an entirely different melody. Melodic strings were replaced with rumbling horns, and deep drums started booming, faster and faster, urging me to action. There wasn't much time.

Bolting up, I vaulted over the fence, making the straightest path back to the capital. Never had my feet traveled so fast, and as I ran, I tried to figure out what I'd do once I reached the dining hall. Being there would accomplish nothing if all I could do was wait for the toxin to take effect. I needed a plan.

Without knowing the exact type of poison, trying to find an antidote seemed a poor use of the few precious moments left. There had to be a way to purge the poison in its entirety, but how?

Oh.

A smile split my face, as the devious scheme came together. Never had I been so thankful for being the test subject for Abin's various hijinks and pranks. The plan, however, required me to make one side stop.

I reached the palace in under five minutes and dashed into the kitchen. "Cooked mustard seeds!" I demanded. "I need mustard seeds now!"

The head cook, a middle-aged man with thick drops of sweat

pouring down his face from the hearth's fire, gasped, looking at me like I had grown horns. His serving assistants backed up several paces.

"Young man," the cook said, shaking his head, "this isn't your personal pantry. You have no right—"

My fist drove into his gut, and the chef doubled over. I couldn't know for sure if he was involved with the plot, but it seemed likely, and right now they needed to take me seriously. My eyes found the smallest servant, a young woman, and I repeated my demand. "Cooked mustard seeds. Now!"

Whatever she saw in my eyes quieted any further protests. She pointed to a jar on the second shelf. Grabbing it, I nodded my appreciation and sprinted back out of the room...

...and ran right into the bulging gut of Alexander. Together we tumbled to the floor, and the jar of seeds flew out of my hands and shattered on the floor.

"Niklas!" Alexander scoffed, on his back. "How dare you assault me. Your insolence—"

Yada-yada-yada. I'm pretty sure he kept chastising me, but I ignored him and scrambled over to the broken jar, scooping up as many of the scattered seeds as I could hold. Two handfuls would have to manage, and I began my quest anew.

King Erik, Damon, Michal, and the queen sat around the royal table, each clearing the last few bites on their plates.

"Niklas!" Michal exclaimed in genuine delight. "I didn't expect to see you tonight. Father, can he join us?"

The king opened his mouth to respond but stopped short when my fists slammed down upon the dinner table.

I opened my palms, showing the dark seeds. "You must chew and swallow these, right now!"

The royal family gawked at me, bewildered by the demand. Ever since catching wind of the plot, Erik's family had been kept under the strongest protection, and two of their guards drew their blades, inching closer to me.

"Niklas," Michal repeated, cautious concern in her voice. "Are you feeling all right?" She rose to place a hand on my forehead.

Damon's eyes widened. "You're covered in blood. What happened?"

"The assassination," I answered. "It's happening tonight. They put the poison in your dinner. You have to eat the mustard seeds, now!"

Erik's face morphed from shock to fear, but then hardened in calculation. His attention turned to the corner of the room, where an elderly servant sat at a small table. "You're mistaken. My meal tester is still fine, and he ate straight from my plate half an hour ago. Where did you get this information?"

I glanced down at my bloodied tunic, my mind racing. The palace had been on alert, so it made sense that the poison would take some time. If the tester died before the royal family ate, it would only make it that much harder to try again.

"Sire," I pleaded, "you must trust me. The food is poisoned. I don't know how or even who did it, but I promise you, your whole family is in danger."

The king had a reply on his lips, but it was his son who moved first. Damon rose from his seat and walked toward me. "Are you certain?"

I swallowed hard. If I was wrong, the king would have me executed before the next sunrise. "Do you remember that 'shadow' you were hunting the day we first met?"

The prince's eyes expanded, and then he nodded. "So we eat these?" he asked, pointing at the blackened seeds in my hand.

My head jerked frantically up and down.

He grabbed a dozen seeds and brought his hand up to his mouth.

I snatched his arm. "Do it together."

If they saw what happened to the prince, it was doubtful the rest of the family would follow my instructions.

Damon studied my face for a moment, but then curtly nodded. "We eat it together." He took some of the seeds, and we went around the table, handing out them out to his father and mother.

Michal took the seeds from me timidly. "What's happening?"

"Trust me," I said with a concerned smile and then looked at the king. "I swear on my family's life, you're all in danger."

Erik's face masked any thoughts. He squinted at the seeds. "Do it, all of you."

Together as one, the royal family dumped the seeds into their mouth, crunching the blackened pods in the rear of their jaws.

The reaction was instantaneous. Eyes bulged, and in unison their chins snapped up, retching hard. Food and stomach fluid sprayed all over the dinner table, as Erik's family discovered the wonders of the affectionately named prank "Abin's Surprise."

Mustard seeds uncooked are fine to eat, and even baked can add a touch of zesty flavor. But eating cooked, whole pods overrides the senses with their pungent, oily flavor. Abin uncovered the secret by making me taste-test every spice in our mother's kitchen when I was four years old.

After a minute, the mass bodily expulsion finally subsided, and the king glared up, murder in his eyes. "You will pay for this insult with your life," he said, harshly wiping colored drool from his beard.

Fun times.

Then my own eyes went wide because there was still one more person who needed help. My head whipped toward the old food taster, but it was too late. With all the commotion of the royal family's gastric issues, we had missed it. His head lay face down on the table, his cheeks ghost white.

The king's gaze followed my own, and he had to steady himself with the arms rests of his chair. "You were right," he said in a whisper. "We almost died."

Exhausted, I collapsed at the table. The prince and princess rushed to my side, helping to hold me up. They guided me to a chair, and I gladly sank into it.

"How did you know?" Damon asked.

Taking a weary breath, I recounted the events of the last twenty-four hours.

"But you didn't discover any leads on who else was in league with the traitors?" Erik asked, frowning.

"No, sire. Matthew took the poison himself before I could question him."

My body demanded to let it rest, the lack of sleep crashing down on me, but my brain frantically hacked away at clearing the weeds shrouding the mystery. This had been too close. I couldn't be caught off guard again.

Desperate and committed as Matthew and his compatriots may have been, he didn't seem to possess either the mental capacity nor the access needed to pull something this extensive off. The head of this group needed to be organized, ruthless, and well connected. Erik had executed almost everyone who met those requirements.

The doors to the banquet hall opened, and Alexander walked in. I sat facing the door, and the chief-toad-in-staff glared and pointed his feather quill at me.

"Your impudence will be tolerated no—" Then he stopped, his mouth agape at the sight of the king and his family.

Anyone else's shock could have been credited to the vile all over the table and the floor, but I had seen Alexander watch dozens of men ripped to shreds by hyenas without so much as flinching. Yet seeing the king and his family merely sitting safely at the table caused him to balk.

His face immediately returned to its usual stoic visage, but in that unexpected moment, I'd witnessed a true emotion from the man — genuine disbelief. The one thing Alexander had not expected entering the hall had been a very much alive royal family.

Harp notes flittered over the air.

One last surge of strength flowed through my veins, and I vaulted the table and dove at the counselor. He was so big it should have been impossible to miss him, but with athleticism that I never would've credited him, he sidestepped my assault. Blame it on my exhaustion. My body slammed into the floor next to him, my skull bouncing harshly on the floor.

Alexander straightened his green robe, sneering at me with his beady eyes. "We will find a most creative punishment for your disrespect, fool."

I rolled over, the room still wobbly from my fall. "It's him," I grunted.

"What?" the counselor asked. "I'm what?" He placed his foot on my neck, draining what little strength I had left. "Quiet now."

And then Damon upper-cut all three of the man's chins. Alexander tumbled back, dazed and bewildered.

The prince stood over me. "Niklas just saved the lives of everyone in this room. If you lay another toe on him, I swear, they'll have to feed you with a spoon for the rest of your miserable life."

The counselor was speechless, glancing to the king for support.

Erik eyed him warily, before turning his attention to me. "What were you saying, musician?"

"He's the traitor," I said, taking Damon's hand to help me up. "The head of the whole bloody conspiracy."

The king glared at Alexander. "And your response to these allegations?"

"Ridiculous," the blubbery man said, his voice squeaking. "How dare he accuse me, your most loyal subject, of treason. He's trying to build upon his victory, use it to undermine me. In fact, it makes sense that he knew about the poison. He probably set up the whole plot!"

The king studied the counselor, and then his lips curled into a hard smile. "Who said anything about poison?"

Chapter 26

Two hours later, the throne room was full. From the highest military officers to the chambermaids, everyone who worked in the palace had been ordered to attend the chief counselor's trial. Only Michal and the king's wife were given permission to miss the proceedings. His daughter had no stomach for what we all knew came next.

Honestly, *I* had no stomach for what came next.

Alexander sat on his knees, both hands tightly bound behind his back, ten feet in front of the king. Even in his disheveled state, the dishonored man still found a way to look down on the rest of us.

Erik sat upon the throne, his three rabid executioners on their feet below him, stretched out toward Alexander. The hyenas were eager to enjoy the thick-marbled meal before them.

Damon and I stood together to the right of the king. Catching Alexander meant I had succeeded in my mission. The traitor was found, and my family was safe. I let those words echo in my mind. *My family was safe.* Without that constant fear of failure coursing through my veins, though, I struggled to keep my eyes from drooping.

The king spread out his hands before the assembly and focused on the counselor. "Well, my most trusted of confidants, we've gathered to hear your defense against the accusation of high treason. Please, enlighten us."

Erik's disgraced counselor sniffed the air and cracked his knuckles loudly. "Let's get this over with. We both know how this ends, no matter what I say."

Rage flashed across the king's face, but cold fury immediately replaced it. "Had I not been good to you?" he asked. "I gave you everything. You were the second most powerful man in all of the kingdom."

Alexander nodded. "True, but as time went on, I realized the second most powerful man could not protect Israel from your childish, foolish rule."

I swallowed hard. No one talked to the king like that — ever. What was he thinking?

"Protect Israel?" the king scoffed, color again rising in his voice. "We're winning the bloody war!"

The traitor didn't flinch at the outburst. "Yes, and even if we obliterate the Philistines, you'll still be the destruction of our people. I've done the numbers. Your rule has caused more harm to our nation than ten wars with the savages."

Erik rose from his chair. "You go too far," he growled, "you craven, inbred, disloyal excuse for an Israelite."

Alexander shook his head. "No, I did not go far enough, but someone else will. Others plot against you, others in this very room."

A wry smile traced the king's lips. "I am well aware of that fact," he said to the counselor and then turned his attention to the assembly. "That is why I have gathered you all here." He walked off the throne and stood over the bound man. "There are those in this room who have lost land, their careers, even their families to my rule. I understand your grief. Yet know that I am at peace with my actions and have always striven to be fair, and whenever possible, merciful. So, I say to you now, anyone who conspired with Alexander has been given a full pardon. The blame and punishment will fall on his shoulders alone."

The people in the court seemed unsure how to respond to his statement. Showing too much relaxation could insinuate guilt. Almost everyone kept their head down, hoping to avoid the king's gaze.

Erik placed a hand roughly on Alexander's shoulder. "However, today I will show you the full punishment for anyone who dares attempt this again. You will all watch the penalty for treason against me and my family."

Then the king whirled toward the throne and threw Alexander forward into the hyenas. At first, the beasts were confused—normally their "meals" were taken to a back room, out of sight of the occupants of the grand hall—but they quickly moved beyond their hesitation and circled the counselor.

Alexander cracked his fingers in defiance one last time before they were upon him.

The next minute seemed to drag on forever, and more than one person threw up as the beasts did their work.

Finally, the king pulled Alexander's dead body away, motioning for the guards to take the corpse to the back room. The hyenas trailed after the soldiers, eager to finish their feast.

"It is done," the king said to the assembly. "Go home to your families. Hold them, love them, but never forget this day."

I doubted anyone in the room would suffer memory loss of the night's events. Suffering recurring nightmares was another matter entirely.

One by one, people silently filed out of the room. Damon and I moved to take our leave, but the king held up his hands as we passed. "Niklas, please stay. We have much to discuss." His son turned around as well, but the king waved him off. "You won't be needed, Damon."

It took substantial effort to keep my shoulders from physically shaking. After witnessing such a powerful statement against angering the king, the last thing I wanted to do was remain in his company. Beyond that, my limbs weighed a ton. How long had it been since I last slept, thirty-six hours?

Still, refusing his invitation could be perceived as an insult, regardless of the reasoning, so I spun slowly and turned to him. "Of course, my king."

Erik smiled warmly, an unsettling contrast to his demeanor from only minutes prior. "Am I destined to be forever in your debt?" he asked, resting both palms on the throne's armrests. "First, you stem the tide of my madness, then you slay the Philistine butcher for me, and today you save my whole family from the plot of that backstabbing coward. I must owe you half of my kingdom by now."

I shook my head slowly. "No sire, I only acted to protect what's important to me. I have no doubt many others would have done the same in my stead."

"Many others should have," the king agreed, "but only you rose to the challenge. Name your reward; anything within my power is yours."

Anything is a big word, especially when coupled with a king's power, but after all that had occurred, more than anything I simply wanted to go to bed.

"Thank you for your generosity, but there is nothing." I breathed in deep, focused on keeping my eyes from drooping. "In truth, I accomplished none of those things by myself. The music always showed me the way."

Erik shifted harshly in the throne, and his face contorted. "What music?"

My eyes wandered up slowly, wondering what had upset him, but then my neck snapped up. Why had I mentioned that? "It's nothing of note, Your Highness."

"What. Music?" Erik repeated though gritted teeth, his dark eyes sinking back into his face.

Blood fled my cheeks. After my victory over the giant, the king had told me he too once heard an invisible melody, but Alvaro had ripped it away from him, replacing it with madness. Nothing good would come from him realizing I now possessed the very thing stolen from him. My weary mind tried to figure out some fictitious story to bail me out of my predicament, but the wheels behind my eyes wouldn't turn, and if I didn't answer soon, I'd be good as dead anyway.

"A harp," I replied, trying to keep it simple. "I hear a harp sometimes. It helps guide my decisions, helps me see things I might otherwise miss." An important thought popped up in my brain. "It helped me save your family tonight," I added, hoping that fact would help him appreciate the situation.

No trace of appreciation appeared in his eyes. He leaned back and stared at me, dissecting me with a leery glare.

"Is everything all right?" I asked and glanced nervously around the empty room, acutely bothered by my privacy with Erik. If only Damon hadn't been dismissed.

The king said nothing.

"May I go, if you wish?"

Again, Erik refused to speak, but his head shook back and forth resolutely.

"When did it begin?" he asked.

I bit my lip. "It started about three years ago." *Shortly after the music had left him.*

I don't know how long Erik made me wait there, but eventually, he tilted his head and opened his eyes wide, an idea dancing in them. "If you'll not accept my offer for a boon, then I shall bestow one on you."

I swallowed hard, fearful of any "gift" the king had concocted in his present state of mind.

"You will receive a commission," he informed me.

"A commission?" I asked, confused. "The only commissions I know of are military positions."

"Exactly," replied King Erik, cracking his knuckles. "We're going to make you a general."

Part Five: Tyrants

In the darkened chamber, the middle-aged shepherd almost missed Erik's body curled up in the bedroom's far corner. He was shivering, taking quick, choppy breaths, and whispering to himself in fragmented musings and accusations. According to the guard posted outside, shortly after the execution of the traitor, the king had again descended into madness, but now refused to see either the young singer or his healers.

Moving gently toward the king, the shepherd knelt down next to the afflicted ruler. "Your Highness," he said in reverent tones, "your faithful servant has returned in your hour of need."

Erik reacted to the voice like a feral dog, lunging at the visitor.

The man didn't flinch. He held up a single, open hand and the manic ruler stopped short, transfixed.

"O favored of all kings," the shepherd continued, "I bring you a great boon."

A trace of awareness floated back into Erik's eyes. "Who are you?" The king moved closer, trying to make out the visitor's features. It took a moment, but Erik recognized the unmistakable birthmark covering the man's cheek. "Doeg, how...?"

Doeg took Erik's shoulder. "For years, Your Highness, I have sought a solution to your affliction, only to discover we were looking at it backwards. You need no longer be bound to this broken state."

A brief seed of hope sprung in the king's eyes, but then he turned away, sinking back into the corner. "No. Every time aid is offered to alleviate this curse—be it Alvaro, Alexander, or Niklas—it only leaves me more dependent, weakened."

"Exactly," Doeg said, excited. "But I come not offering a balm to soothe, but a power to control."

The king glanced back, skeptical but attentive.

"What Yahweh intended for punishment, also opened a door up to untold power." The shepherd took out an eight-pointed bronze star hanging around his neck. "As I served you from afar, I came across an avatar, an ancient being, to aid in your rule." He brought his hand closer to the king's face. "May I?"

Erik's eyes narrowed, but he nodded slowly.

Holding the bronze medallion tightly with his right hand, Doeg dropped his head, speaking quietly in an unrecognizable tongue. When he finished, the shepherd reached out with his left palm.

The king recoiled at his touch and rolled his neck. After a moment's pause, he opened his eyes wide. "The noise," he said, his voice growing stronger, more coherent. "It is still there, but now it's muffled, not as demanding."

Doeg rose to his feet. "And soon you will come to understand it, learn from it," he promised. "From today onward, you will never again fear the tyranny of the voices, for they will be your steadfast guide." Offering his hand, he helped the king gain his footing. "However, in my absence, troubling rumors reached me of a young warrior, another shepherd, who, by the accounts of your own people, could soon challenge your rule."

A hint of a smile began playing on Erik's lips as he gazed into a bedside mirror. "That, my faithful servant, will soon take care of itself."

Chapter 27

General Carmi accompanied me to the barracks where my new troops awaited. A gust of wind blew, and the battle-seasoned commander quickly fixed quite possibly the worst comb-over in all of Israel. Damon and I had named it the Carmi Special.

Yet today, I found no humor in the general's presence, because the king had personally assigned him to assist with my initiation as a general. He was Erik's longest tenured officer and the closest thing the king had to a friend. For the foreseeable future, I wanted to avoid anything to do with His Highness.

Since revealing the presence of the mysterious music to the king three days ago, I had felt like a scared mouse forced to eat from the same food bowl as the house cat. Every day, Erik found some new excuse to keep me around his court. He refused to address me directly, but his eyes always drifted in my direction, as if at any moment I might morph into a deadly cobra and strike.

Part of me wanted to simply tell King Erik the whole story, how I didn't even know what Alvaro was doing until after the anointing, but if finding out about the music put me on the king's manure list, how would he respond to hearing that I'd been anointed? I had enough axes hanging over my head already, thank you.

My solace came in the belief that if the king wanted to kill me, he'd have done it already. My family wasn't powerful enough to organize any sort of retaliation, which left me wide open for immediate disposal. I briefly entertained trying to escape the capital, but if he caught me attempting to flee, an execution was sure to follow. My best bet was to accept the assignment and hope his anger blew over.

Of course, the small wrinkle in that plan was I had never even been an enlisted soldier in our army, let alone a commander. Beginning as a general seemed like a poor starting place on multiple fronts.

On a merrier note, at eighteen I must have been one of the youngest men ever to make general. Kudos to me.

So together I walked with Captain Comb-over, wondering how large of a battalion the king had issued me. Our army had grown since the tide had turned against the Philistines, many families suddenly revealing eligible soldiers for conscription. Go figure; when certain death is taken off the table, more people are willing to fight. Success breeds friends.

"You've already been replaced," the general said off-handedly, stripping me from my musings.

"What?" I asked.

Carmi kept his eyes ahead. "The king has found a new favorite for his court, a foreigner from Edom. He's discovered a way to keep Erik's madness at bay." The general paused, a smile tugging at his lips. "You're expendable."

I rolled my eyes. If Carmi intended this news to be disheartening, he obviously didn't spend enough time in the king's presence. I would gladly welcome someone else enjoying Erik's "favor" until the day they dropped me in the ground.

We reached the edge of town where my new troops waited, and the other shoe dropped, along with my stomach. I'd be spending time in my grave sooner than anticipated.

General Carmi started chuckling under his breath.

After seeing the state of our army before the battle with Goliath, I had substantially lowered the bar for what I considered a field-ready military. The men standing before me had not only found a way to slither below it, they somehow managed to dig a whole bloody canyon under it.

Three groups of men stood before me. To my left waited a group of shepherds, most of whom were either five years too young or thirty years too old to rightfully go near a battlefield. They collectively cowered from the other two groups. In front of me, some three dozen men sat cross-legged in a long row, prisoner shackles tethering them all together. Finally, to their right waited the last group of my "platoon," fifty filthy, craven, dung-eating Philistines.

"This has to be some kind of joke," I said through gritted teeth.

The commander's laugh morphed into unabashed mocking. "Oh it is a joke, and it's a punch line I've been waiting to hit you with for two and a half years, *god-slayer*," he sneered.

Turning on the man, I clinched my fists tightly and then pointed to the shepherds. "How is this even happening? Those boys aren't old enough to be enlisted, and the men are old enough for military exemption!"

A cruel smile appeared on his lips. "You have no one but yourself to thank for such a battalion," he replied, sweeping his hands across my troops. "Your great deeds caused Erik to see sheepherders in a new light. He issued a nationwide invitation to any shepherd who wanted to fight alongside the mighty warrior Niklas. These are the men who volunteered."

I narrowed my eyes. "These are children."

"So were you," the general said, enjoying every moment of this travesty.

"Then what about them?" My arm lashed out to the criminals. "Since when did conscripts come with shackles, not armor?"

Carmi's face hardened. "Watch your tone, boy." We stared each other down before he turned to the men bound on the ground. "War takes its toll on any nation. We needed to find a way to reduce the deaths of Israelite men, so we decided to find a better use than the gallows for these turncoats, cutthroats, and traitors."

Traitors? My work had just led to the execution of Alexander, their leader, and now they were being forced to serve under me. Awesome. I took several deep breaths before asking about the last group. "And them?"

"Them," the general repeated. "Our recent victories over Philistia have caused some of the Philistines to defect. Why waste our own blood when such an ideal alternative exists."

"And you trust them?"

He barked a laugh. "Trust them? Pharaoh's beard, no!" He placed his hand roughly on my shoulder and leaned close to my ear. "But they aren't my troops." He pushed me forward. "Enjoy your new assignment, General Niklas."

It took considerable effort not to turn around and pull my blade on Carmi. Stuffing down my anger, I fought to keep my voice level. "Do I have any commanders beneath me?"

His eyes lit up. "How could I have forgotten? Benaiah!" he bellowed. "Where did you disappear to, you runt?"

Sitting with his back to us, a boy jumped up in shock. When he turned, I found not one of the shepherd youth, but a most unusual looking man. He had a thick brown beard, but most ten-year-old boys had a larger build than him. He stood up and couldn't have been more than four and a half feet tall, with bean-pole arms and knobby knees. He scrambled up to the general with a roll of paper in his arms; his head hung low.

"I'm sorry, sir," he muttered. "I was trying to organize the troop manifests."

"Good luck with that," the general said, dismissively. "Niklas, meet Benaiah, your second-in-command. His father and younger brothers each have received the medals of courage from the king himself. He comes from the highest of lineages." He smacked the small man on the back, and the impact threw him to the ground. "Which makes me believe Benaiah was adopted."

The short man slowly pushed himself to his feet, cowering from Carmi. He inched his neck up toward me. "It's an honor to serve under you."

I hesitantly extended my hand. "Yeah."

"Well," Carmi said, "I'll leave you to your work. I'm sure you're eager to see what your men can accomplish." He turned and left, snickering.

About ten million different emotions threatened to boil to the surface, all of them fighting for supremacy. This assignment managed to insult everything I stood for, while simultaneously scaring the undergarments off me. After all I had done for the kingdom, for the king, Erik had just handed me enough noose to hang myself a dozen times over, and he found a way to use Philistine turncoats to do it.

My attention turned to the shepherds. I could at least comprehend why the youth had taken up the call. Everyone glamorized battle at their age, especially given the opportunity to fight alongside the famous Hero of Elah, but what were the older men thinking? They knew how war's glamor turned to vapor the moment you traded blows with someone trying to take your life.

I brought my hand to my mouth and slowly rubbed my chin, evaluating the mess this situation left me in. A commotion stirred at the back of the group of shepherds as someone pushed his way forward. My brother Isaiah emerged, waving as he approached.

"Niklas!" he exclaimed and wrapped his arms around my shoulders. "The king accepted me into your army!"

My arms never returned the embrace, and he pushed back from me a bit. "What's wrong?"

Everything, I answered silently. How did Isaiah get dragged into this? It was bad enough that I'd gotten myself into this trap. Right now he needed to be as far away from me as possible.

If I took these men into battle, they were all dead, which meant I needed to ensure that these men never left the capital. If the whole point of this charade was to get rid of me, the cleanest solution was to take myself out of the equation. I needed to run.

"Nik," a woman's voice came from behind Isaiah. Deborah, the granddaughter of a judge herself, walked up to me. She wore a dress hemmed in brown, with her grandmother's purple sash around her waist and held her blacksmith mallet in one hand. "Our glorious general!" She turned to my brother, arching one eye. "Do we have to bow to him?"

My mouth hung open. "You're a woman..."

Deborah nodded. "Very observant. I can see how your visual prowess will prove invaluable on the battlefield."

"...in the army," I finished.

Her eyes hardened, and she clasped her fingers tightly around her hammer. "Yes. King Erik's invitation explicitly stated any shepherd, blacksmith, or trades *person*, regardless of age, class, or citizenship status was able to enlist. I arrived with Isaiah, and while the recruiter originally had his doubts, the king's edict was clear. I was allowed to serve."

The expression on her face dared me to challenge her. "Of course," I replied, not wanting to start a full-on fight. "With your experience in your dad's forge, you probably have more experience dealing with blades than the lot of us."

She nodded curtly, releasing the handle of her mallet. "Exactly. I'm glad I didn't have to knock some sense into you."

I plastered a smile across my lips and told them I needed a moment to inspect the rest of the troops. Walking away, I set my mind to escaping. Erik had stacked the deck against me. Deborah could handle herself—probably better than Isaiah—but this whole assignment was a tinderbox waiting to be engulfed in flames. My flight had to happen soon, before the king could light the first spark.

I passed the prisoners, trying to ignore them, when one of the bound men called out to me. "Niklas!"

My neck craned to locate the owner of the voice. At the far end of the prisoner chain, Yashobeam, the barbarian slave who had assisted me in my first Seraphim mission, waved at me as much as his metal bindings would allow.

My lungs constricted. What was he doing here? He was supposed to have gotten the children to safety and disappear. If Gabril had found out I had spared them…I shivered. Nothing good came from the former slave's presence.

Pulling him to his feet and unchaining him, I dragged him away from the rest of the criminals. "Why are you here?" I demanded through a harsh whisper.

"I joined with the other foreigners," he stated, brushing away a greasy lock of hair from his face.

"No," I said, grabbing his dirty tunic. His stench almost pushed me back. Didn't this man ever bathe? "Where are the children? You promised to protect them."

He started picking at his teeth with a crusty thumbnail. "I promised I'd get them to safety, and I did. They're with a family to the north of all the fighting. It's as safe as you could hope for. Trust me, not you nor anyone else wanted me raising anyone's children, even a filthy slaver's."

Frustration guided my hands to grasp the handle of my dabar. If he had come back to blackmail me, the only hope the children or I had of surviving was to end his tenure in my service immediately. "I'm not in the mood for games. What are you doing here?"

He glanced at my knife. "I'm here to join your army," he repeated. "After we parted ways, I looked into the famous Niklas. You're quite war hero. Even the Philistines talk about you with respect. When I heard about the call to join your army, the opportunity seemed too..." He glanced to the sky, searching for the right word. "...intriguing to pass up."

"But you're a foreigner?"

"Yes, an Amorite," he said.

"Then why are you chained up with the prisoners?"

He began chuckling. "I wanted to see the rest of the troops, but the guard wouldn't let us intermingle. So after I punched him in the stomach, he bound me with the prisoners. Mission accomplished."

I must have gawked at him for a good thirty seconds. "You're insane."

He shrugged and resumed picking at his teeth while surveying the troops. "You know this platoon's a farce, right?"

Biting my lower lip, I nodded.

"So what did you do to get stuck with a suicide assignment?"

"I saved the king's life."

He barked out a laugh.

"The king sees me as a threat," I explained, glancing off into the countryside, "and he's willing to sacrifice all of you to get rid of me. I'm going to take that opportunity away from him."

Yash's eyes narrowed slightly. "What do you mean?"

"I'm going to run. Flee the capital tonight, that way there's no reason to keep up the charade and this company won't have to die."

The ex-slave shook his head. "It may help the wool herders over there, but you'd be signing a death warrant for hundreds of people. Without this assignment, Erik promised to execute the prisoners, the foreigners, and for good measure, all of their families as well. The men all know this ends only one way for them, but they're willing to accept it if it keeps their families safe."

His statement hit me like a punch to the gut. These men had placed themselves on the executioner's block to protect their families, just like I was trying to do. If I left, I took their opportunity to do that with me. Yes, I wanted to keep Isaiah and Deborah safe, but I couldn't do it at the cost of hundreds of innocent people—even if most of them were Philistines.

It took a minute for me to form the words, but I finally turned to him. "I guess I'm staying."

Chapter 28

My mousy second-in-command was exactly where I'd left him, pouring over the scroll of our manifest.

"Benaiah, wasn't it?" I asked from behind him.

He jumped at the sound of my voice and spun around. "Apologies, General," he said. "The dark glances of some of our new troops have left me a touch uneasy. But yes, Benaiah, son of Gabek."

"As in General Gabek?"

He nodded but kept his eyes downcast. "One and the same."

"Did you serve under him?"

Benaiah shook his head. "Father never thought my service necessary, sir."

My eyebrows arched. "So how'd you end up with this assignment?"

He rubbed his hands uncomfortably together. "I missed Alexander's execution, due to stomach issues. The next day Erik informed Father of my new role."

I felt sorry for the man. Though probably ten years my senior, he seemed more like a terrified younger brother, making the constant honorifics sound weird. I patted him on the back. "You'll do fine. This is all new to me as well. We'll learn together."

He gave me a weak smile. "Thank you, sir."

"So how many troops do we have?"

Benaiah glanced down at the parchment. "One hundred and seven. Forty tradesmen, thirty-five pardoned criminals, and thirty-one foreign deserters."

I arched an eyebrow, running the math several times. "That totals one hundred and six?"

"Yes," my squirrelly commander said, "I didn't know how to categorize the woman." He bit his lip. "She's petite but quite intense."

"Indeed," I said. "Classify her as a shepherd."

I took a deep breath, wondering about my first order of business. I doubted my Seraphim training could be directly applied. Our tactics specialized in subterfuge and assassination, and I had the sum of zero large-group infantry expertise. Still, it stood to reason that most of these men had no training of any sort, so basic combat skills would be a good place to start. "Can you call them to attention for me?"

"Of course," he said. He turned toward the troops but then back toward me. "How do I do that?"

My shoulders sagged. "I'll take care of it."

I stepped up to the center of our forces and yelled, "Good morning! I'm your new general, Niklas."

Each group responded differently. The shepherds moved a little closer to me, a mixture of interest and concern on their faces. The Philistines moved closer together, unsure of how to respond. None of the criminals, except for Yashobeam, even acknowledged I had spoken.

"It's an honor to lead you," I continued. "I'm eager to see what we can accomplish together."

Isaiah raised his hand as if we were learning arithmetic from our father, not a part of an actual army.

Groaning under my breath, I acknowledged him. "Yes?"

"Why are there criminals and Philistines here?" He dropped his voice. "Are we supposed to kill them?"

The convicts responded aggressively to his question, barking for him to try, and my brother shuffled back closer to the other shepherds.

"You have all been assigned to my command. We're all on the same team."

Now it was the shepherds' turn to cower together. They stared anxiously at both the criminals and foreigners.

Of course they were scared. The Philistines had terrorized our people for hundreds of years. They were the evil nightmare that kept us awake at night. Now we were supposed to simply turn off years of conditioning and fight alongside them as if they were a neighbor from the next village over? Good luck with that.

We needed to keep moving, keep everyone's focus on something else, something more productive. I turned to Benaiah. "What armaments are we working with?"

"None as of yet, sir."

I blinked several times. "*None?*"

He held up the scroll. "The orders said Israel is currently out of stock, and they'd be delivered as soon as possible."

I clenched and unclenched my fists half a dozen times, fighting against storming the castle singlehandedly and calling horse manure to Erik's face. He could save us all a lot of trouble and just turn me into hyena kibble on the spot. It'd at least not be a massive waste of my time and energy.

The men stared blankly back at me, waiting, expecting some plan, some direction.

I had no answers for them. How do you train an army without weapons? I'd bet every sheep in Israel against Erik actually allowing blades to be delivered to our group, and even if they did eventually show up, they'd be all but useless in the hands of untrained soldiers.

What did we have to work with? Convicts whom no one trusted, Philistine deserters conscripted into the army with their families at sword point, and shepherds who specialized in herding wool, not advancing against infantry lines of battle-tested soldiers—hardly the ideal components of a mighty army.

No matter how you ran them, the numbers didn't add up to more than arrow fodder. We were in trouble.

Three long notes of a lyre drifted over the troops. My teeth ground against each other in annoyance. The blasted music started all this trouble in the first place. It always heralded my life becoming needlessly more complicated; first the lion, then the giant, next the assassin, all of it.

All of it…

My mental wheels started groaning, inching forward. I'd survived all of those adventures, completed all of those tasks, and you could hardly qualify me as the normal candidate for deeds of renown. I was a shepherd, untrained in anything but mischief and mayhem.

I surveyed the troops again. If they didn't believe they had a chance in battle, we were all as good as dead, so we needed to start with something they already had some history with. I swept my eyes over the shepherds and noticed Isaiah, leaning on his shepherd's staff.

A sly smile danced across my lips. Someone could do a lot of damage with a five-pound, five-foot-tall slab of wood, as long as that someone knew what he or she was doing.

My voice boomed with new confidence. "Each of you has come here for a different reason. A few of you joined for glory, to fight with me, the supposedly great Hero of Elah. I tell you now to spare you the disappointment later: I will fail to live up to the legend. Most of you, however, are here under duress, trying to save either your own life or protect the lives of the ones you love.

"I imagine you have doubts about how this will work, but I promise you, by the time we're finished, you will become a part of something far greater than anything you've ever seen before."

One of the convicts still sitting on the ground turned his head up to me. "Where are the weapons? The armor? The supplies?"

Men from every camp nodded, wondering the same question.

I visibly winced but quickly regained my poise. "We haven't received them yet, so we're going to improvise."

A young shepherd stepped forward. "We're not planning on giving the criminals and Philistine butchers weapons, though, right?"

With that one question, all the unsaid suspicions and mistrusts erupted among my men.

"Say that to my face, you little runt!"

"A Philistine killed my brother. We should gut you all right here!"

"Come and try!"

"We're all dead anyway. We might as well speed the process up!"

I watched the groups move closer together, on the very cusp of an all-out brawl. They were angry, yes, but their rage was rooted in something far more insidious.

They were afraid. Afraid of each other, groups they'd been conditioned to hate. Afraid of this all being an elaborate death sentence. Afraid for themselves, afraid for their loved ones. The lack of weapons only fed that fear, turned it into something all too real. And when people are afraid, they divide themselves into two groups: *us* and *them*.

Yet the only way this would work was if we did it together. They needed each other. They needed to believe, to have some hope that they could possibly survive this. They needed inspiration.

I whistled, and its harsh piercing ring quieted the uproar. "Hear me," I bellowed, placing myself between each group. "From today on, we are family. It doesn't matter where you were born, who you have wronged, or what you have accomplished. Today, each of you are brothers."

Deborah coughed harshly.

"Or a sister," I conceded. "I know we don't trust each other. We will. I know you don't believe in each other. You will. By the time we're finished, we will be something far greater than anything we could be separately. Starting today, we are soldiers, one and the same."

"What about the weapons?" the original criminal asked again, though this time less condescendingly.

"Swords are powerful," I agreed, "but training is even more so. We don't have blades to fight with, so we'll fight with what we know." Turning to my brother, I motioned him near. "Isaiah, give me the staff."

He moved cautiously toward me and handed me the familiar stave.

I held it high above my head. "This will be our weapon, our expertise, and our victory. This will be our battle cry."

"A blade will beat a stick any day," one of the younger Philistines scoffed, tugging on his handlebar mustache.

Pulling my dabar from its sheath, I threw it at his feet. "Come at me then and prove it."

He eyed me and then the knife warily.

"You will not be punished," I promised. "And if you win, you are free to go home to your family." I was fairly sure I didn't have the authority to make that call, but he could never have known that.

He picked up the blade, thinking for a moment, and then approached.

I held my ground, beckoning him closer.

The man slashed out with the blade several times but never came near my chest.

"Fight me," I said resolutely, "or sit back down."

Anger flashed in his eyes, and he dashed forward. My staff first struck his ankle, redirecting his momentum to the ground, and then darted to his wrist. His fingers lost their grasp on the weapon, and the knife fell from his clutches.

The wood gently touched his chin, and he conceded defeat.

"What's your name?" I asked my opponent, reaching out my hand.

He stared at it for a moment and then grasped it. "Gadi."

"Gadi, let me train you." I addressed the rest of the troops. "All of you, let me train you, and together we will become something new. You were once shepherds"—I tossed the staff back to my brother—"now you will be warriors."

"You were once criminals." I unlatched the first prisoner. "Now you will be honored soldiers.

"You were once deserters, enemies of us and our God." I turned to the Philistines, forcing the words to come out, "Now you will be our countrymen, our people!"

Again, they shouted together, though this time in a unified voice. They believed.

Now the only person left to convince was myself.

Chapter 29

Three months later, the "Woolen Warriors" were on the march. The other platoons had given us the nickname as an insult, but our troop wore it as a badge of honor. Many of them had once been shepherds (and one day they may be again), but today they were soldiers, capable, in sync, and formidable. Today, they were an army. They were *my* army.

Our first mission had come down from the palace last night, an order to patrol a valley near Gath. Apparently, the Philistines had been acting up, roaming the countryside near the borders. We were to scout the territory and report back to Damon's much larger force behind us. Shortly after being assigned the Woolen Warriors, the prince also received a military commission. Erik had decided his son required experience leading an army, though by odd happenstance, there were somehow enough weapons to properly arm his troops.

We set out, and by early evening we had reached the east side of Israel's border markers. I had directed our men to move slowly, cautious for anything out of place. Since promoting me to general, Erik had made no direct moves against me, and in fact had brought me to sing again in his court several times, but the palpable tension still lingered in any conversation we shared. His family never noticed it. Michal still openly flirted with me in front of her father. Most dads threaten to kill their daughters' suitors in jest. It's all levels of creepy when you realize he means it.

Yet so far, no trap had been sprung; no knife had appeared to stab me in the back. Our expedition had been blissfully uneventful. The fields were empty, and there was no sign of any major activity from the Philistines or anyone else. All was well.

Then the children started screaming. Their voices were shrill and terrified, and three of them sprinted out of the wheat fields and straight into our soldiers.

The two girls, probably between six and eight years old, saw Deborah and ran into her arms. The boy, a year or two younger than the girls, wrapped his arms around Benaiah's legs, clutching them until his knuckles went white.

I hurried over to the oldest-looking girl and bent down to her. "What happened?"

"Philistines," she said through heavy sobbing. "They attacked our farm house and..." She trailed off, burying her face in Deborah's dress.

And then they did what marauders do, I answered myself. "Gadi!" I called out to the mustached Philistine in our ranks. Since our short sparring match, he had become one of my most competent soldiers.

He worked his way to the front of the line. "Yes, sir?"

"How well do you know this territory?" I asked.

"Extremely well," he answered. "My family lives on the border about ten miles south."

I nodded. "I need you to take three men and scout further ahead. Do not engage the enemy's soldiers, but if you meet anyone else, try to figure out what happened here."

"Yes, sir." He grabbed three men and sprinted off into the fields.

They returned an hour later, panting.

"The Philistines have begun mobilizing again," Gadi told me. "They're testing the borders, seeing how much they can get away with."

"And where are their troops now?"

"Behind the walls of Gath," he shook his head. "We'll never be able to breach them."

I rubbed my face in thought. By now, Damon, who had also been promoted to lead a different contingent of forces, should only be a mile or two behind us, and he'd have a better idea of the next course of action.

Turning to Benaiah, I told him, "Send word to the prince about what we've discovered and find out what our next orders are."

He nodded and went off to find our fastest runner. The messenger was not out of sight before a man riding a horse met him. The two exchanged words before he pointed toward me.

As he approached, I recognized the prayer shawl. The rider was Damon.

"Friend!" I called out. "You have good timing. I'd love some help with our unruly neighbor to the west."

The prince never greeted me back, his face carrying heavy regret. "We need to talk," he replied, his voice grim as he dismounted from his horse.

The two of us wandered out of earshot from the troops. "What's wrong?" I asked.

He stared at me. "We have a problem." He held out a scroll.

I took the parchment and unraveled it. The king's seal was on the top, our military orders. How did he know what he wanted us to do when he hadn't even heard our report yet? I opened the instructions. By the time I was done reading, my hands were shaking.

This had all been one giant, glorified, grotesque trap.

"He intends to use us as bait," I said quietly.

Damon clasped my shoulder. "I know. I tried to argue with General Carmi, but he'd hear none of it. There are over two hundred soldiers behind Gath's gates, and he's convinced if we find a way to crush them, we'll have the Philistines on the verge of collapse."

I crumbled up the order, throwing it to the ground. "My one hundred cannot hold against two hundred. They'll slaughter us from attrition alone. These are good men, strong men, loyal men. They don't deserve this." There had to be an out. My eyes lit up. "Can you rescind the order or at least wait until your forces reach us? As prince, you must have some power, some sway."

My friend shook his head. "I can't contradict a higher general, especially one who's been given the authority over the whole army."

My shoulders sank.

"But..." he continued as I looked up. "I can remove you from your post."

"Remove me as their leader?" I asked, confused.

"Yes," he said. "If I relieved you of your command, it'd be my duty to take your place. It might make Captain Comb-over reconsider this idiotic plan."

I'd be lying if I said the offer wasn't tempting. Survival is quite a powerful motivation. Yet right behind the desire to live came thoughts of my brother and Deborah, and all the hundred-plus soldiers under my command. They were my responsibility. I had called them family to inspire them, but now I meant it. On top of that, there was no guarantee that Carmi would change the order with Damon in command. The risk was too great, my responsibility too high.

I shook my head. "No. My place is here with my men. We'll figure out something to incite the Philistines and hold them off. Just make sure the reinforcements are ready behind us."

The prince put his hand on the hilt of his sword, weighing my decision. "You are a brave man, Niklas. When you survive this, I'd be happy to see you marry my sister."

I blinked at him. "Where did that come from?" For the most part, Damon had been completely apathetic to my relationship with his sister.

"I'm not blind," he said chuckling. "Be warned, though. She's a bit of a man-eater. She may be more deadly than the Philistines."

"I'll keep that in mind."

We clasped arms.

"God will be with you," he said, in a kind but serious tone.

"Here's hoping," I answered, crossing my fingers. "But I'm more concerned with you making sure your troops are ready."

He smirked and gripped a prayer tassel. "We'll both be there."

After the prince had mounted his horse, I ran my fingers through my hair. We needed a plan, some kind of advantage. Now that I'd gone and boasted about surviving, I'd better find a way to make good on it. I trusted our men's ability, but by sheer numbers alone the Philistines could wear us down simply by overwhelming force. We required a scheme, but for that we needed more information. I called Benaiah over to me. "Do we have any maps of the terrain?"

"Yes, General."

"Get them."

Five minutes later, Benaiah, Gadi, and I knelt over a map. "Gadi, tell me everything you can about the area."

"The city's here," he answered, pointing to a square on the map. "Its gates are made of cast iron, and its walls are twelve feet tall and made of limestone and brick. It'd be pointless to attack."

"Seeing as I left all my siege equipment back home, I agree," I said with a touch of irony. "What's around the city?"

"There are a couple of smaller settlements here." He drew two x's east of the city. "And then just a bunch of farmland. There's a river directly to the south, and a dried-up quarry to the north."

"Tell me about the quarry."

"I don't know much," he replied. "We used to mine copper there, but it ran dry a decade ago."

I thought of the Seraphim headquarters and all the empty mine shafts. Superior numbers would be useless in such small quarters. "And you're sure they're abandoned?"

He shrugged. "I can't guarantee it, but it'd be a safe wager, yes."

Nodding, my finger tapped the quarry on the map. "This is where we'll fight. It will give us defensible ground, and once Damon's troops get here, a place where we can get them in a pincer hold."

"And if I may ask..." Deborah's voice came from over my shoulder. "How do you intend to convince the Philistines to leave the city?"

A very good question. My brow furrowed as I looked at the map. We needed to get them angry, make them upset enough to leave the protection of the city's fortifications. A small, foolhardy thought bloomed in my mind. "Gadi, wasn't Goliath from Gath?"

"Yes."

I stood up, wiping the dust from my knees. "When I fought the blowhard, we made a wager." I took a deep breath. "It's time to let them know I've come to collect."

Chapter 30

I strolled nonchalantly up toward the city of Gath. My face wore a broad smile, contrasting mightily against the utterly terrified but completely rational part of my brain, reminding me of everything wrong with a plan that centered on me egging on an entire city of embittered, angry, and humiliated soldiers. Its heavy iron gates were locked shut, and at least fifty men stood at the walls of the city, almost all of them holding bows notched with arrows. I stopped just short of where I suspected their arrows could reach, then took one more step back. Better to be safe and appear a touch wary than prideful and a touch killed. This plan had enough opportunities for a gruesome death already.

For a moment, I let them take me in before I spread my arms and yelled in a loud voice. "Philistines! It is I, the Hero of Elah himself, Niklas. Two years ago, I met your champion Goliath in armed combat. Though to call him a champion seems a bit of stretch, considering I slew him with a nothing but a stick and a bag of pebbles."

I took several steps forward, playing on arrogance, and continued. "Before the match, Goliath made a wager, that if he won, we Israelites would become your slaves, but if our champion won, you would become our servants. For a while, I thought such a prize of pathetic, weak, and cowardly people below my consideration, but after some thought, I have decided to make you our personal manservants. We have two hundred years of latrines that require cleaning, and you all already smell like feces."

Dead calm drifted over the air. The metal bars of the city remained tightly clasped, and the archers on the walls held their positions

Maybe I should have gone with ordering them to build leper colonies.

Then the gate of the city opened, and as if a giant horde of locusts had been unleashed, enraged troops began sprinting toward me.

Two thoughts occurred to me as I turned and ran. First, this was a plan for the ages. I mean really, as far as schemes go, focusing the wrath of hundreds of furious soldiers on myself without any backup was so incredibly genius.

Second, and significantly more concerning, was the fact that as the troops flooded out of the city, it dawned on me there were considerably more than two hundred soldiers stationed in Gath.

Swearing under my breath, I quickly processed how that information changed things. I pegged their numbers at around five hundred, and five-to-one odds meant we were laughably outmanned, no matter how much of a terrain advantage we commanded, shortening the time we could expect to hold out until Damon's men could get here.

Yet if we fled after unleashing a force this size, there's no telling how much rampant destruction their warriors could cause before we managed to halt them. On top of that, Erik would simply execute us for desertion once we returned home.

No, our only hope was bunker down until the reinforcements arrived.

I ran onward, placing a decent distance between the murderous horde and myself.

Two miles to the north of the city, I finally reached the quarry. Isaiah and Gadi were coming up to meet me, a panicked look in their eyes.

"Get back down to the other troops," I howled, throwing my hands at them. "Five hundred bloody Philistines are about to come busting through those trees!"

"Five hundred?" my husky brother squeaked.

"Yes," I said, grabbing them both by the shoulder and hauling them down to the rest of our forces. "We'll have to hope our lines can hold until Damon gets here."

Gadi pulled me back, halting our progress. "But that's what we were coming to tell you. Damon's not coming."

"What?" I balked.

The soldier shook his head, pulling on his mustache. "One of our messengers just returned, informing us that your back-stabbing king recalled them back to the capital."

My stomach forced its way up my throat, choking off all the words of rage burning to spew out. Erik had set this whole thing up by ordering a nearly impossible task before abruptly thrusting it into the category of preposterous. My fingers ran through my hair, pulling firmly against its roots. Heavy guilt replaced fear. I had led my men to their deaths. The king may be the puppeteer pulling the strings, but they wouldn't be in this mess if they'd been assigned to someone else's command.

Should we sound a general retreat? At least some of my men might survive the next hour. The quarry below me appeared empty. Our troops had done well, hiding themselves in hopes of springing themselves on the Philistines unaware. But now it left them trapped. They'd never make it out before the Philistines ran through them.

We needed help; some advantage we could use to leverage against the impending onslaught. Damon was gone. All other forces who could possibly help were marching in the opposite direction. This deep into Philistine territory, no town would offer their assistance.

No one could reach us here.

Except...my gaze turned to the sky. "Hey," I shouted to the evening clouds. Isaiah and Gadi frowned, confused by my outburst, but I continued on with my demands. "We need your help. Now! Something, anything, to turn the tide."

Nothing.

My voice got raw. "Please. I can't protect them."

The heavens gave no answer.

No music drifted over the breeze to guide my actions.

We were alone.

My shoulders sank, and my back slouched down. Apparently His interest in battles only extended to lions, giants, and traitors. Those facing marauding armies need not apply for divine intervention.

My gaze stared off beyond the cusp of the quarry, where excavated boulders stood at the edge of the deep pit. How do you let a hundred men know you've failed them?

A faint, murky idea pushed against my anguish. My eyes focused, looking at the top of the pit, and more importantly, at the huge balls of stone and earth resting at its edge, directly over the caves. Rocks that size could crush almost any force.

It'd have to be timed almost perfectly, and there'd be an awfully good chance it would crush us too, but at this point, it at least had the potential for us to get out of this mess alive. Still, those boulders were huge, and I had no idea how to move them.

Spinning to look at a still bewildered Isaiah, I pointed to the cliffs. "Isaiah, I need you to be the hero."

His eyebrows arched, but I continued, speaking frantically. "Run and grab ten men, and then head up to those bluffs. Once the entire Philistine force descends into the pits, I need you to drop those boulders on them."

He looked at the cliff and then back to me, mouth agape. "How are we supposed to move the rocks?"

"I have no idea," I replied honestly, again pulling both him and Gadi into the quarry. "But I believe in you."

Who knows what series of emotions went through Isaiah's mind as he processed my request, but pride swelled in his chest as he gave me his answer. "I'll do it. We'll find a way, somehow."

Nodding curtly, I turned to Gadi. "Go into the caves and let the men know the plan. Make sure they know not to leave the protection of the mine shafts, no matter what happens, but to stay at the mouth of the cave. That way, when those rocks fall, it'll be a death trap for anyone caught outside, but they will be safe."

The sounds of trampling, hurried footsteps echoed from behind us. They'd be here any moment.

We reached the quarry's floor and Gadi and I took off in different directions, repeating the orders. Isaiah and his group scrambled up the quarry's side, and I noticed Deborah with the cohort following after him. I breathed a sigh of relief. At least if this went south, there'd be a chance those two could escape.

Benaiah waited at one of the mine shafts. He handed me my staff, and I pulled out the dabar from its sheath. No sooner had I set myself at the mouth of the cave than the first wave of enraged soldiers appeared over the edge of the cliff. They poured down into the quarry, looking like hundreds of ants swarming down their hill.

"Will this work?" Benaiah asked, his small form visibly shaking next to me as he clung to his own staff. While he at least knew how to swing the slab of wood, combat would never be his strength. Still, it felt appropriate to make my stand beside him.

"I have no idea," I answered honestly, giving him a wink, "but if we survive the night, I promise when we get back, I'll spend the first hour bragging about your battle prowess to your father."

A nervous smile appeared on his lips, and he tightened the grasp on his staff. Two other men joined us, with two more behind them waiting in support.

Then the bloodthirsty warriors were on us.

A lanky, shirtless Philistine bum-rushed into our line, sword raised. His sword came down, and I sidestepped to the right, the blade hitting the ground where my thigh had been just a split second earlier. My staff whipped out and down, smacking his jaw and then finishing him off with the improvised additions the Woolen Warriors had fashioned to our staffs.

Erik had never supplied our regiment with weapons, so we started thinking outside the box. The wooden staves of a shepherd gave us the advantage of distance, but obviously lacked the deadlier finishing power of a sword, so to compensate, we had modified our staffs with sharp iron spear tips, courtesy of our resident female blacksmith.

Benaiah intercepted the next enemy's sword with his staff, holding it off with both hands above his head. I jabbed the butt of my weapon into a soldier's stomach, knocking the wind out of him, before hurling him back with a hard blow to his chin.

"Don't let them get that close before attacking," I reminded my lieutenant. "We can't let them press into the cave!"

He jerked his head up and down in acknowledgment, and the

next wave of fighters was on us.

Nothing can fully prepare a man or woman for war. Sparring is singularly focused by design, giving the combatant plenty of time to analyze and deduce his opponent's next attack. On a battlefield, there are simply too many moving pieces to track, leaving one's attention only on the nearest, most direct threat. It's chaos; always one wrong move away from a life-ending misstep. The best anyone can hope for is that their training has become reflex after life-saving reflex.

I don't know how long we stood at the mouth of the cave frantically fighting for our lives, but we held our ground. Several times one of our men took a hit, but then one of our reinforcements rotated in, keeping the Philistines at bay.

Eventually, there was a brief pause in their onslaught, but then two identical men with axes appeared, each easily a full foot taller than me. Both of their heads were shaved, and they approached the entrance of the shaft with malice and sadistic excitement.

Benaiah and the other two men took a step back in hesitation, but I held my ground. "Well come on," I goaded them. "I've never killed giant *twins* before. I might as well check that off my bucket list."

Their grins turned down, and they charged straight at the cave. Stepping out of the shaft's entrance to give myself a bit more maneuvering room, I drove my knife toward the abdomen of the warrior on my right.

He recognized the attack coming and dodged it by inches. His brother immediately swung his axe down at my extended form, and I only just spun out of its reach. I grabbed its handle so he couldn't pull it back up, and pushed my blade deep into his neck.

His strength abruptly left him, and he fell forward.

The other brother still had plenty of strength, though, and uncontrolled rage bellowed from his lungs at the death of his twin. He began swiping his axe out in wide arches, faster than I ever would have believed possible. The offensive came so rapidly that it was all I could do to avoid a fatal attack, diving back and forth in the open field of battle with little care for my surroundings.

Finally, his blows came slower. His anger still fumed but, with his body finally exhausted, he bent over, and I used the momentary weakness to strike, attempting to inflict the same neck wound that killed his brother. A second before my attack reached him, he stood up erect, and my blade pierced his chest instead.

It was a killing strike, but apparently, his body hadn't been informed yet because the barbarian still had the strength to bring his axe up from the ground and gouge out a chunk of flesh from my torso's side.

I screamed in pain, and together we fell to the ground, me to my knees, clutching the wound, him to his back, with the light finally expiring from his eyes.

Glancing around, it dawned on me that our battle had ended with me exposed from the protection of the cave. My wide eyes whipped around, and I realized how many Philistines still waited in the quarry. Bodies lay all around me, but their numbers did not seem to be lowered in the least.

Several of their soldiers moved in to finish me off. Struggling to get back to the cave, one of them pushed me back down. Fire erupted from my injured side, ending my feeble attempt at retreat.

I was done. There was no energy left to fight. We had lost.

A bare-chested warrior stood over me with a sword, glaring down. He raised it high above his head, and I forced myself to watch the blade's attack.

Instead, my eyes witnessed a piece of debris the size of a fist strike him in the jaw. Both our eyes traced its path back up, and what seemed like enough rock to build a mountain followed right after it. A boulder the size of a cow crushed my would-be executioner deep into the ground.

Other rocks now fell all around me. Philistines all around the valley were shouting in distress as boulders rained down on them, splatting them like bugs, and those who avoided being crushed now fled in full retreat.

Isaiah had done it. He'd saved the day.

I bent over, still in excruciating pain and unable to escape, but now at peace with the situation. My men would survive.

The first rock hit me in the back, driving me into the quarry's floor. The next one hit my head, and everything went quiet.

Chapter 31

"He's waking up," said a familiar but unplaceable voice hovering over my face.

Each of my eyelids felt like a fattened calf weighed them down, but I managed to open them. Yashobeam and my brother knelt down beside me, torchlight illuminating the mine shaft.

For a moment, my mind was hazy on how I'd gotten here, but then it came flooding back. "How did I survive?" I asked through a raw, dry croak. There's no way I could have lived through that avalanche.

Yash flicked his head to the right. I turned my head and found Benaiah standing next to him, his shoulder in a sling.

"He managed to pull you back in before you got squashed," Isaiah explained through a broad smile.

I nodded gingerly to the lieutenant. "Now I'm really going to have to talk you up to your father."

He chuckled at the thought but then grimaced as his bandaged body shifted.

"And the Philistines?" I asked.

"Dead or in full retreat," Yash answered.

I pushed myself up with my elbows. "It worked. Isaiah, you genius, you pulled it off."

He shook his head, but his chest puffed up a bit. "I only figured out what was needed for it to work. Deborah and the prince figured out how to build the needed equipment."

"The prince?" I asked.

Damon walked up, a hand resting on the hilt of his blade. "I relinquished my command," he informed me. "The stresses of leadership must have finally gotten to me. I've officially enlisted in the Woolen Warriors and happened to reach the quarry in time to lend a hand." He winked and flicked his nose upward. "He must have liked my choice. Though I believe the young lady would have managed it without me. She's got quite a bit of moxie."

"The smartest thing any of you boys have said all day," echoed Deborah. She walked up, her clothes miraculously smooth and spotless compared to the rest of the troops. "You may be teachable yet." She curtsied. "Your Highness."

I glanced up at the earthen ceiling. We'd done it. Against immeasurable odds, we'd made it through. "We survived," I concluded softly.

Yashobeam glanced down at me, his tone even. "Most of us."

My eyes narrowed. "What?"

Benaiah limped forward. "Eleven men died, sir." His head hung low. "Gadi was one of them."

"He fought well," Yash said, "but once the Philistines realized some of their own were fighting for us, they went berserk and started focusing on those soldiers."

The weight of exhaustion moved from my eyes to my heart. Eleven men meant more than ten percent of our troops had died during the attack. Part of me knew that the fact any of us lived qualified as an unmitigated success, but that didn't change the fact that for the first time, someone had died under my watch. I had failed to protect them.

Damon knelt down next to me. "You did well, more than anyone could have asked or expected. Mourn those you lost, but honor them by living. We're not in control of everything. That's Yahweh's job. Ours is simply to do our best with what we're given."

His words made sense, but it brought up new thoughts, insidious new thoughts. If *He'd* simply sent help, given us some kind of advantage, none of my men would have died. A fresh wave of anger boiled in my blood.

I looked at my friend and feigned a smile. I didn't agree with everything the prince said, but he was right about honoring the fallen by living. Sulking would only get in the way of that, and the men deserved the very best after what they just accomplished. I also happened to know the person who had the obligation to honor them.

Isaiah helped me up, and I addressed the forces around me. "Gather our fallen men and prepare to march. We're heading back to Gibeath." A tight smile crossed my lips. "The king owes us a party."

***

The rising sun had just started warming our backs when we reached the outskirts of the capital. We thought it best not to tarry any longer than necessary in Philistine territory, and once we began our march, it seemed pointless to make camp so close to our destination. Plus, we could only get the needed supplies for our victory celebration at the capital, and I intended to make good on my promise to deliver a party for the ages.

However, the journey had pushed us to our limit, and even our stoutest warriors were beginning to drag their feet. Benaiah's eyes kept drooping, his neck snapping up, waking himself back to life.

"We're almost there," I encouraged him. "Another half an hour and you'll have a real bed to sleep in, and in half a day we'll have enough food to carry us into the next month."

"Bed," he mumbled in dreary desire.

Damon walked on the other side of me, but then he stopped, a perplexed expression covering his face. "Someone's coming out to meet us."

The prince was correct. Three unrecognizable specks had left the city gate, heading directly toward our troops. After a few more seconds, it became clear they were on horseback, and after a minute my own befuddled expression covered my face. "Is that…"

"Michal," Damon completed my thought. "It's my sister. General Carmi's with her, along with…" He paused. "Doeg?"

My face scrunched up. "Who?"

"Father's new advisor," the prince answered, frowning. "He's an

Edomite informant who spent years spying on the Philistines. His official title is Chief Shepherd, but he almost never leaves Father's side these days."

Huh. Edom was a small tribal nation to our south. They shared distant ancestry with Israel, and while occasionally they claimed to be allies, their lone guiding star was to fight for whatever side served them best. Erik had chosen an unsettling advisor.

"Why would they be out this early?" I asked, concerned about their presence.

The prince shrugged his shoulders. "I have no idea. My sister hates mornings."

Two minutes later, our two groups met, and my company halted before their approach. The princess looked as beautiful as ever. Carmi appeared bored, while Doeg rode next to him, sneering.

The first thing I noticed about the head shepherd was the large birthmark covering the right side of his face, almost as if a broken mask had been grafted over his cheek. One fist clenched a staff, its purple tassels marking him as the king's chief herdsman. Around his neck, he wore a bronze eight-pointed star, and as Doeg stroked it, he glared down at me with open contempt.

Oh yay, another advisor of Erik's already hates me. I wonder if that's a prerequisite for the job?

Still, picking a fight served no purpose. Right now all I wanted was a day's worth of sleep, followed by a week's worth of feasting.

"Michal!" I exclaimed, pointedly ignoring the shepherd's dark stare. "What brings us your delightful presence this early in the morning?"

Her face beamed as she dismounted her horse, and she sprinted toward me, throwing her arms around my neck. "Niklas, I have the most wonderful news!"

The force jostled my wounded torso, and a sharp cry escaped my lips. The princess quickly evaluated me. "Are you hurt?"

I gently raised my hand to calm her. "A flesh wound from the battle. Outside of possibly being a touch lighter than when I left, I'm fine." I touched her cheek gently. "Why are you here?"

She again beamed. "The news! Word has already spread about your victory over the Philistines. As a reward, Father's finally approved of our marriage. Isn't that wonderful?"

I blinked in shock several times, before Michal's features shifted to concern. "You're happy, aren't you?"

My head inclined in a single nod. "Of course," I said, forcing myself to smile. "It's great news."

As her joy returned, my mind started running full speed. *Why now?* Yesterday Erik had sent me to my death. One victory couldn't have erased that much distrust. And how did he already know about our results? We had come straight from the battlefield. None of this made sense.

General Carmi coughed and readjusted his feeble comb-over. "The king has prepared a celebration to commemorate the engagement. He has asked you enter after the rest of the troops, in hopes they too may play a part in the festivities."

The commander wouldn't meet my eyes, but shared a knowing look with Doeg.

Unease blanketed my thoughts. What weren't they telling me?

"Oh, say yes, silly," Michal chided, wrapping her arm into mine. "We have enough to talk about with the wedding planning and all the...things that come after it." She winked at me playfully and drew her body close to mine, whispering in my ear. "My father plans to kill you as soon as you enter the city."

My head turned slowly toward her, my eyes wide.

She held my gaze for a moment, before abruptly laughing again. "You can use that thought to keep you warm at night until then."

Feigning awkward embarrassment, I inwardly tried to digest the information she had just given me. After everything we had just accomplished, all we had survived, now he chose to drop the executioner's axe?

Reason told me I should be scared, cautious, and calculating, but truly, one emotion dwarfed all others—indignation. I was sick of living in fear, sick of hiding from a madman more concerned with holding on to power than protecting his own people. Most of me wanted to simply stomp into the capital here and now and challenge him to his face.

Yet as tempting as that scenario was, if I walked behind the city walls with these men, they'd fight to protect me and promptly be slaughtered. I wouldn't risk their lives to simply make a statement.

Immediate flight also wasn't possible. If I ran now, Carmi would simply send troops after me, and exhausted as I was, they'd catch me in no time. I needed to stall, divert their attention, and then figure some way out of the noose.

"Darling," I drawled at Michal, "could you do me one favor? I'm disgusting at the moment, covered in blood and wearing a tunic with more holes than seams. Would you ask your father to give me a couple of hours to clean myself up before we start the celebration?"

The princess untangled herself from me and sniffed the air, curling her nose up. "You are a little rank. A bath would do you good," she commented and went back to her horse. "General, please take me home. A few extra hours works nicely. It will give me more time to prepare."

The general and his companion traded a skeptical look.

"Your young Grace," Doeg said, stroking his starred necklace, "His Holiness's orders were quite specific in this matter. We are all commanded to return to Gibeath at once."

Michal scoffed. "I'll handle my father. I'd rather not spend the day clinging to my future husband while he smells like the back end of one of your sheep. Let us go. The longer we tarry, the longer Father has to wait." She pressed her ankles into her horse and started trotting back to the city, the issue decided.

Captain Comb-over glared at me. "Arrive no later than noon," he said, and then he and the shepherd turned their horses and followed after the princess.

Damon came up next to me and pressed his arm around me, avoiding my injured side. "We're going to be brothers!" he exclaimed.

"It would appear that way," I said, keeping up the pretense. The best thing I could do for my men was to get my troops into the city and hope Erik planned to keep them out of the way. Once they were gone, I could make my escape.

"Benaiah," I called, and my second-in-command's weary head snapped up.

"Yes, sir?"

"You heard our orders. Lead the men into the city. Your father should see you at the front of the line, returning in command and victorious."

A new wave of energy rippled through the little man. "As you wish, General Niklas." He quickly called out for the march to resume, and soon the sounds of my soldiers' footsteps faded into nothing.

The prince waited with me. "This will be a joyous day. We should call the rest of your family to celebrate as well."

My expression flattened. "The only thing waiting within the capital's walls is a quick death."

Damon face scrunched up. "What are you talking about?"

"Your father plans to murder me as soon as I enter the city. It's what Michal whispered in my ear. He's planned to ever since the day Alexander was executed."

"No," my friend replied, discomfort in his posture. "He can be harsh, but you're Israel's hero. You slayed the giant, you help keep his demons at bay, and you're coming home the conquering hero. Why would he even think that?"

I shook my head in disbelief. "Yesterday, he betrayed our entire regiment to the Philistines just to kill me!"

"No." He brought his finger up to my face and then pointed it at the capital, "Carmi acted alone and out of vain jealousy, but I'll be with your platoon from now on. He won't be able to pull another stunt like that again."

Watching him make excuses for the king was painful, both because I knew the truth, but also because I knew no son wanted to imagine the worst about his father.

The only way he would believe me was if I told him everything, about the music and the anointing. I had sworn to Alvaro to keep it secret or forfeit my life, but after everything that had happened, how close I was to death already, I simply didn't care anymore. Screw His rules. I couldn't carry the weight of it by myself anymore.

"Three years ago, Alvaro anointed me," I said simply.

"What are you talking about?" the prince asked, confused.

I told him everything. About the ceremony, the music, the consequences for my family if I failed, all of it. The story came out fast and emotional, the isolation of it all dropping like a metal weight off my shoulders.

By the time I finished, the prince had braced himself against a tree, uncertainty dancing in his eyes. Then abruptly—and quite frankly inappropriately, he started chuckling.

My eyebrows furrowed. "Why are you laughing?" I asked, through a growl.

He coughed down another laugh, holding up his hand apologetically. "It's just kind of funny, you, being the chosen one of Yahweh. Do you even believe in Him yet?"

Fresh ire rose in my blood. "Yes, I believe in Him. I'd be a fool to deny all that's happened. I don't doubt that's He's up there, I just have some serious reservation about *what* He's doing up there."

His gaze shifted to a more serious expression, and he placed his hand on my shoulder. "Belief *in* something is not the same as believing something *exists*."

It was my turn to chuckle, though there was no mirth in my laugh. "Look where all this has got me. Your father literally has his hyenas chomping at the bit to make themselves a Niklas steak."

Damon nodded, sympathetically. "Let me talk to my father, help him see reason. Even if what you say is true, he'll listen to me. Give me an hour, please. Let me make this right."

At this point, I'm not sure anything could make me trust the king, even if Damon could make him promise to let me live. Yet there was nowhere else for me to go. Bethlehem would be the first place they'd look for me, and the last thing I wanted to do was drag the rest of my family into the king's war path. In fact, anywhere in Israel would pose a risk, so unless I planned on leaving the country, this might be my last chance to stay in Israel and survive.

I clasped his outstretched hand, shaking my head in skepticism. "Do what you can. I'll be here until half past eleven, but then I have to leave if there's any chance for me to escape."

"I'll take care of it," the prince promised, returning the pressure on my palm. "Trust me." He turned and ran toward the city.

I watched him until he turned into a speck, and then I went down to the river. Even if I had no intention to celebrate my own engagement party, Michal had spoken true about my odor. Plus, a quick dip in the water would feel good.

I quickly undressed and dove into the clear, crisp stream. The water felt amazing, washing away the dirt, grime, and blood that I had accumulated over the past several days. After scrubbing myself down, I simply lay floating on my back, bobbing up and down on the stream's surface, staring at the sun.

Part of me wanted to dwell on everything that could go wrong, all the ways Erik could make the final days of my life truly painful, but for now, all I could do was wait. I needed to relax, a moment to let my mind off the hook for making every decision.

Eventually, I got out of the water, and after slipping back into my undergarments, decided a quick nap might be a good idea. Resting again may not be in the cards for quite a while, and Damon could wake me when he arrived. I laid down next to the stream and shut my eyes, sleep coming faster than I would have imagined possible.

Shuffling feet woke me, and my eyes snapped open. My temporary peace evaporated, and I grabbed my long knife resting next to me.

The prince stumbled forward. He was covered in heavy bruises from his neck to his forehead, and blood dripped from his sword hand. I caught him just as he tumbled to the ground.

"What happened?" I asked, quickly evaluating his wounds. None looked life threatening, but after years studying fighting, I knew together they could be more than his body could handle.

"My father," he said, looking up at me through swollen eyes. "I confronted him about the plot, and he went..." The prince shuddered. "He tried to kill me with a spear. I had to fight through a dozen of his personal guards just to get here."

My eyebrows arched. "The Seraphim?"

Damon's head barely twitched. "No, he calls them the Acolytes. Doeg is their leader. He's some kind of occult fanatic and said he's on a divine crusade, sent to root out all who stand in the king's way. He convinced Father that you're trying to steal the throne." His eyes opened wide. "They'll come after me. You have to run, now, while there's still time. An anointed can't be allowed to die. It'd be catastrophic." His breath quickened at the thought, but then he let out a final sigh and fainted from exhaustion.

Seeing my best friend beaten to the point of unconsciousness broke me. Unrestrained tears flowed down my cheeks, and I held him there. This should never have happened.

I turned to the sky, and rage intermixed with my sorrow. "You did this!" I screamed to the heavens. "He's one of your most loyal servants, and he might die because of all of this!" My body visibly shook from the fury, as I tried to think beyond the anger.

I couldn't let anyone else get hurt because of me. If the prince was right, a search party would be arriving soon, and they'd be his best chance of surviving. No matter how upset the king may have been, no citizen in Israel would want to be responsible for letting Erik's son die.

His best chance was for me to get as far away from him as possible before he could attempt to argue on my behalf again.

But where did I go? No one else deserved to be dragged into this mess. Except...

I set my jaw. One man did deserve it. The one who started all of this. It was well past time to finally pay Alvaro a visit.

Chapter 32

It took the better part of the day to reach Ramah, Alvaro's hometown. Though even calling the backwater collection of huts a "town" seemed a bit of an exaggeration. The village had no walls or gates, and the houses were spread out much further than any typical settlement. Close proximity naturally created a hedge against raiding parties, but judging by their distance apart, Ramah had been spared from such terrors and the residents enjoyed a bit of breathing from neighbors.

My chief problem was having no idea how to identify the judge's home. The village had no tabernacle or gathering place, which meant I needed to find one of the residents to ask for directions. The first home I passed had a bare-chested young boy, probably no older than five, tending a garden outside his house.

Approaching him, I asked, "Do you know where the judge lives?"

He stared at me blankly for a moment, and then his nose crinkled. "The judge?"

"His name is Alvaro," I elaborated. "Old guy, talks to himself."

The boy's face lit up. "The animal man," he said and pointed to the far north edge of town. "He lives on the other side of the hill."

I nodded my thanks and headed in that direction. I had passed a dozen houses before I came upon the last home of Ramah. The sight of it stopped me in my tracks. The animal man indeed.

Alvaro's house was modest, a two-level square, but surrounding it for a good quarter acre were animals of every sort. There were the usual farm beasts: an ox, a rooster, and several sheep. But beyond that, there were dozens of types of non-domesticated animals: red foxes, turtles as long as my thigh, and a bird I'd never seen before. It had long legs like a stork, the deep beak of a pelican, but with feathers which seemed to be dyed bright pink on its back.

The property had no fence, but the animals seemed quite content to stay near the home. The whole scene was altogether peculiar.

I walked up to the house and noticed the flaming bush engraved into the door, Alvaro's sigil. *People of the Voice*, Matthias had called them. Well, the founder of this organization had some explaining to do. Clenching my fist tight, I swung at the door, pounding harshly against it several times.

Shuffling could be heard from inside, and as the door swept open, I parted my lips to lay into the ancient geezer.

Instead, an aged woman with long, full, silver hair appeared, smiling sweetly at me. "Niklas, you're finally here."

My mouth stayed agape for a good three seconds, backpedaling on my anger, and then my mind reengaged with my tongue. "I'm sorry, I came to see the judge, Alvaro."

"Yes, yes," the kind old woman said, "my husband told me you'd be stopping in sometime this afternoon. I've been baking honey fruit bread all day for you." She swatted my shoulder. "He failed to mention you'd be so handsome."

I blinked at her several times, unsure of how to respond.

She chuckled at my discomfort and waved me in. "Come along, dear. I promise, my days of chasing young men are long past. You have nothing to fear from me. Oh, and I'm Abela."

I didn't move. "Thank you for the offer," I said, "but my business with your husband is quite urgent. If you could just tell me where he is, I'll be on my way."

Abela turned her back to me, shuffling deeper inside the house. "He'll be back eventually, sweetie. Come in and have some food."

Taking several steps inside the home, I pleaded again with her, trying to keep the frustration from my voice. "Please, this is a matter of the highest importance. Lives may depend on it." My own being chief among them.

The old woman craned her neck around, staring at me with amusement. "Conversations with him usually do," she said, unimpressed by my plea. "Yet the fact remains; he is not here. My husband never told me where he was going, so unless you feel the need to run around the region hunting him down with a great chance of missing him completely, I'd suggest you enjoy a meal and take a load off your feet. You're already drenched in sweat."

I glanced down at my tunic. Her words were true; the journey here had left me covered in salty perspiration. And assuming she was telling the truth about not knowing where her husband was, the fastest way for me to find him probably meant staying put.

My head bowed. "I'm grateful for your hospitality."

"Good," she said simply, and then moved to her kitchen area to set several small loaves of sweetened bread on a plate. She walked back over and gave it to me.

The dessert was fresh, and the smell sent shivers of excitement all across my face. It'd been a good month since I had anything other than military rations, and at least three more since I'd had a home-cooked anything.

Settling down on a soft mat, I said thank you before biting into the sweet goodness. My lips devoured the four desserts in under a minute.

Abela clucked her tongue a couple of times in amusement. "I'm glad you liked it." She went back to her counter and brought out five more loaves.

I took my time eating these, my stomach quickly filling up. Once finished, I set my back against the wall and closed my eyes, wondering how long it would be before Alvaro arrived.

No sooner had my eyelids closed, she clucked her tongue again. "Dearie, while you're here, could I ask your assistance in something?"

Glancing up at her, I nodded. "What can I do for you?"

The old woman pointed to the ceiling. "My husband and I can't get to the roof of the house anymore, and it's been ages since it's been cleaned off. Would you be a saint and sweep it for me?"

I paused in thought for a moment, but then quickly agreed. It was a small request, and the woman had just fed me. She handed me a broom, and in short order I had cleaned off the roof from what looked like several seasons of wear.

Entering the main floor again, I quickly retook my place on the mat. This time, my eyes didn't even have a chance to shut.

"Love," Abela said innocently, "would you be so kind as to do me another favor? A mole has been tearing up my garden something fierce, and I can barely walk through it without fear of catching my ankle in one of its holes. Could you take the spade in the garden and fill them for me?"

My lips puckered at the idea. Moles could be a real terror in a garden, and who knew how long it could take to patch its excavations. With my very existence on the line, it seemed a poor use of time, but looking around, I realized there was also literally nothing else I could do. A little bit more hesitantly, I agreed to the chore and set about filling the divots.

Two hours and one thousand divots later, sweat again poured down my face, and the sun had begun to set over Alvaro's property, and still there was no sign of the judge. Abela had her back to me when I walked back into her home, chopping away at vegetables in the kitchen.

She clucked her tongue in joy. "Oh good, you've come just in time. I'm just preparing the ingredients for our stew, and I could really use some help with the carrots. Would you be a gem and come help?"

I laughed at the ludicrousness of the last three hours. Less than ten miles away, King Erik was preparing a bloody witch hunt to come and gut me alive, and instead of spending the day plotting, gaining information, or running for my life, I had accomplished nothing but a set of menial chores.

Snorting loudly, I planted my feet in the door. "I do not mean to be rude, but while your hospitality is appreciated, I believe my time may be better used elsewhere. My..." I struggled for the appropriate word. "...situation is time sensitive, and if I don't do something about it soon, things will get messy, quickly."

Her neck craned back to me. "Sweetie, we might as well be honest about your 'situation.' The king found out about the second anointing and will stop at nothing until you are dead. The whole kingdom will be on the hunt for you. The mess is already here. We simply need to figure out how to clean it up."

I gawked at her. "You knew?"

She raised an eyebrow. "Alvaro is my husband. We discuss everything."

Ire started building. "Then why have you had me running around like your personal manservant all afternoon! You know how much danger I'm in."

"Indeed," she agreed, "but until my husband returns, there isn't a single productive task that will change that reality. However, there is plenty of other productive work to be done, so we might as well be about it."

I shook my head back and forth. "You don't understand."

Her own head tilted sympathetically. "Dearie, my husband's life has been directly threatened no less than twenty-three times." She nodded to a series of dash marks etched along a ceiling beam. "We started keeping track after the third year of our marriage. Once, one of the threats lingered over us for half a decade."

I stared at the lines. "Twenty-three?"

She waddled over to me. "Yes. And do you know what we've learned after all of it?"

"What?" I asked, quietly.

"We're not in control." Abela placed a soft hand on my shoulder. "We have a role to play, but it has severe limitations. We found it best to simply keep handling the other small things on our plate and deal with the rest as they come. It's why my Alvaro took up care of the animals. It's a small part of the world he can do something about."

For a long while, I simply stood there, internally fighting against her counsel. There had to be something I could do, some way I could fix this. Yet nothing came. No insight. No magic plan. Nothing.

Finally, my hand met hers on my shoulder. "Where are the carrots?"

Together we cooked and ate dinner, and by the time the dishes were cleaned and put away, night had set over Ramah.

Abela laid out a sleeping mat for me in the corner. "Alvaro should be back by morning, and then we'll see what comes next."

Part of me wanted to stay up and wait for him, but the excitement of the day had left me exhausted. I crawled beneath the covers, and sleep descended over me within moments.

Abela's whispering woke me.

"What news from the capital?"

My eyes snapped open, the morning sun burning them. I blinked several times to push through the irritation and saw Alvaro standing in the front doorway with his wife.

"Erik knows he's here. The king will be on us before the hour."

My stomach sank. I should have stayed on the move. Throwing the covers off me, I pushed myself up.

Alvaro's eyes shifted over to me. "It's worse. The Philistines plan to attack Bethlehem. They'll be there by this evening."

Bethlehem? The news drove me from my bed. Within a second I was on my feet, and within another my long knife was pressed against Alvaro's throat. "You promised that if I found the traitor, Bethlehem would be safe. That my family would be safe!"

The judge stared back at me. "Niklas," he said softly, "you never found the traitor."

Part Six: Traitors

The man stood on a cliff, overlooking Bethlehem. In a matter of hours, a Philistine horde would rampage through the city, forcing the faux god slayer out of hiding. His chief weakness, his need to defend others, was pathetic in its predictability. When he arrived, the man would finally eliminate the root of all his troubles.

He took an even breath. "Today, we destroy Niklas."

Chapter 33

His statement rocked me back on my heels. My blade left the judge's throat, and I took several steps backward.

"The traitor was Alexander," I stated, shaking my head in disbelief. "He had the means, the motive, all of it." I moved toward him. "He confessed."

Alvaro rubbed his neck. "The counselor was only a piece of something larger. The man could manage numbers well enough, but he'd never be able to lead something of this scope. Someone else has been pulling the strings."

"But the music," I argued. "I've only heard it once since Alexander confessed. How was I supposed to find him without it?"

The old man's bony shoulders sagged. "I do not know."

Stumbling back, I caught myself on the wall. After everything that had happened, all that I'd accomplished, none of it mattered if my family still was destined to die. This had all been one giant setup, an elaborate, predetermined failure.

My eyes rose steadily to the judge, and I pointed harshly to the sky. "For three years, I've fought for Him. I slayed lions and bears, I put down Israel's enemies again, and again, and again. I battled giants, assassinated slavers. At every turn, I was one poor choice away from death, and still, I pressed on. I tracked down the conspiracy to the best of my ability, and I saved the entire royal family. All because you promised that if I succeeded, my family would be safe."

I took several steps forward. "And after all of that, after surviving every crow-begotten swine assignment alone, now He throws my family under the cart?"

The judge's cheeks flinched, and then he arched an eyebrow. "Alone?"

I started laughing. "Yes, alone! The music sent me against a lion—alone. It had me battle Goliath—alone. I've had to snatch victory from the jaws of certain defeat more times than I can count—alone! You sent me into a den of vipers with no means of victory, and now my whole family will pay the price of my failure." My voice got quiet, a small snarl escaping my lips. "Then I'll truly be by myself."

The house was silent.

"Oh dearie," Abela finally said through a small sigh, "tell me you're not that naive."

Emotionally done, I turned my gaze to her. "What?"

"Are you some kind of supernatural being? Blessed with innate strength and wisdom?"

My chin moved back and forth. "Of course not, that's what I'm telling you. I'm just a normal guy, and He sent me against all of that."

She shuffled closer to me, slowly taking my hands in hers. "No, He walked *with* you *through* all of that. Answer me this, what are the odds you would survive any one of those things again, let alone all of them?"

At first, her question seemed irrelevant. If I fought ninety-nine more lions, I'd probably end as lion kibble every other time, double that for the giant, and probably triple the odds for me against surviving the bear. My feet scuffed the floor. "Answering 'not good' seems like it may be a bit of an understatement."

She clucked her tongue in amusement. "Exactly."

"But my family…"

"Is still alive," she finished. "There is still time."

"For what?" I asked, turning to Alvaro. "The king is on his way here with every intent to flay me alive. Even if I got past him, Bethlehem is defenseless. They'll be slaughtered."

"Maybe," Abela answered. "Maybe not. Predicting the future is a fool's game, even for my husband, and he cheats." She turned toward Alvaro, a look of humor on her face.

"Is it still possible to save them?" I asked him, terrified of his answer.

The judge focused on the ceiling for a solid minute before he returned his gaze to me. "I have no answers. At the moment, He's gone quiet. The traitor is still loose, but Bethlehem still stands. It could go either way. Understand this, though: being anointed doesn't make you invincible. Even if you try to help them, there are no guarantees you or your family will survive, even if you go to them."

Fear mixed with hope. We still had time, but zero leads. If Alexander wasn't the main man hiding in the shadows, who else could it be?

I inhaled sharply as it dawned on me. Doeg. Damon had told me Erik's new advisor had served as an informant against the Philistines. He must have been a turncoat twice over, feeding us information for a longer con. Now he wielded enough power to eliminate any left in his way, including one meddlesome shepherd. After escaping the noose in Gibeath, he probably sent the Philistines to Bethlehem in hopes of luring me there.

I could return to the capital and attempt to capture him, but by then it would be too late to save my hometown. I shook my head. No, first I needed to protect my family. Then the man from Edom and I would have a reckoning.

I met the judge's gaze. "I'm going to Bethlehem."

Alvaro nodded, a rare, understanding smile on his face.

"How do I get past Erik's troops, though?" My forehead furrowed. "If I go around them, by the time I reach Bethlehem, the battle may be over."

The judge's eyes wandered up back to the ceiling, and he chuckled to himself. "Let me take care of Erik and his men. It's been too long since the two of us talked."

I grimaced. "He must realize you anointed me. He'll kill you for it."

"Possibly," Alvaro agreed, "but as my much wiser wife said" —he

229

paused, letting her enjoy the compliment—"the future is a fickle thing. We shall see what we shall see."

I surveyed both of them. At least two people remained in my corner. "Thank you."

Abela winked playfully at me. "Save your family, sweetie."

My shoulders squared. It was time to go home.

Chapter 34

The journey to Bethlehem took five hours, giving me plenty of time to think through the best course of action once I arrived. It also allowed ample opportunity to dwell on all the ways things could go horribly, irreversibly, wantonly, and terribly wrong. Forcing my mind to focus on the former took considerable, consistent effort.

At first, second, and fifteenth glance, the current pieces on the board certainly left my hometown in an unfavorable position. Our city had several hundred people living within our walls, with at max around 150 men, which meant depending on the number of soldiers the Philistines decided to bring, we could be outnumbered anywhere from two to one, all the way up to ten to one. Beyond that, while most of our men had some form of military experience, they didn't have access to armor or weapons, meaning they would be significantly underequipped for a fight. Numbers and weapons alone usually determined the outcome of a battle, so right from the onset, we were already under the wagon.

We did have two significant factors in our favor, though. First, while Bethlehem was nowhere near the most fortified city in Israel, her walls were tall and thick, and I doubted the Philistines would have been able to drag siege equipment halfway through our nation, meaning if they wanted to sack my hometown, they'd have to do it the hard way. Second, and even more important, we'd be fighting on home turf, with not only our own lives on the line but also our families' lives as well. Survival is a powerful motivator, and if properly harnessed, can almost double the ferocity with which someone will fight.

Part of me wanted to run straight for the capital, alerting our commanders of the Philistines' attack. However, the small hiccup in that idea was that I was a wanted convict, which would delay reinforcements being sent, if they believed me at all. I'd end up stuck in a prison cell, which seemed like a less-than-useful spot, given our current situation.

Thus our best chance of surviving meant buying time. We needed to fortify the city and hold out until someone else could escape and bring back help. It wasn't the ideal solution, but given all the factors in play, it was the best we could hope for. I just needed to get to the city and warn them before the Philistines arrived.

As I sprinted up the last hill, my heart sank at the first sight of Bethlehem. Thick, black smoke billowed from the north, south, and west gates of the city and a force of at least two hundred Philistines waited outside of Bethlehem's western walls.

I was too late.

Crippling despair overwhelmed all other thoughts. Image after image flashed through my mind; every member of my family dead or enslaved, our home in flames, and everything we had built destroyed. From atop the hill, I couldn't make out details, but it didn't appear any more battles raged within the city. Had Bethlehem already been sacked? Were the Philistines marching home with the spoils of their victory?

Alvaro had given me no promise of success, but I had assumed I'd at least be able to try and protect my city. Those hopes, along with any semblance of surviving this crucible unscathed, now floated away like the smoke over the city.

My teeth began to grind against one another. If I had failed to protect my family, the next best option meant ensuring the Philistines paid for their actions. One man could not slay an army, but if I followed them, eventually, there'd be an opportunity to butcher every commander in their forces.

I glanced back down to Bethlehem, a counter idea blossoming.

While the odds were slim, if the attack was truly over, there may be a few survivors in need of help. The enemy may have left some warriors behind for such an event, but it was worth the risk if I saved just one person. I swallowed my thoughts of revenge and headed down to the city.

The east gate didn't have the burning smoke and was on the opposite side of where the Philistine soldiers would have left from, so I rushed toward it hoping not to draw any unwanted attention. The iron bars were clasped tight, but I had discovered how to scale them during my nighttime escapades growing up.

About twenty feet from the gate, a voice called out, immediately halting my advance.

"Come any closer and we'll set this entrance ablaze as well!" a man yelled. He had an Israelite accent.

"No, we won't," another person—a woman—contradicted him. "Not for just one soldier. We'll simply shoot you dead."

"Oh," said the man, "what she said then."

My mouth hung open. I recognized the female's voice. "Deborah!"

"Niklas?" she called back, appearing on the other side of the gate. "You're here, thank God."

I ran toward the gate. "You're alive! Is everyone else safe?"

She swung the gates open and threw her arms around me. A dozen other men waited with her, guarding the entrance. "So far no one's been killed, but a couple of our people got burned in the fires."

"When I saw flames I assumed the worst. How'd the Philistines light them?"

Deborah bit her lip and straightened out her grandmother's purple sash. "They didn't. We did."

My eyebrows arched in confusion. "What?"

One of the sentries walked up. "It was genius. We only had about a half-hour warning before they showed up. We didn't have time to fortify the gates, so she suggested we set up a trap.

"We placed carts full of oil-covered wheat at each of the entrances, and when the invaders ran in to move them, we lit them up like a bonfire, their arms a solid substitute for kindling. We killed a dozen of them at least."

"More importantly," she explained, "it bought us time to figure out what we should do next."

Grabbing both her shoulders, I grinned ear to ear. "And you called me the Magistrate of Mischief! Good show. So what's the plan?"

My question brought a scowl to her face. "They're trying to figure something out in the courtyard right now."

I nodded. "Let's go then."

"The village elders are in charge," she said, ruefully. "Women and children are required to stay silent. I'd rather be helping with the defense."

I barked a laugh. "You just singlehandedly drove back their first attempt at invasion. You're going to be a part of the planning. Come on."

She sniffed the air in amusement and followed after me. "What happened to you, though?" she asked. "Yesterday started off with Benaiah saying you were officially engaged to the king's daughter, and it ended with a one-hundred-silver-piece bounty on your head. Erik disbanded the Woolen Warriors, sending us all home."

My face contorted. "Yeah, the last twenty-four hours have been anything but simple or particularly enjoyable. We'll have to sort it out afterward, because if we live to see an afterward, we'll have done pretty well."

Her head bobbed in agreement.

"How many of our soldiers are here?"

"Bethlehem had the largest representation in our platoon. I'd say at least twenty."

I made a mental note of their presence. It wasn't much, but at this point, I'd take any advantage we could get.

We entered the city's center, and despite our ridiculously dire situation, a smile grew on my face. My whole family waited in a corner, alive and well. One of the most powerful emotions surged through my veins: hope.

The ten village elders sat in a circle, reviewing the situation.

"We can't make a stand against them," said one of the men about my father's age. "The best chance for our families is to surrender and beg for mercy. Assuming that's even an option after the fire stunt we just pulled at the gates."

Another elder scoffed, significantly older than the first. "Elder Moses, we could have been waiting with biscuits and honey for them when they entered, and they'd still have tried to slaughter us."

"Then we flee," Moses said, a nervous motion rolling through his shoulders. "Run until we reach the reinforcements from King Erik."

My father shook his head from the other side of the circle. "They would run down every child before we were a mile outside the city."

The courtyard was silent, as everyone realized our options could be counted on one finger, and that finger was about to be cut off by the enemy horde standing outside our gates.

I cleared my throat. "Gentlemen, it appears the only recourse left is to fight until someone can come back with reinforcements from the capital."

Every head turned toward me, and a chorus of whispers flickered through the courtyard.

"The Hero of Elah."

"He defeated a lion."

"The god-slayer."

It took effort not to roll my eyes. I had hoped that specific name would never catch on, but honestly, right now, a bit of overblown grandeur might prove useful for morale.

Elder Moses stood up, pointing at me. "You're the reason they're here! You're the source of this whole bloody mess!"

"What?" I turned to my father, my hands up in surrender. "I just got here."

It was Isaiah who answered, walking up and weakly waving at me. "It's Lahmi—remember, the guy we tried to steal the swords from. Apparently, he was Goliath's younger brother, and he's come for a little family vengeance."

My fingers clenched several times. "You've got to be kidding me. This whole thing is about a grudge?"

Isaiah shrugged his shoulders.

Moses started visibly shaking. "We should give him to the Philistines. See if it's enough to satisfy their anger. If we bind him now and—"

He never finished his insidious thought. My father's fist swung into the man's abdomen, doubling him over and sending him to his knees. "I would like to suggest we temporarily remove Elder Moses from this council. It appears he's gone delirious due to an acute bout of ineptitude. Does anyone disapprove?"

No one opposed the motion, and Dad flicked his head to Abin and Sham. They dragged the still wheezing elder from the town's center. "I move to place the city's defenses under the care of my son, seeing as he has commanded troops successfully against the Philistines in the past."

"Agreed," said the oldest elder, and the rest of the council quickly approved the motion.

"Well, Niklas," my father asked, "what should we do?"

It's a strange feeling when your father places the lives of everyone you love into your hands. It seemed best not to screw up the new responsibility.

The fires at the gates wouldn't keep them at bay much longer, and without a plan in place soon, they'd overwhelm the entrances in short order. Squaring my shoulders, I asked for an accounting of how many men we had who were capable of fighting, along with any weapons.

My original estimates were close. We had 126 men who could be used on the battlefield, but we had virtually no military-grade weapons. The lone bright spot was the spear-tipped staffs of the Woolen Warriors, seeing as the king didn't have the right to force them to return weapons of their own making.

"We have another problem," one of the villagers said. "We brought all our flocks inside the gates when we heard about the Philistines. They've clogged up a good quarter of the streets."

Grimacing, I rubbed my eyes. Just when I thought the days of sheep making my life more miserable were behind me, the blasted animals find fresh opportunities to get in my way. I ran a hand through my hair, cursing the beasts' entire existence, an idea growing in my head. We had farmers with long, sharp harvesting equipment: hoes, pitchforks, scythes. We had confined spaces. We had things to get in the way. Put it all together and...

"Isaiah," I called, a devilish grin creeping up onto my face.

He came over, and I drew a diagram of the city, explaining the plan. After several moments of gawking, he bit his lower lip. "I don't know if it's possible."

"I'm open to other ideas, if anyone else has one."

No voices offered a competing plan.

"It'll be like one of your puzzle games. Do you think you can figure it out?" I asked my brother.

He took a deep breath. "Maybe, but I'm going to need time to set this up."

My face scrunched. "How much time? The fire can't keep them out indefinitely. Philistines are as dense as granite, but they'll figure something out soon."

"An hour, at least," he responded, still shaking his head over the map. "And I'm going to need everyone's help for this to work."

Sixty minutes was practically an eternity from a battle perspective, and I wouldn't have anyone else helping to stall. How do you hold off an entire army by yourself? Especially one so personally bent on your destruction.

"Oh." I answered my own question, not at all thrilled about the idea coalescing between my ears. "I know something that will keep them occupied."

For it to work, though, it required pulling every emotional string available. I'd need to take along the one man who had humiliated Lahmi more than me.

In the corner of the courtyard, Eliab waited with his wife and my four-year-old niece. He was my only brother with a child, and my plan would put him at tremendous risk. Yet it was our best chance. "So Eliab," I called to him, "are you up for offering our old friend Lahmi a rematch?"

Chapter 35

Eli and I carefully weaved our way around the burning wreckage at the west gate, leaving the protection of the city's battlements. We came out with our right hands held high and a green arm band tied around them. We also carried our respective weapons in our left hands: his heavy, gargantuan axe and my spear-tipped staff. It was a regional sign for a parley between two conflicting armies, and our first risk in this grand plan of mine was expecting the Philistine malcontents to honor our request to talk. We'd know in a matter of moments, as their arrows would have little trouble reaching us on open ground.

No archers moved to the front of the lines. I inwardly breathed a sigh of relief, but my posture remained resolute. Showing weakness to a predator only provokes them to attack faster.

Moments later, a group of five bare-chested Philistine soldiers strode out to meet us, and though they were still a long way off, Lahmi's ridiculous black mohawk marked him as one of their group.

Eliab shook his head next to me. "It's such a horrible haircut," he commented. "How has no one ever told him he looks like a rooster?"

I barked out a laugh. "Or the ugliest peacock on the planet."

We walked on, the momentary levity contrasting with the growing apprehension of our task.

"This isn't your fault," my brother said to me, keeping his eyes fixed ahead.

I swallowed uncomfortably. My actions had directly led to the tenscore of Philistine butchers standing outside the walls of our hometown.

He stopped walking. "Niklas, hear me. You didn't bring this up-on us."

I halted, but I refused to turn and meet his eyes. "Trying to steal their swords, picking a fight with Goliath, leading an army against them, what have I done in the last three years that *hasn't* brought this avalanche down on us?" I bit my lip. "I never thought about the consequences of my actions, and this is the cost. You were right all along."

"No, I wasn't," Eliab replied and walked up next to me. "Do you know why I stopped fighting?"

"Because you didn't want anyone else to get hurt," I answered, waving my hands at the horde in front of us. "You didn't want this manure show."

"It was more than that," he said, placing his hand on my shoulder. "When the Philistines laid the trap for our men, when they killed Abraham, I realized that if we continued fighting, more of us would fall, and their deaths would be my responsibility. Fear made me forget that doing the right thing can get messy, but a bit of a mess can't stop us from pressing on. You helped remind me of that."

Setting my jaw, I stood up a bit straighter. This was the right thing to do.

I glanced at him, a twinkle in my eye. "So you're saying the Hero of Elah and the Bear of Bethlehem need to get their hands a little dirty."

He grinned through his thick beard. "Exactly."

His pep talk ended as our Philistine counterparts stopped a dozen feet in front of us. I recognized several of the other men in the group. This was largely the same crew that transported the swords, which meant Lahmi probably hadn't brought an official army. These men were little more than a group of thugs, hoping for a bit of payback. Our chance of survival ticked upward. Near perfect discipline was required in defeating an organized army, but a swift punch to the face often disbanded bullies.

"Lahmi," I sneered, my voice dripping with arrogance, "how many times does my family have to kick your back end before you realize picking a fight with us always ends the same way?"

The Philistine leader's fingers tightened on his sword, but he kept his composure, smiling to his men. "I told you, didn't I? The mighty Niklas is not the nightmare our people discuss in whispers. He doesn't command the beasts of the field or disappear within the shadows. He's an undersized, loudmouth, two-bit, walking rodent."

The rest of his compatriots laughed, growing more confident with his insults. We couldn't have that. For this to work, we needed to get him off-balance.

"So what would that say about your brother, Goli-lady, or whatever his name was?" I leaned against my staff, feigning boredom. "Apparently, he got himself killed by an 'undersized, loudmouth'...insert lame insult, etcetera, etcetera."

Rooster Hair took a harsh step forward, glaring down at me. "Watch your tongue," he snapped, baring his teeth. "Your whole nation is nothing but a collection of cowards and miscreants. You and I both know you got lucky, end of story."

My right eyebrow rose to Eliab. "Didn't this guy run from a fight with you a few years back?"

Eli stared up at the sky, thinking. "Yeah, I believe he scurried home with his tail between his legs, and after talking such a big game, too." He effortlessly tossed his hulking axe behind his shoulders, draping his arms around it. "A shame really. I hadn't gutted a decent Philistine in a while."

Lahmi's demeanor tensed, his eyes darting between myself and my brother. "You and your whole family will be dead by sundown."

It was now or never. "Why wait?" I asked, moving inches from his face. "If you're convinced our family has just been lucky, how about a rematch? You can fight either me or my brother. I'd hate to see any more of your troops unprettied by a little fire. We can do it with the same terms as last time; winner takes all."

The Philistine took several controlled breaths. "No."

My eyes went wide at his rejection, and their leader smiled at my shock. "There will be no fluke to save you today," Lahmi said. "We will grind your little, insignificant town to powder. But worry not, I come bearing good news. We're giving you another hour before we attack again."

My forehead furrowed in confusion. Why would he give up military intelligence before an attack?

"Why?" the glorified thug asked my unspoken question, turning to his companions with a sick grin on his face. "Because we have some friends on their way to join us. Do you remember meeting a certain slaver a year ago? It turns out his business associates didn't take too kindly to his murder, and they're coming with another two hundred men. Once they get here, the real fun will begin."

It took substantial effort to keep from yelping. How did anyone else know about the slaver? There were dozens of Seraphim operatives. There's no way they could have known it was me who had killed him.

Still, a more pressing concern demanded my full attention. Our trap barely had a chance of success against the numbers the Philistines currently commanded; another two hundred would equate to a guaranteed death stroke, no matter how well we executed the plan.

Delight appeared on Lahmi's face at my obvious distress. "Well, I'll allow you two to enjoy your last pathetic moments with your family." He shoved me back roughly. "See you soon."

And with that, he and his men turned around and started walking leisurely back to their troops.

My head snapped to my brother. "Against that many troops," I whispered harshly, "we don't stand a chance. This battle needs to start now."

Eliab rested his axe on the ground. "But Isaiah won't be ready."

I shook my head back and forth in protest. "Better half-prepared against a manageable force than completely helpless against what's coming when their reinforcements get here."

Eliab kept his eyes on the Philistines walking away. "Go back and warn the village. I'll provoke the idiot to fight."

For once, I got to shut down one of my brother's plans. "No," I said forcefully. "You're the one with the family. You go back. I'll pick the fight."

We glared at one another, neither willing to leave the other behind. Whoever stayed to incite the battle would never make it back to the city. Even if he managed to put down Lahmi and his men, the uncircumcised army behind them would finish the job.

"Whatever," I finally said, "The oncoming onslaught of rampaging Philistines will take care of the warning issue anyway. They're not an organized army, so if we can tick them off enough, they should break ranks and counterattack." I rolled my neck. "Together then?"

Eliab bit his lip as he thought on my compromise, but then he shrugged his shoulders in agreement. "Let's do it."

We needed to get their attention. I figured bum-rushing them would accomplish the task, but Eli beat me to the punch. He lifted his axe high above his head and then threw it end over end at the Philistines. It spun through the air until its heavy blade cleaved into the back of the soldier to the Lahmi's right, immediately dropping him like a sack of grain. Then the Bear of Bethlehem roared his defiance and ran forward.

Not to be outdone by one of my own siblings, I too bellowed my rage. "Lahmi, you mentally underdeveloped man-child! We're settling this here and now!"

Eli's assault left them in shock for a good two seconds, but they quickly regrouped, flanking each other and preparing for our attack. I also noticed that the Philistine horde responded with expected rage, and a swarm of two hundred soldiers rushed down to slaughter us. We probably had less than two minutes before they were on top of us, at which point we'd be outnumbered one hundred to one.

We engaged Lahmi's men at a dead sprint, both attacking the soldiers on the left. Eli didn't have a weapon, but his muscle mass more than made up for it. He tackled the man on the edge, sending them both spiraling to the ground five feet behind his impact spot. I cut off Lahmi and the other two soldiers. Our best chance was for me to hold them off long enough for Eli to take care of his dance partner and then he could help me with mine.

Lahmi stared at me, holding his sword in guard position over his chest. "You only expedited your death."

"Probably," I admitted, "but at least this way I get to drag your unseemly corpse with me. I killed your brother. I wanted to make sure I got a complete set before I died."

His sword lashed out, and I deflected it with my staff, yet before I could counter, one of his partners' blades dove toward my stomach. The blow missed me by inches, but then Lahmi used his free hand to jab my nose. I recoiled, the shock knocking me back, and soon it took all of my concentration to keep the unrelenting stream of attacks from removing one of my limbs. I'll give Lahmi's team this: they knew what they were doing. Two constantly lashed out with attacks, while the last one waited for an opening.

I wouldn't last long like this. I needed to take one of them out, now. The only way I'd pull it off was to create an opportunity, which meant leaving a hole in my defense. I started parrying their attacks upward, leaving my lower body exposed. The soldier in waiting saw the opening and lunged.

At the same time, the tip of my staff's blade dove down, correctly anticipating his attack, spearing the assailant and plunging him to the ground.

In response, Lahmi's other guard unleashed a sudden strike at my upper hand, cutting the lower part of my palm.

I screamed as searing pain sliced through the side of my hand, and the staff dropped from my fingers. The soldier pressed his attack, thinking me defenseless, and I threw out one hand to grapple over his sword's hilt.

His hand went to my throat, suddenly cutting off my airflow.

My left hand, however, went to my back and grabbed the handle of my long knife. Pulling the blade from its sheath, I drove the weapon into his side, and his body went slack.

I noticed the motion flicker a half-second before Lahmi's sword lashed out at my belly. I jumped and spun away, but not before the blade tore into the meat of my thigh, propelling me down to one knee. The intensity of the pain momentarily blinded me, and a heavy kick to the chin sent me spiraling backward.

By the time I regained my bearings, Lahmi stood over me, his blade sharply pressing against my neck. "It's over," he said through a laugh, manic joy covering his face.

My last thought was that I'd die looking up at that ridiculous mohawk.

Chapter 36

Lahmi placed a palm over the butt of his sword, a breath away from plunging its blade through my throat.

Then a rock hit him in the forehead.

Truthfully, calling it a rock is a misleading description of the projectile. A small boulder, roughly the size of a newborn lamb, flew through the air and crashed into the side of the Philistine's head. The blow ended his life on impact, the force of it causing his body to spin away from me. His blade scraped against my throat as it was whipped away. The cut burned, but it was shallow enough not to be life-threatening.

On the other hand, the marauding horde of screaming Philistines, now only a few hundred feet away, definitely fell into the life-threatening category.

Eliab came shuffling up. His was tunic covered in dirt from his scuffle, and he reached out his hand to help me up.

Taking it, he quickly placed me on my feet. I tested the weight on my injured leg, and sharp pain erupted up and down the limb. It would hold up, but I wouldn't be winning a race anytime soon.

Which unfortunately was what this very situation called for. I grabbed my brother's shoulder and tried to push him toward the city. "You have to go. Now! My leg will only slow us down."

The statement brought a genuine smile to his lips. "You're an idiot," he said, shaking his head, and then as if I weighed no more than an infant, he tossed me over his shoulder and started running at full speed back to Bethlehem.

My personal pack mule sprinted forward, giving me the horrific opportunity to evaluate the army bearing down on our city. Our stunt had certainly accomplished its purpose. We were close enough to see the murderous intent on every warrior's face, their screams of wrath getting steadily louder as they closed the gap between us. It was no sure thing we'd reach the city's center before they overtook us.

Even if we did, our hopes could still be dashed if we hadn't given Isaiah enough time to set up the ambush. Organized army or no, the Philistines would pick us apart if the battle devolved simply into man-to-man fighting on even ground.

Part of me wondered if it would be worth telling Eliab to stop at the city gates, and have the two of us make one last stand at the entrance in an effort to give our brother precious extra seconds. However, the sheer number of Philistines would sweep over us like the tide, and our sacrifice would be no more of an inconvenience than a couple of pebbles holding back the sea along the beach.

By sheer will, my brother safely brought us under the western archway of the city, the enemy soldiers now only twenty feet behind us. Bethlehem's gates had been torn down in the earlier attack, so there was nothing to stop the horde from entering the city. However, we had added new burning barricades in front of all the side streets to the north and south, forcing us all east into the heart of Bethlehem. The road we sprinted down led straight to the city's center, and if all had gone according to plan, the fruit of Isaiah's work would be waiting for us there.

Yet little by little the Philistines gained ground on my brother and me. The long street was barren, which meant we'd have zero support if they caught us.

"Over here!" called a voice.

Eliab immediately veered to the right as we reached the heart of the city. A moment later, he was ducking behind a hole in one of the blockades. Two men from our town appeared, quickly pulling the bulwark back in place, creating a barrier between us and the horde.

My brother has taken several steps further down the street before he dropped to his knees, exhausted. The sudden change in momentum cast me over his shoulder, and I skidded to the ground, as a half dozen different injuries on my thigh, torso, and palm all reminded me of their presence.

The makeshift barricade protecting us bucked hard, and the two hundred odd men trying to murder us howled in frustration and fought to pull it out of the way. Our Israelite compatriots braced it from our side, but they were laughably outnumbered.

The momentary perception of safety vanished. If the situation didn't change in the next ten seconds, we'd all be cut down.

"Now!" cried Isaiah's voice from a rooftop up above.

A new sound boomed through the narrow alley behind us—hundreds of thin, black hooves beat against the ground, being driven directly into the murderous horde. A shout of defiance went up from the men of Bethlehem as they rushed in with the herd. The trap had been sprung.

With my official role in the plan finished, hope battled against despair. One voice clung to the fact that despite how dreadfully things had started with Lamhi, so far the plan was technically working. The other voice pointed out how laughably dismal our chances still were of pulling this off.

I slammed my fist against the dirt. There had to be something else I could do.

Rising to my feet, I called out to the two men who had saved us. "Which roof is Isaiah on?"

The man pointed me to the correct house, and I offered to help a still wheezing Eli up.

He waved me off. "I'll be right up. Go on ahead."

Reaching the roof, I found Isaiah standing at the edge of the house, gazing down at the chaotic, battle-ridden streets. Deborah waited next to him.

"No!" he yelled to another man on an opposite roof, flailing his arms. "Don't release the second herd yet. There are still some more funneling in!"

Deborah noticed me as I shuffled forward, and her eyes grew large. "You're injured!"

I grunted something and checked my leg. Fresh blood continued to trail down my thigh, and the cut on my throat probably looked unsettling as well. "I wanted to see how the battle was going."

"No," she chided, shaking her head back and forth, "you thought you'd somehow be able to help, even though letting yourself bleed out would thoroughly negate any assistance you could bring." She bent down and began tending to my leg.

While she did her work, I surveyed the chaos below us.

From up above, it almost seemed like nothing more than one of Isaiah's puzzle games.

The streets we had just run through were now clogged with hundreds and hundreds of sheep. The blockades had been arranged to funnel both the invading army and also the herds to the center of the city. Interspersed with the livestock, we had dozens of men wielding either spear tipped staffs or long, sharp pieces of farm equipment. The Philistines had superior weapons, but they were designed for the open field of battle, where a warrior fought directly with another soldier. Here, at least several waist-high, fur barricades separated each soldier from their opponent, and their swords were too short to adequately engage our defenders. If they focused on pushing their way closer to our troops, the loss of concentration meant a quick stab to the gut.

Still, the enemy's sheer numbers would eventually wear down the advantage. Which is where the second part of my brother's plan came in.

"Shouldn't we—" I began before Isaiah cut me off with a quick wave of his hand.

"Wait for it," he said. "Or it's all for nothing."

Two of our men cursed loudly after being cut down by Philistine attacks. The longer we held off, the more of our men would be killed.

The last sheep brayed as it was herded into the jammed street.

"Now!" Isaiah bellowed again, and suddenly hundreds of women stood up upon the roofs, all of them holding objects of substantial weight: ceramic pots, bricks, and the like. Among the women, dozens of slingshots whirled around the heads of young teenagers. Then, together they walked up to the edge of the roofs and rained down their rudimentary projectiles upon the Philistine forces.

Our opponents never saw the aerial onslaught coming. They took hit after hit to their skulls and shoulders, many falling unconscious and being trampled underneath the flocks. Others were distracted enough to fall victim to our men on the ground. A few women had even dumped scolding hot water upon the invading force, the unlucky warriors screaming as the boiling liquid burned their faces.

The battle was going our way.

I reached out and grabbed Isaiah's shoulder. "You did it!"

He ran a hand through sweaty hair, finally taking his eyes off the streets. "What happened out there? I thought you were trying to buy me time, not expedite the battle."

"Everyone's always complaining," I said through a grin, but then my face darkened. "We had no choice. Lahmi informed us that there's another Philistine contingent coming to back them up. If we didn't provoke the attack, their combined forces would have ruined any chance of the plan succeeding."

Isaiah nodded slowly. "Okay, but then what happens when the reinforcements get here? This trick is only going to work once. How do we hold off a second invasion?"

"A very good question," I said, again turning my eyes to the battle. "If we can finish this fight against the first assault, we have a chance at demoralizing their second wave. They'll be expecting to either join forces with Lahmi's group outside of the city or simply add a secondary surge of fighters in the siege. If, however, they get here and we've already killed off Lahmi's troops, they'll be a lot less eager to try and sack the city. It may even turn them back entirely, and at the very least, it should buy us more time. We simply need to finish the battle before—"

A deep horn bellowed, and my stomach dropped. I craned my neck westward, and the first line of Philistine reinforcements appeared on a hill five hundred yards outside the city.

I stared up into the sky—at *Him*. "*Seriously?*"

Isaiah ignored my rant and swallowed hard, his pudgy cheeks losing all color. "If they make it through the gates, they'll bust right through the trap, and we'll be dead within the hour."

It took every ounce of willpower, but I pushed past the latest wave of terror and frustration to think clearly. The gates needed to be protected or all this was for nothing.

Swearing loudly, I swept back to the ladder. "I'll find some men to hold the entrance as long as possible."

Deborah reached out and grabbed the back of my tunic, pulling herself in front of me. "Some men and one woman." She made it to the ladder before I could argue.

We reached the bottom of its rungs to find Eliab entering the house, apparently coming up to check why the horn had been blown.

I raised my eyebrows. "Are you ready for round two?"

A weary laugh escaped him, but his head bobbed up and down once, and he fell into step behind Deborah and me. We wove our way through the back streets of the city, picking up five more men as we worked our way back to Bethlehem's west entrance. Deborah had her staff and her hammer, Eliab still carried his axe, but I had lost my stave in my battle with Lahmi, leaving me with nothing but my long knife. The other men carried items which fell more into the category of household tools than military-grade weapons.

"So what's the plan?" asked Deborah as we made it to the city gate only to find the second wave of Philistines less than two minutes from entering the town.

"Fight until they butcher each of us" seemed like a morale killer, so I pointed to carts blocking the southern streets. "Let's re-barricade the entrance."

The six of us set out to moving the carts in front of the gateway, haphazardly stacking wine casks, sacks of grain, and anything else we could throw on top of the wagons. It was far from structurally impressive, but the bulwark would buy Isaiah a few more moments at least.

We braced ourselves against the barricade, and moments later screaming enemy forces slammed into the other side. The carts bucked, and everyone but Eliab was thrown back. We all quickly regained our positions, and for a moment our structure held. However, the Philistines started pulling down the objects on top of the carts, leaving openings in our makeshift barrier. Openings where pointy things like arrows and swords could get through. Immediately blades began blindly thrusting through the unobstructed windows, and soon one of our companions took a sword to his shoulder. He fell to the ground, moaning.

This couldn't get much worse.

Then a new sound erupted to our right. Twenty feet away from us, the barricades from a side street to the north shook violently, as men fought to tear it down from the other side. Burn it all! The slavers must have sent warriors through the north entrance of Bethlehem as well. With no one holding down that blockade, they'd be through in a matter of seconds, and our meager defense would be crushed immediately between the two forces.

Retreat served no purpose beyond an arrow or spear to the back. Fortifying my balance, I called for Eliab to pick up his axe and let them through. Confusion covered my brother's face, but his body sagged as he stopped bracing his cart, and he swooped down to grab his weapon. At least this way we'd have an opportunity to finish a few more of them off before they entered the larger battle.

The five of us stood side by side as the Philistines now easily tore apart the barricade, and soon our handful stood opposite a fresh horde of invaders.

Against all odds, a smile found its way onto my face. This certainly wasn't how I'd have chosen my end, but unlike with the lion, the giant, or any other of my recent near-death experiences, I found comfort in being surrounded by friends and family.

The north bulwark crashed to my right and ripped away the idle thought. We needed to engage this first group head-on before we were flanked. Raising my weapon high above my head, I screamed in defiance at their presence. The slavers roared back, bursting forward in an angry line of death.

Chapter 37

I focused on the warriors in front of us, pushing the fall of the northern blockade from my mind, but it was impossible to overlook the dozens of spears they unleashed into the air, all of which hurtled toward us.

The sheer number of the projectiles seemed overkill for our feeble defense, but as they sailed over our heads, raining down not on us, but into the advancing Philistine troops, I decided they were the appropriate amount. The unexpected onslaught took the Philistine slavers behind us completely unaware, cutting through almost all of the warriors who had already entered the city.

Confusion rippled through my body, and I craned my head to see nearly one hundred familiar men rushing forward, Yashobeam and Benaiah leading the Woolen Warriors' charge.

"How?" I gawked, as my trained, experienced troops fortified the entrance.

Yash just shrugged his shoulders, but Benaiah smiled broadly at the question. "The prince sent us to check on rumors of a Philistine invasion force."

"But how did Damon find out?" I asked, thoroughly baffled. "And beyond that, I heard the king disbanded our contingent of soldiers?"

"Orders did not bring us here," Yashobeam answered solemnly,

"I am just searching for a new place to die." He flicked his nose over to the gates. "Are those Philistine slavers?"

I nodded. "Apparently they wanted a little payback for a certain assassination a few months ago."

A rare smile crept up Yash's cheeks. "Oh, today someone will enjoy a little payback." He swung up his massive oak club and went to join the rest of our troops, now guarding the gates of the city.

My mind started evaluating the turn of events. While we were still outnumbered, now we had the advantage of both a defensible position and having the Philistine troops separated. For the first time since reaching Bethlehem, I could imagine us winning the battle.

Part of me wanted to stay and direct the fight here, but Benaiah was more than capable of commanding our group, and my time would be better spent returning to Isaiah and figuring out how to leverage these new military pieces to their full potential.

I turned to Deborah. "Can you lead fifty of our men through the city and bring them to reinforce those fighting deeper at the city's center?"

"We'll take care of it," she promised, and then she started bellowing to some of the men not yet engaged in combat. In a matter of moments, half of our soldiers were following her back through the city.

I turned to my lieutenant. "Keep the rest of the men here and hold the gate, but if the Philistines retreat, send two dozen down the central street to help the villagers still finishing the first force."

With the orders given, my attention swept to Eli, who had used the momentary reprieve to find a stool to sit on. "Catch your breath," I told him, "you've earned it. I'm going to let Isaiah know what's happened and figure out how to end this."

He nodded. "I'll be right behind you. I just need a second."

I sprinted back down beyond the southern street—or, more aptly, hobbled quickly—making my way back to the house Isaiah was using for our giant puzzle game's operational command. The initial surprise of the attack had knocked the Philistines on their heels, but I feared the ferocity with which they would retaliate once they regrouped.

Reaching the house, I quickly mounted the steps of the ladders, only to find the roof empty.

Huh. Had something gone wrong below that caused Isaiah to leave his command and help with the battle? I ran to the edge of the house to get a look into the streets. The congestion of the flocks had lessened, and smaller groups of Philistines and Israelites had taken up fighting below. By the number of shirtless corpses on the ground, the invaders had taken heavy losses, but with the advantages of the surprise and preparation gone, those remaining could do some serious damage to our under-equipped defenders. Deborah and her men couldn't get here fast enough.

Still, Isaiah wasn't among the pockets of fighting.

Then I saw it. A black feather, neatly stuck beneath a heavy stone. Kneeling down, I picked it up and frowned. It looked like—

"Nikky," said a deep, mocking voice. I spun and found Almon, the Seraphim's muscled, idiot enforcer, standing behind me. The hems of his brown tunic were covered in mud, and he idly played with the necklace hanging around his neck, a dozen or so black feathers strung together—each representing a successful assassination he had performed. Ever since the night I humiliated him during the drinking game, I had kept my distance, figuring he was the type to repay grudges by taking the cost out of his opponent's teeth.

"What are you doing here?" I asked, keeping a defensive stance.

He bared his teeth as he smiled. "Gabril sent me to deliver a message." He pointed to the feather in my hand. "We have your pudgy brother."

My chest tightened. Why would they take Isaiah? We are so close to surviving this, it didn't make sense for them to get in the way now. "Did the king send you to capture me?"

Almon let out a sadistic laugh. "Maybe. Maybe not. Gabril's orders are for you to come with me peacefully and alone, and he promises to let your brother live. If you put up a struggle, I'm to kill you on the spot, and afterward, the Seraphim will personally pay a visit to every other member of your family." He took several steps forward. "Honestly, I'm hoping you take option two."

I clenched my fists, furious at their betrayal and terrified for my brother's safety, but I needed to think clearly. The Seraphim obviously hadn't come to aid in our defense, which meant the best case scenario was they'd stay out of our way and let us work. If I didn't go to Gabril, he'd unleash them against us in efforts to get to me. I had several close acquaintances in the Seraphim, but by its nature, we each operated independently, and who knows which agents Gabril had brought with him.

Yet surrendering to this big idiot equated to wrapping the noose around my own neck, if he actually intended to let me live that long. And after they dispatched me, I doubted they'd let Isaiah survive as a witness. All options left pretty much everything to be desired, with mine and my brother's death essentially assured.

Still, the only way to change the variables was to get closer to the source of the problem, and there was a time limit before they decided Isaiah's life was no longer needed.

"I'll go with you," I said quietly.

Almon swept out his arms toward the ladder. "After you."

I held his gaze, and he didn't even try to hide his intentions.

Taking a deep breath, I walked past him.

Before I had taken two steps beyond him, he sprung his attack. I couldn't see him, but I knew how men like him would fight. He was used to being the biggest, baddest man in a brawl, dominating his opponents by his sheer mass.

Unfortunately for Al, I had spent my whole life fighting older, larger brothers, and I knew what to expect.

Visualizing his hands reaching out to grab me from behind, I ducked beneath them with my back turned. Then I whirled around, my hand already clutching the knife in my belt. I propelled myself upward between his outstretched arms and dug my blade in a curved pattern from his chest to his shoulder.

His strength faltered immediately, and I was able to knock his legs out from him. Together we fell to the ground. My body pinned his to the roof, and I kept my hand on the hilt of the blade, using it like a handle protruding from his body.

"Where did you take him?" I demanded, digging my knife deeper into his shoulder.

He bellowed at the pain, but when his eyes focused, they blazed with spite. "I'm not telling you anything, you soft, holier-than-thou pig."

"Oh no," I said, shaking my head and then routing the blade around in his shoulder, inciting fresh howls of agony. "Damon is the holy one in the group. I'm more of the black sheep. Now, where is my brother?"

He spat in my face.

As much as inflicting the maximum amount of pain into him would be personally enjoyable, unchecked rage wouldn't help Isaiah, and a dead prisoner couldn't tell me where they took him. Still, it seemed one of Almon's more endearing traits was insolence. How did I get him to reveal where they were holding my brother?

I inspected the thug's person. Outside of a disconcerting lack of hygiene, he had nothing on him to offer any clues of their location, unless, of course, they were holding Isaiah in a pigpen. His filth left grime on my legs, and I wiped the bulk of it away on his tunic, but then slowly brought a hand up to my face. His calves were caked in mud.

I grabbed hold of his face and forced him to focus on me. "Are they by the river?"

His eyes went wide in shock at my question.

"Thanks," I said smugly. "I'll make sure to let Gabril know you were particularly helpful."

Quickly pulling the knife out, I hesitated with what I should do with him. Leaving an embittered enemy alive that you've already bested *twice* is not exactly the best chance for a victor's long-term health, but who knows if he really was just acting on Gabril's orders? Calling him an uncivilized, backwoods cretin was an insult to the uncivilized, backwoods cretin community, but he may well be technically innocent in this. Plus, with his current wounds, any concern about his revenge would be a long time coming.

I got up off the ground and left him there, moaning like a small child.

The next question was whether to recruit someone else for the rescue? Running back to the entrance and getting reinforcements from the Woolen Warriors or Eliab would waste precious time, and every capable man around me would be engaged with a Philistine enemy. On top of that, the riverbank wouldn't give me an opportunity to mount any kind of surprise attack.

Descending the last step, I decided it was best to go by myself—

I never saw the attack coming. The blade pierced my side from behind, plunging deep into the fat of my back.

I cursed at my own stupidity. It had been one of the first lessons the Seraphim taught us. When you fail to be mindful of your surroundings, you're playing inside your own coffin.

I pushed off the ladder, trying to put distance between myself and the unknown attacker. There wasn't much *oomph* in the action, the injury sapping what little reserves of strength I had left. I half succeeded, knocking back my opponent, but then promptly fell to the ground floor of the house, the knife still lodged in my back.

Gasping against the pain, I tried to push myself back up to defend myself, but the wound kept me on the floor.

Dizziness clouded out all other concerns, and my vision went dark.

Chapter 38

Being dead hurt—a lot.

My back throbbed with a deep, burning sensation, while my thigh demanded attention with an acute, throbbing ache. Uneven rocks lay under me, and my face was smushed uncomfortably against cool, moist stones. The constant sound of a stream burbled quietly behind me. They had taken me to the river, which meant—

Snapping open my eyes, I quickly scanned the landscape.

To my left, a shirtless Philistine crouched next to Isaiah's horizontal form, harshly shifting my brother's body back and forth. I couldn't see either of their faces, but Isaiah's reactions to the other man's prodding meant he was at least still alive.

Despair immediately overtook any relief as I caught sight of the other three men along the riverbed. Gabril stood with his back to me, his raven-feathered cloak blowing in the wind, and his scarred, bald head bobbed in conversation with two other Seraphim. One of his thugs noticed I was awake, flicking his nose at me.

Gabril turned around slowly. "The god-slayer awakens."

I forced myself to sit up, pushing through the painful protests of a body begging me to remain still. I checked the injury on my back, and though my tunic was sopping wet from blood, fresh bandages were wrapped over the wound. Beneath the wrappings, I felt an unnatural, unrecognizable lump.

My eyebrows arched in confusion. "Why am I here?"

The Seraphim leader shook his head. "An oversight." He pointed his thumb at the warrior still checking on my brother. "Philistine mercenaries are fine for arrow fodder and hired muscle, but an overabundance of brains was never one of them. Almon was ordered to bring back a corpse, not another hostage. This Philistine thug didn't understand that. Worry not, though. We'll correct his lapse of judgment momentarily."

As much as I wanted to object to his plan, between my injuries and absence of a weapon, we both knew there was nothing I could do to stop him from carrying it out. He must have come at the king's request, which meant he saw me as simply another target that needed to be eliminated. My brother, on the other hand, was innocent in all of this, and there was still a chance for him to survive.

I weakly put a hand in the air. "I obviously don't agree with the king's order, but I understand it. You've captured me. The task is complete." My voice changed, carrying a hint of desperation. "Please, let my brother Isaiah go. He's never been a part of this. Erik doesn't want him, and you'll gain nothing by killing him."

For a moment, it seemed like Gabril was weighing my request. Then he turned to his two Seraphim subordinates and cocked his bald head. "Apparently, we're here on orders of the king."

"That's news to me," said the shorter of the two warriors in mock confusion.

"What?" I asked, pushing myself up straighter.

Gabril's hand flashed behind his back, and a short knife flew through the air, slicing a fresh cut across my bicep.

I hissed, and he approached me, hard determination in each stride.

"I do not take orders from a mad dog," he said, ice in his voice. "Years ago he would have been thrown down, if not for one incessant, pathetic saboteur of my plans." His foot kicked out, grinding into my wounded thigh. I recoiled, which set aflame all my other wounds. "How could one boy find so many ways to keep a dying nation alive?"

The fresh round of agony kept me from asking what he was talking about, but he read the question in my eyes.

"For years, I watched our country limp along like some kind of stray, broken dog. We've begged for scraps for so many generations. We barely remember how to take what is rightly ours, and all the while, we're encircled by predators waiting to devour us whole."

He began pacing over me, speaking as if giving a lecture to a student. "When Erik was appointed king, for a fleeting moment I believed he could be the answer, the one to build our country into something strong, something to be feared. Yet he insisted on following that feeble charlatan Alvaro, choosing belief in an imaginary friend over forging our own destiny. Then, as soon as he wizened up, the insufferable goat went crazy on us. He needed to be the first one to go.

"Yet if I killed him outright, we would only make the same mistake again, electing some new fool to take his place. Our nation needed to be shown how desperate, how miserable their lives really were. We needed a powerful enemy to strip away their delusions."

"The Philistines?" I whispered, shifting uncomfortably. The hard lump beneath my bandages kept awkwardly shoving into my back.

"Oh, they may be dumb," he continued, sneering toward the Philistine guarding Isaiah, "but they are a nation of warriors, proud and easily provoked. We'd had border skirmishes for years. The bow was already drawn back. It was simply a matter of unleashing the arrow."

My head shook back and forth in disbelief. "No, Doeg has been orchestrating this."

"The Mad King's new magician-sheep herder?" Gabril barked a laugh. "Hardly. He's either a fanatic or an opportunist, but either way, he's nothing more than another example of Erik's weakness for superstition. No, this kind of work needed to be done with flesh and blood, not with parlor tricks and loaded dice."

The commander stared off into the distance. "The operation was supposed to be precise and final, one battle to upend the power structure, to show the true weakness of our king." He bent down and picked up a handful of small stones. Without warning, he threw them in my face. "Until some boy came with a bag of pebbles and ruined over half a decade's worth of planning!"

I brought my arm down from protecting my eyes. "You staged

the fight with Goliath…" My voice trailed off.

"Your fluke victory infused our people with the most insidious of diseases: false hope."

My head shook back and forth again. "But we turned the tide against the Philistines. We're winning the war."

"This isn't about the Philistines!" he bellowed. "They're not the real problem. If it's not them, it'll be another nation. At our core, we are weak, infirm. For us to survive, we needed to remove the diseased flesh."

Pieces started falling into place. "It was you!" My eyes wandered up to him. "You were the one behind Alexander's plot to assassinate the king!"

"I *will* save our country, no matter the cost," he answered coldly.

"So why come to Bethlehem?" I asked, waving my hands around. "Some chance at revenge?"

"Oh no," Gabril said, "If it were simply a matter of killing you, you'd already be in the grave. I didn't realize it until the day Erik executed Alexander, but it was no longer enough to simply murder the king. The mighty Niklas had become a symbol to the people, a legend more influential than our current ruler. They failed to recognize what a pathetic creature you are, nothing more than a product of dumb, unfathomable luck. If I simply killed you, your legend could haunt our nation for decades. I needed to destroy you."

My head craned toward Bethlehem, smoke still rising from the city. "You sent the Philistines today."

"If the mighty Niklas failed to protect his own hometown"—his hands swept over the city—"the tales of his power would be found out as nothing but the phony hoax they always were. Your renown destined your people to die."

The Seraphim commander shook his scarred head and walked back to his two accomplices, kneeling down to unwrap a thick blanket roll. When he stood back up, Gabril clutched his two long, curved knives, stuffing them neatly into his belt.

My mind raced to process all of the information he had just told me. The fact that he had vocalized his plans in front of Isaiah meant there was zero chance he'd allow my brother to live. In fact, with all of this legend nonsense, he probably intended to kill my whole family just to ensure no one ever remembered my name. Alvaro's warning had been right all along. If I didn't stop the madman now, Bethlehem and my family would perish.

Glancing around the cliff, I tried to find any advantage to swing the situation in our favor, but the circumstances I was working with left no opportunity for success. On an even playing field, Gabril would crush me in a fair fight. He literally taught me everything I knew. During the two years I had trained under him, I had scratched him a grand total of three times, compared to the literal hundreds of lacerations he had cut into my flesh. He was a focused, ice-cold force in battle. Beyond that, he had two more trained, armed, Seraphim with him. There was only one way this ended.

And what was that poking me in the back?

My arm reached behind me, gently placing my fingers beneath the bandage wrappings. They found an unmistakably familiar object.

What? How?

Gabril's attention fixed on me. "This could have all been avoided, really. You had potential, an unmatched determination. We could have worked together. You simply chose the losing side." He cocked his head. "Do you know where your weakness comes from?"

"Nope," I said, carefully pulling out the object beneath the wrappings, "but I'm pretty sure you're going to tell me." As long as he kept talking, I had more time to unravel the final mystery. The Philistine guarding my brother finally turned toward us, giving me a good look at his marred face, his one good eye intensely focused on me.

"Mercy," Gabril answered. "Instead of letting the weak be devoured, you stand with them. It saps you of strength and leaves you powerless to defend yourself."

Mercy? It had always been about mercy.

Gentle strumming of a harp flowed over the air.

My hand grasped tightly to the object's handle bound in the wrappings, and I nodded resolutely to the familiar Philistine with a clover-shaped burn mark on his cheek. The exact same Philistine whom I had offered medical treatment after he infiltrated our village. His wrists were still encircled by the faded scars of infection I bandaged years ago.

It was time to put an end to this. I pulled out the dabar hidden beneath the bandages. "Mercy will get me killed?" I repeated, cracking my neck. "Let's test that theory."

Chapter 39

Gabril's eyes locked onto my blade, shocked by its appearance.

I cocked my head to the side. "We can thank superstitious, imaginary friends for this little surprise."

The commander blinked, but then a mask of composure spread across his face, and he retreated to his comrades. Isaiah clamored up, bruised but standing tall, and both he and the Philistine took a spot to my right and left.

"What exactly is happening?" Isaiah asked in a whisper, gripping tightly to the spear-tipped shepherd staff our new Philistine friend had returned to him.

I flicked my nose toward Gabril and his Seraphim accomplices. "They're the bad guys."

My brother squared his shoulders and took an uncomfortable breath. "Got it, and just to be clear, they're probably going to try and kill us, right?"

"Yeah."

Our Philistine turncoat carried a nasty looking hatchet and stared at the three men in front of us. "They are capable warriors."

I nodded, trying to analyze our situation.

I knew full well the quality of training our opponents possessed. In a fair fight, either of Gabril's two stooges would have been a manageable task for me one-on-one. However, a fair fight was out of the question. A quick inventory of my injuries left me with deep gashes on my leg, arm, and torso, a knife puncture in my lower back, and a literal chilling amount of blood loss. Beyond that, Gabril was on a whole different fighting level than the rest of us. While my brother had made huge strides in combat during his time with the Woolen Warriors, the chances of him being a match for either of Gabril's stooges was slim. Our defector was a complete wild card.

Yet if we tried to gang up on one of them, we'd leave ourselves wide open to the attacks from the others, meaning our best and only shot depended on three individual matchups.

There was one other factor in our favor: Gabril's rage. The man never showed emotion, and his cold, ruthless logic was as quiet as a winter night. Yet instead of simply killing me when I was unconscious, he had chosen to let me wake up. He needed me to know he had beaten me, the one who had stood in his way. Like pretty much all of my enemies, his hatred was personal, and blinding rage may give us an edge in the battle.

I glanced back and forth between my partners. "I'm going to need you two to handle Lackey A and Lackey B. I'll take care of the ugly one."

Isaiah swallowed hard and fixed his eyes ahead.

The Philistine's head bobbed once, and a question bloomed in my mind.

"By the way, what's your name?"

The turncoat looked at me, blinking several times.

"We're fighting alongside each other with our lives on the line. It seems appropriate."

"Zalmon," he answered.

I placed a hand on his shoulder. "Thank you, Zalmon."

He shrugged. "I'm just balancing the ledger," he replied, returning his attention to our opponents. "Plus, these guys are tools."

I chuckled. "You're a good judge of character." I cracked my neck again. "On three."

Gabril and his men braced themselves, but before they could discuss a plan, I shouted, "Three!"

Adrenaline surged through my body, and I sprinted forward, flanked by my brother and Zalmon.

Gabril smirked as I rushed toward him, raising his twin knives to defend his torso and neck. My long blade whipped out at his exposed right leg, but I had to pull it back to parry the two quick swipes he sent at my cheek. Ducking underneath them, I dove into a roll and spun back around. The abrupt bouncing around lit every scrape and scar on my body ablaze with pain.

Taking two short breaths, I advanced again, this time lunging forward with the intent to grab onto one of Gabril's arms. I caught hold of his left wrist, but before I could bring my knife up to strike, again I needed to retreat, using my knife to block his other blade's attack on my stomach. My weapon intercepted his and managed to redirect the thrust, but the sharp metal still scraped my side.

I back-stepped several paces, breathing deeply.

Gabril raised an eyebrow. "You always were a competent student. You're wounded, so you know the longer this fight drags out, the smaller your chance of success becomes. You realize the difference in our ability, so you willingly risk personal protection to gain an opening for an attack. Finally, you understand that while killing me is unlikely, you may be able to wound my legs in an effort to give your allies an edge in a later fight."

His utter dissection of my thinking sent a wave of shivers climbing up my spine. My thrown-together plan was built on the assumption that the difference in our fighting capacities would only expand as the effects of my wounds wore on me. The sooner we finished, the better the chance of success. Yet the difference in combat ability between us had started at insurmountable and was now growing into full-blown absurdity.

My eyes checked on my companions. Zalmon and his opponent still circled one another warily, and Isaiah had chosen to grapple with his adversary, using his bulk to his advantage. If I waited for either of them to defeat their opponents, there'd be a small chance together we could handle Gabril. However, the far more likely outcome would be the commander defeating me first, and then he'd have free reign to help his buddies, making short work of my allies.

The best chance they had of surviving was getting Gabril as far away from them as possible. After all the talk about needing to root out my influence in Israel, I doubted the Seraphim commander would let me out of his sight, giving me the advantage of dictating where we fought.

My legs sagged, and I dropped down to one knee, panting deeply.

Gabril shook his head in disappointment and took a couple of cautious steps forward. My hand whipped up, throwing a palm full of sand and gravel into his eyes. He grunted in frustration and brought his blades up to stop an attack, but I used the momentary opening to turn and run full speed in the opposite direction.

He grunted and unfiltered rage could be heard in his voice. "Today we finish this, you insignificant speck!"

I had made it a dozen paces when my biggest fear was confirmed. He still had knives to throw. A short blade dug into the meat of my back shoulder, before falling to the ground. It felt like someone had driven a prod iron into my skin, but my running gait only faltered for a moment. Regaining my stride, I continued on.

Apparently, he had exhausted his supply of projectiles because now his footsteps pounded from behind me.

Pouring every ounce of energy into our race, I concentrated on nothing other than placing one leg immediately in front of the other. Up a hill. Down a hill. Through a valley. Soon, I stopped paying any attention to my surroundings and focused only on the chase.

What felt like an eternity later, my legs finally failed me. A foot struck uneven ground, and my body skidded out of control. Tumbling upon an unyielding rock bed, I rolled awkwardly several times before I finally came to a stop.

"A coward's choice." Gabril's voice came through labored breaths. "Running halfway to the capital just to be gutted all the same. I expected better from you."

"I've always had a knack for disappointing authority figures," I said. "It's a spiritual gift."

Flipping myself over, I found Gabril standing a cautious distance away from me. He needn't have worried. I had no energy left to defend myself.

With the adrenaline wearing off, every one of my wounds reminded me of their presence. My bag of tricks had been depleted, my body was broken, and any friends to aid me were as far away as

I could get them.

Taking in the surroundings, I pushed myself up to a crouch, and an ironic grin touched my lips. Our chase had taken us to the very same outcropping where I had killed the lion years ago, where this adventure had really begun.

My attention flickered back to my former commander, who now towered above me, one attack from completing his mission.

"I'm assuming this whole game of tag was a pathetic attempt to save your brother," he said, unsheathing one of his long blades. "But even if he manages to survive my men, I'll make sure he ends up just as dead."

His threat sparked fresh rage, but my body was done. Isaiah would have to find some way to protect himself without an overly complicated scheme from his younger brother. Barring Yahweh himself coming down and striking Gabril dead, you could count the number of breaths I had left on one hand.

This was the end.

Defeated and callous, I almost missed the harp strings being plucked on the evening air. A brief seed of hope blossomed in my chest, yet unlike the battle with the lion, no superhuman strength flowed through my limbs. In fact, keeping myself upright became a labor of legendary proportion.

Then I noticed it. The final wrinkle.

Five feet behind Gabril was the entrance to the snake pit I had fallen into after my victory over the lion.

The Seraphim leader may be near unbeatable against a sword or a knife, but even he couldn't fight five hundred Israeli vipers. The guy upstairs had given me a chance to take Gabril out, to complete my mission. Of course, the one small hiccup in the ingenious plan was it required me to make the trip with him.

"Don't worry," Gabril said, misinterpreting the conflict in my eyes, "you'll see your brother soon. Your whole family, actually."

At least he made my decision easy.

Flinging myself up, I wrapped both of my arms around his waist and began barreling forward. The reaction caught him off guard, but he recovered within a breath and buried his blade deep into the muscle of my back. The wound slowed me down, but we had already reached the edge of the hole. With one last desperate burst of energy, I howled and pushed us into the pit's mouth.

Gabril realized my intentions a moment too late, and together we tumbled down into the shaft. We rolled down end over end, the knife in my back coming free and falling out of reach. The angle of the ramp increased the further we slid, and by the time we stopped, the sounds of hundreds of vipers could be heard slithering below us.

The commander had fallen further down the shaft and froze, his Seraphim training analyzing the situation. He tried shifting his body weight and slid another few inches into the hole. Any moment now, he'd be within reach of their fangs.

"You won't get out of here," he said through seething breaths.

In defiance of the unholy pain spreading throughout my body, smug satisfaction covered my face. "That was never the plan."

He roared and reached for me, but again the movement betrayed his position on the ramp. He descended further and harsh, angry hissing and snapping erupted from the pit. The commander squirmed and cried out, sliding deeper, and more snaps followed.

Israel's chief traitor didn't last long. In less than a minute, Gabril's groaning ceased.

Which left me alone, trapped in a hole, with hundreds of deadly, enraged vipers half a dozen feet below me.

Yet in spite of those merry facts, the faintest hint of a smile traced my lips.

The conspiracy had been stopped, which meant Bethlehem and my family were safe. For the first time in what felt like years, I breathed deep and free. I hadn't failed them.

Remembering my injuries dampened the celebration a bit. The sheer number of cuts, bruises, and punctures covering my body bordered on ludicrousness, so unless the secret to escaping this pit involved me flopping my damaged limbs around like wet blankets, this shaft would serve as my crypt.

Passing out seemed like the best option. At this point, I had earned a little rest, and with a bit of luck, I'd be unconscious when the end finally came.

My eyes had closed for half a second before a familiar, concerned voice snapped me from my slumber.

"Niklas!" a man cried out from above me.

My neck flopped over, and I looked up. Eliab and Abin knelt at the top of the tunnel.

"Little brother," Abin said, a broad smile on his lips, "why are you always in this pit?"

Chapter 40

"But why didn't you run back to Bethlehem?" Deborah asked, shaking her head. She smoothed out her lavender dress, sitting suspiciously close to Isaiah. Their hands never touched, but they always remained next to each other. Isaiah got the girl — good for him.

"I didn't want to drag anyone else into my mess," I answered.

My father stretched out his injured leg. "We had already survived two separate attacks by the Philistines and an infiltration by the Seraphim. I'm pretty sure we'd have handled one more enemy."

"Everyone's a critic," I said, hobbling over to the counter to grab a piece of bread. "Next time, I'll leave the hero decisions to you all."

Abin scoffed, bringing his cup to his lips. "Not likely."

I leaned against a structural pillar, watching my family and friends. Two days and sixty-three stitches later, I was sore, exhausted, and absolutely giddy. Finally, the mission was complete.

After I had been captured and taken to Gabril, Deborah and Benaiah took charge of our forces, and within the hour the Philistine invaders were either defeated or in full retreat. We had lost three dozen men, including seven Woolen Warriors, but Bethlehem had weathered the attack and come out the other side wounded, but whole.

Erik was still after me, but according to rumors, after he encountered Alvaro, he and all the men with him began prancing through the streets of Ramah, singing songs to the moon like a band of sun-addled fools. They didn't come to their senses for the better part of twenty-four hours and then quickly retreated to the capital. The old geezer had given me enough time to slip away unnoticed.

I still hadn't heard word from Damon, but considering he managed to send the Woolen Warriors to our aid, it seemed safe to assume he would be fine. After finishing off the slavers and enjoying a night of long overdue celebration, my troops scattered to the wind, hoping to avoid the king's ire for aiding me. Zalmon the Philistine slipped out with them.

"When are you leaving?" Eliab asked from behind me.

My eyebrows arched.

He grinned and shook his hairy head. "I noticed the travel pack in the corner. An extra set of clothes, your lyre, a few coins."

I shrugged and quieted my voice. "Unless we want to chance round three of 'Everyone Tries to Sack Bethlehem,' I can't stay here. Erik's return to the capital is only temporary, and he'd raze the entire city just to get to me."

"We'd fight for you, all of us," my brother stated. "We're willing to do whatever it takes."

"I know, and I appreciate it, truly, but if I leave, no one gets hurt, not our people, not the innocent soldiers Erik would bring." A sly grin spread across my lips. "Or myself."

He pondered my words for a moment and then nodded. "Where will you go?"

Abin belched loudly, and my whole family erupted in laughter.

"First, I'm going to visit an old acquaintance for a bit of advice, and after that..." I paused. "It's safer for everyone if you don't know."

For a while, we watched our family in silence.

"So when will you leave?" he asked again.

"It'll be easier once everyone is asleep," I replied. "Plus, Mom's making rack of lamb tonight. There's no sense in missing that."

I chose wisely. It was the best meal I'd had in years.

Epilogue

By the time I slipped into his tent, the dead of night had already blanketed the small town. I managed to get a couple of hours of sleep before its owner awoke and began moving through his morning routine.

Matthias, the bald and jovial priest, almost stepped right on top of me before he noticed my presence.

"Bah!" came an expected, humorous outcry.

I rose and let him get a good look at me. "Matthias, good morning."

The priest's eyes furrowed, but then a wide smile spread across his lips as he recognized me. "Niklas," he said in an exuberant but hushed voice.

"The one and only," I replied and matched his audio level, knowing his son still lay asleep in the corner. I motioned toward a couple of sitting pillows. "I would love to have a quick chat."

"Of course," he answered and began tending a fire. "Let me get some tea started."

Once we both were seated and brimming cups warmed our palms, I asked my last unanswered question. "Is it over?"

Matthias cocked his head to the side. "Is what over?"

"My mission. Alvaro said my assignment was to find the traitor before he destroyed Bethlehem. We thwarted the conspiracy three days ago."

"Ah," the priest said, closing his eyes. "You're wondering if Yahweh is done with you."

"I really hadn't thought about it in those terms, but yeah, am I released from the anointing?"

Matthias peeked out with one eye. "Do you want to be?"

Considering that in the last seven days I had faced off against three separate barbarian armies, lived through a landslide of boulders, endured two independently organized assassination attempts, and been impaled more times than I could count, the answer should have a been a resounding, "Absolutely!" Yet despite all of that, my family was now safe, Gabril had been defeated, and our nation was secure. I took pride in having a role in that.

"So He's given me a choice?" I asked.

Genuine delight appeared on the priest's face. "I often forget how suspicious others can be of Him. Dear boy, you've always had a choice, which is an entirely separate thing than being chosen."

"But the anointing," I protested. "Alvaro's charge to protect our people, to uncover the conspiracy..."

"And you could have ignored it, refused to take up the mission. Yahweh isn't fond of removing people's free will. I imagine for Him it'd be too close to cheating."

"So He's" —I nodded upward— "not done with me?"

The priest mimicked my gesture. "*He's* not done with any of us."

We sat in quiet reflection for a good five minutes. "But why me?"

"Why any of us?" the priest replied, amused.

My face scrunched up, unamused.

"Why you?" Matthias said, slightly more serious. "You were a shepherd before all this started, correct?"

Laughter escaped my lips. "Not by choice. I hated sheep. They're dumb, defenseless, cowardly, stubborn, always a step away from doing something that will get them killed, and all the while they're ungrateful for your help, like they're doing you the favor."

The priest spread his hands. "I believe you just answered your own question." When I didn't respond, he continued. "Our people, all people really, can be stubborn, defenseless, and ungrateful. Yet Yahweh still chooses to watch over us. It's an exceedingly rare trait to follow in His footsteps, to fight for people who may never show appreciation. He obviously saw that potential in you."

Huh. I had never really looked at life like that.

I fidgeted. "So what do I do now?"

"Whatever you want," Matthias replied. "I imagine you'll know when He has need of you. Would you mind if I asked a more personal question?"

I nodded. "Anything."

"Do you ever talk to Him?"

My neck rocked back at the question. The concept of a conversation with the guy managing the cosmos seemed bizarre. During some of the more trying moments of my adventures, I unleashed some fairly combative words at Him, but it was a far cry from actual dialogue. "He doesn't seem to be one for talking," I replied.

"Maybe you're simply not listening closely enough," Matthias said, and then he winked at me. "Food for thought. So where will you go now?"

Again, I was tempted to vocalize my plans, but I held myself back. "I'm not exactly in Erik's good graces at the moment, and knowing would put you and your son in danger." I began rising to my feet, and he joined me.

We stared at one another for a moment, and then his eyes lit up. "Oh, I believe I have the perfect parting gift for your travels."

I shook my head. "I've packed everything I need."

"I doubt you have something like this." A spark of mischief danced in his pupils.

Intrigued, I agreed with a bob of my head.

He moved to the far corner of the tent and pulled out a long, heavy bundle. "Two and a half years ago, men from the army dropped this off after a particularly bull-headed young shepherd defeated an even more bull-headed foreign braggart. It's been sitting here as a religious relic ever since. Seems like a waste if you ask me."

My eyes widened as I slowly unwrapped the package, recognizing the golden handle. Beneath the cloth lay Goliath's massive sword. "There is none like it," I said solemnly.

He gestured for me to pick it up, and my fingers curled around its hilt. In one motion, I pulled it from its sheath and swung it in the air. Whether I had simply gotten stronger, or something more supernatural was at work, I lifted the blade easily with one hand.

"Thank you," I said and bowed low. "This is a gift for a king."

Matthias shook his head. "It's a gift for a hero."

A heartfelt goodbye later, I walked out of the tent as the first light of sunrise fell over the street. I left the village of Nob from their western entrance, mentally fortifying myself for my most audacious, absurd, asinine scheme yet. There was only one place known where Erik's powerful arm could not reach, and where his agents would not have the power to attack.

Setting my feet firmly forward, I headed for Philistia, the home of the Philistines.

END OF BOOK ONE

Acknowledgments

Growing up takes a village. Becoming an author is no different. I can confidently say this book would never have become a reality without a host of friends and family providing encouragement and inspiration along the way. My mom dragged me to Barnes and Noble. My father first identified my fascination with narrative by giving me a mixtape. "You've always loved the songs that told a story." Rachel, my sister, challenged me to write down the worlds I imagined while daydreaming. And countless friends read poorly edited drafts of Tyrants and Traitors. Without your support, none of this would be possible. Thank you.

About The Author

Joshua McHenry Miller, a native Michigander, grew up living in two worlds: the cozy suburbs of Detroit and the urban jungle of Pontiac. A lover of story in all forms, he's spent over a decade honing his writing, and his debut YA novel, Tyrants and Traitors, is being released October 10th, 2016. When Josh isn't writing, he's starting a church and working as a community developer in south-central Madison, WI.

Want to learn more about the author of Tyrants and Traitors? **Check out his website at <u>joshuamchenrymiller.com</u>.**

Want to be Joshua's best friend for a day? **Leave a review of Tyrants and Traitors on Amazon, Goodreads, or your favorite book platform.** One of the most helpful things you can do for a debut author is provide positive reviews, so if you get a moment, Josh would love it if you wrote one up!

Other great books from Blue Ink Press

Dandelion on Fire
Sherry Torgent
Benjamin Franklin Gold Award Winner

Everyone knows the legend — Greene Island is cursed. 17-yr-old Hardy Vance doesn't care about curses. All he wants to do is graduate from high school and head to college on the mainland. But Hardy has a knack for finding trouble. When he gets stuck doing community service with a girl that has a secret, their lives quickly become entwined in a murder mystery that leads straight back into the island's dark past and the dreaded Curse of Viola. It's up to Hardy and the supernatural abilities of his friends to uncover the horrible truth using the only clue left behind. A dandelion seed.

Chronicle of the Three: Bloodline
Tabitha Caplinger

Zoe thought the loss of her parents would be the most difficult thing she'd ever have to endure. When she began seeing things she couldn't explain in her new home of Torchcreek, Virginia, she was sure the grief was driving her mad. Instead, Zoe discovers she is part of an ancient bloodline, one destined to prevent the powers of darkness from condemning the world. But Zoe, the daughter of the three, isn't just another descendant–she's the key to humanity's salvation. In this first installment of the supernatural fantasy trilogy The Chronicle of the Three, Zoe Andrews learns that not all shadows are harmless interceptions of light. Some are a more sinister darkness that wants to torment the soul.

Made in the USA
Lexington, KY
18 February 2017